Even at his slow pace Aleister almost tripped a few seconds later when his toe hit a large soft object.

He knelt down to see what it was. He realised it was a human form. Someone drunk or sleeping, he almost hoped. But they weren't drunk or sleeping. There was blood oozing from their skull; he could feel its stickiness.

It was a dead person, recently dead, and he was pretty sure who it must be, though in the dark it was hard to make out the features. He knelt there for a few seconds, his fingers in the blood.

A huge explosion of fireworks rocked the air. Coloured wheels rotated above, flares soared, rockets glared. There was light enough to see now, and there could be no doubt who the dead man was.

* *

REMEMBER, REMEMBER

A Victorian Mystery

by

SHELDON GOLDFARB

Published by UKA Press 2005

2 4 6 8 10 9 7 5 3 1

First published in Great Britain in 2005 by the

UKA Press

PO Box 109,
Portishead
Bristol. BS20 7ZJ

www.UKAuthors.com

A CIP catalogue record for this book is available from the British Library

ISBN: 1-904781-43-8

This book was prepared for print by the UKA Press
Cover design by Peter J. Merrigan

In Memory of My Father

TABLE OF CONTENTS

Remember, remember
The Fifth of November,
Gunpowder treason and plot.
I see no reason
Why gunpowder treason
Should ever be forgot

— traditional rhyme
for Guy Fawkes Day

CHAPTER ONE

Something is Amiss

The first thing that Aleister Lister Smith noticed was wrong was that Mr Rawlins wasn't bellowing, glowering, or doing much of anything at all. He did not even seem to be paying attention, standing by his desk at the front of the class while the recitations droned on.

'*Possum, potes, pot* – '

That was Biggs, stumbling over a Latin conjugation. Biggs was always stumbling. But by this point Mr Rawlins should have been saying something.

'Biggs!' he would say, and Biggs would stop, hesitate, not be sure whether to try another conjugation or just admit defeat.

'Biggs,' Mr Rawlins would usually say, 'have you studied this material at all, or have you just been wasting your time reading novels?'

And the funny thing was that Biggs never read novels. He studied all the time, but nothing ever sank in. Aleister felt sorry for him.

But this time Mr Rawlins was just letting things continue. Aleister sneaked a glance at him. It wasn't always safe to do this: Mr Rawlins might catch your eye and ask you to take over, and then if you didn't know the conjugations, you'd be the one in trouble.

Of course, Aleister usually knew the conjugations. He was Mr Rawlins's star pupil in the fourth form at Shrewsbury School. Still, there was never any guarantee that the schoolmaster's wrath wouldn't land on you: even star pupils were not immune; it was best to keep your head down. But now there was an uneasy silence in the class. Biggs had broken down completely, unable to remember the first person plural, and Mr Rawlins was saying nothing. The other boys shifted uneasily on their wooden benches and played with their steel nib pens. Aleister risked another glance at Mr Rawlins. He seemed lost in thought.

Finally, the unusual silence must have registered. Mr Rawlins snapped out of his daydream.

'Biggs,' he said, much more mildly than usual, 'have you finished?'

'No, sir,' said Biggs. 'That is, I was not quite sure how to proceed, sir.'

'No,' said Mr Rawlins, 'a common problem.'

He surveyed the class. Everyone shrank into as small a piece of human existence as was possible, hoping not to be called on.

'Smith,' Mr Rawlins said at last. 'Lister Smith.'

'Yes, sir,' said Aleister.

'Finish up. I ...' Mr Rawlins paused, looking strangely absent. 'I have to go.'

And with that Mr Rawlins waved vaguely at Aleister, at the class, at the heavens – it wasn't clear what he was waving at, really – and left the room.

Aleister stood up. This was highly unusual. Not that Mr Rawlins would ask him to take over the class; he had done that before; he was the star pupil after all, almost a monitor. But to walk out in the middle of recitations; that was unusual.

Aleister hurried to the front of the class and noticed Mr Rawlins's big, bulging briefcase. It was overflowing with the boys' Latin assignments. Mr Rawlins carried it with him everywhere, but now he'd forgotten it. Well, Aleister would deal with it later. Now he had to revive the class.

'Johnson,' he called out, knowing he could depend on the boy in the front row, 'continue for Biggs.'

Johnson timidly cleared his throat, then began: '*Possum, potes, potest. Possumus, potestis, possunt.*'

'Good,' said Aleister. 'Next we'll turn to the chapter on the fourth declension ...'

After the class, Aleister wondered what to do about the briefcase. Perhaps Mr Rawlins had meant to leave it behind. But no, that didn't seem reasonable. He should bring it to him, though he'd hardly ever been to the schoolmaster's rooms, and never except when he'd been ordered to. Still, it seemed the thing to do.

Aleister struggled to close the briefcase. He had to push the assignment papers down into it, and even then the ageing clasp would barely fasten. Finally, he picked up the battered old thing and, staggering a bit because it was so heavy, made his way to the masters' section of the school.

He walked down the tiled corridor, glancing up at the walls with the portraits of headmasters on them. Butler, Kennedy, Moss. They stared down at him, almost frowning, he thought. What are you doing with your teacher's briefcase, they seemed to say?

Finally, he reached Mr Rawlins's office. The heavy oak door was partly open, and he could hear voices coming from beyond it.

'You've got to help me, George,' a strange voice said. 'I don't know what I'm going to do.'

'I really can't see how I can help,' a very familiar voice said. It was Mr Rawlins. He must be George, Aleister realised. It had never even occurred to him that Mr Rawlins had a first name.

'But what will I do?' the strange voice said.

'Perhaps you should just confess everything,' said Mr Rawlins.

'I can't confess. It would mean my job.'

'You should have thought of that before you acted so foolishly in the first place.'

'But George, think of the scandal. Think of the family.'

Aleister listened, fascinated. What scandal? What sort of thing should the stranger confess? The heavy briefcase hardly seemed heavy any more.

'You're no family of mine,' Mr Rawlins was saying.

'George!' said the stranger. 'How can you say such a thing?'

There was silence from the room. Aleister began to think he should not be standing in the hall, listening. He stepped forward and knocked timidly on the half open door.

'Who's there?' Mr Rawlins roared out.

'It's just me, sir,' said Aleister, peering around the door. 'You forgot your briefcase.'

Aleister took a tentative step into the office, lifting the briefcase up in front of his chest as proof. Mr Rawlins peered at him from behind his big oak desk in front of a bookshelf full of worn-looking books. The stranger, a tall nervous-looking man, stood on the far side of the room.

'Who is this?' said the stranger. 'Has he been eavesdropping? What will we do with him? Or can he help us somehow?'

'Oh, do try and compose yourself, Arthur,' said Mr Rawlins. 'Go for a walk in the grounds. That may calm you. Just don't fall in the river.'

The stranger seemed about to say something. He looked half offended and half terrified. But in the end he said nothing, just stood there stroking his grey side whiskers and staring at Aleister long enough to make him uneasy. Then he somehow slid out of the room.

Aleister moved slightly to let the stranger pass, and then stood in front of Mr Rawlins, still holding the bulging briefcase. It was feeling heavy again, but Aleister wasn't sure where to put it.

Mr Rawlins seemed lost in thought.

'Sir,' Aleister stammered out.

Mr Rawlins looked up, then waved in the direction of an uncomfortable looking wooden chair.

'Put the briefcase there, Lister Smith. Good of you to bring it.'

Aleister gratefully deposited the briefcase on the chair, then turned to go. He hesitated, though, wanting to know what the stranger's visit meant, but not knowing how to ask. One never asked anything of Mr Rawlins. He did the asking.

He could feel Mr Rawlins looking at him now.

'Is there anything else, Lister Smith?'

'Oh, no, sir. I was just wondering. I mean ...'

Mr Rawlins looked at him. He had a way of doing it that made you feel like a tiny ant about to be stepped on by a bear. Mr Rawlins even looked like a bear, a big brown bear in his brown suit with his brown hair.

'What were you wondering, Lister Smith?' the brown bear asked.

'About the gentleman who was here,' said Aleister.

'Ah, yes,' said Mr Rawlins, shaking his head ever so slightly. 'The gentleman who was here. My impecunious brother-in-law.'

There was a pause. Aleister felt a bit flustered.

'Well,' said Mr Rawlins at last, 'what were you wondering?'

But Aleister no longer knew what he'd been wondering. He also didn't know what impecunious meant.

'I just ... that is ...' he said.

'You weren't really eavesdropping, were you, Lister Smith?' said Mr Rawlins. 'I think I know you'd never do something as improper as that.'

'Oh, no, sir,' said Aleister, blushing a bit, and feeling suddenly guilty.

'Well, you'd best be off, then,' said Mr Rawlins.

15

Aleister nodded and hurried out. He wondered if he had committed some terrible crime by listening at the door. But he hadn't really listened long, and he had been almost unable to help himself. He hadn't sinned too terribly much, had he? Anyway, what really occupied his mind was what he had heard about a scandal and confessing – what did it all mean?

And Mr Rawlins had a brother-in-law – that was another surprise. Did it mean he had a wife? Aleister tried to imagine a wife for the stern schoolmaster; it seemed an impossible task.

But there was another way to be a brother-in-law: perhaps Mr Rawlins only had a sister. Even that seemed hard to grasp, though. Mr Rawlins had always just been Mr Rawlins, the terrifying teacher. Did terrifying teachers have first names and families and impecunious brothers-in-law?

And what did 'impecunious' mean anyway?

Aleister headed back along the corridor, thinking to go back to his room in the dormitory, where he could look 'impecunious' up in his dictionary. At least he could figure that out.

As he walked, he began musing about the word. He wondered if it was Latin. Impecunious. 'Im' and 'pecunious.' Well, there was the Latin word *pecunia*, meaning money, and 'im' would mean 'without' – was Mr Rawlins's brother-in-law without money? It didn't seem likely: weren't people without money always dressed in rags and looking half-starved? He'd seen them in picture books. But the brother-in-law had been dressed normally and had looked well enough fed. Aleister shook his head. Perhaps impecunious meant something else. Perhaps ...

Suddenly, a voice broke into his reverie.

'Boy,' it cried out. 'Boy. Come here.'

It was the impecunious brother-in-law himself. Aleister stopped and looked up at him. He definitely wasn't wearing rags. Aleister didn't like him, though.

They were stopped at the end of the corridor connecting the masters' area with the classrooms. Behind the brother-in-law was the masters' washing-up room. It looked like he had been putting water on his face. Aleister could see a drop or two still there.

'Don't stand there like a statue, boy,' the brother-in-law was saying. 'Where are you headed?'

'Nowhere, sir,' said Aleister.

'Shouldn't you be in class?'

'It's between classes, sir.'

The brother-in-law seemed to consider this. Aleister began to feel uneasy. He wished he could get away and go to his room and read *The Count of Monte Cristo*. He was halfway through and just getting to the part about the Count's revenge.

'Come with me to the garden,' said the brother-in-law.

'Sir?'

'This way, is it?' He pointed to a pair of glass doors at the end of the hall.

Aleister nodded, and then followed as the man headed for the doors.

'But,' said Aleister, 'I'm not allowed in there; it's for the masters only.'

Ignoring this, the brother-in-law flung open the glass doors and motioned for Aleister to follow him onto the terrace, beyond which Aleister could see the lush green of the forbidden garden.

'I mustn't, sir,' said Aleister.

'Oh, it's all right,' said the man. 'And you can call me Mr Talbot. That's my name: Arthur Talbot. Mr Talbot.'

'Pleased to meet you, Mr Talbot,' said Aleister, 'but I still don't think – '

'Come along, boy,' said Mr Talbot. 'It's stuffy in here. I need some air.'

Tentatively, Aleister stepped out into the garden. It was a

17

well-manicured lawn surrounded by high hedges. A white bench stood invitingly at the far end.

Mr Talbot breathed in deeply, as if he'd been holding his breath under water.

'That's better,' he said. 'Nice air you have here, boy. What's your name anyway?'

'Lister Smith, sir,' said Aleister. 'Aleister Lister Smith.'

'Hmm. That's a mouthful. Posh parents in London, no doubt.'

'In India, sir.'

'India. Of course. Bombay?'

'Calcutta, sir.'

'My family was in India, you know. My grandfather was in the Company. The East India Company. Back when they ran things, back when we were going to make something of India. Now we think railways and the telegraph will fix everything. Such nonsense.'

'Yes, sir,' said Aleister, a bit hesitantly. He wasn't quite sure what Mr Talbot was talking about or why he was talking about it to him.

'My grandfather made money in India, you know. That was in the days when you could make money there, before all the foolish reforms were introduced.'

Mr Talbot snorted in a mixture of nostalgia and disgust. He seemed to have forgotten that Aleister was there. Aleister looked around the garden. It seemed a much nicer place than the dusty piece of ground where the boys were supposed to play. Not that Aleister much enjoyed the games anyway; he'd rather be up in his bed reading an exciting adventure story.

Mr Talbot suddenly noticed Aleister again. 'So what do you do here, boy?'

'Sir?'

'Study, I mean. What do you study?'

'Latin mostly, sir,' said Aleister. 'Virgil and Horace. And this year we're beginning Greek.'

'Don't suppose you know much about insurance.'

'No, sir.'

'That's what I'm in. Insurance. The Saviour Assurance Company in Manchester. Have you heard of it?'

Aleister shook his head.

'No,' said Mr Talbot, 'why would you? It's not quite the East India Company.'

Aleister was not sure what to reply to this, or whether indeed any reply was called for at all. Mr Talbot seemed to be one of those people who liked to carry on a conversation all by themselves.

'How old are you, anyway?' Mr Talbot asked suddenly, but before Aleister could tell him that he was fourteen, a bellowing voice from the direction of the glass doors interrupted.

It was Mr Rawlins. 'Lister Smith,' he said. 'What are you doing here?'

Aleister turned around to face Mr Rawlins, but could not think of anything to say.

'Come here this instant,' said Mr Rawlins.

Aleister walked sheepishly over to him. He did not have far to go; he had not gone far into the garden.

'You know pupils are not permitted in this area,' said Mr Rawlins; 'why are you in here?'

Aleister again was at a loss for words; it had seemed so nice in the garden, but he knew he wasn't supposed to be there.

Mr Talbot came to his rescue. 'It was my fault, George,' he said. 'I brought him out here.'

Mr Rawlins glared at his brother-in-law. 'Why would you do that?'

'Well,' said Mr Talbot, 'I'm not entirely sure. I needed someone to tell my troubles to.'

'And you were going to tell them to a child?'

'Well,' said Mr Talbot. He paused and gestured towards Aleister as if he was going to refer to him by name, only he seemed to have forgotten what it was.

'Aleister,' said Aleister.

'Aleister seems like a very bright young boy,' said Mr Talbot.

'Arthur,' said Mr Rawlins, 'I think you should just get on the first train back to Manchester.'

'But wait a minute, George.'

'Arthur ...'

'No,' said Mr Talbot, 'hear me out. Suppose – I don't know, suppose I were to take young Aleister to Manchester with me.'

Mr Rawlins could only sputter in reply. Aleister looked wide-eyed, wondering what Mr Talbot was talking about.

'Suppose I got him some work in the insurance company,' said Mr Talbot. 'Apprentice clerk, something like that. Then he could nose around a bit for me.'

'Nose around?' said Mr Rawlins.

'Find things out,' said Mr Talbot. 'Find out who's been ... you know, troubling me.'

'You're mad, Arthur.'

'But what am I going to do, George?'

'Not take away a pupil entrusted to my care.'

'It wouldn't be for long. I can tell he's a bright boy. He might find out who's behind things right away.'

'And what would you do then, Arthur? Even if you found out who it was, what would you do?'

'Well,' said Mr Talbot, 'I don't exactly know. But at least then I could discuss things with the person, and maybe work something out.'

Aleister was bursting with curiosity. 'Who is this person?' he said. 'How are they troubling you?'

Mr Rawlins and Mr Talbot looked at each other.

'You see?' said Mr Rawlins. 'Look what you're beginning here.' He shook his head. 'Lister Smith,' he went on, 'go back to your room and study your Horace. Arthur, come with me.'

Aleister headed back into the school. He felt vaguely

disappointed. What strange adventure had he just missed out on?

He ventured a glance back and saw the two men engaged in discussion. Mr Talbot was shaking his head. Mr Rawlins shrugged and seemed about to follow Aleister into the school. It looked like Mr Talbot would stay in the garden. Perhaps he really needed the fresh air if he lived in Manchester. Aleister had heard that the smoke in Manchester was so thick you couldn't see your hand in front of your face.

He could see Mr Rawlins gaining on him, and hurried beyond the doorway where he was lingering. Down the corridor he went, along towards the dormitory. He didn't really have to study his Horace; he knew the assigned passages already. He could read *The Count of Monte Cristo*, but suddenly that seemed like a bore. It would be more fun to live an adventure than just to read about one.

When he got to his room, he threw himself down on his bed. His head ached strangely. Maybe he would take a nap. He felt tired and worn out.

CHAPTER TWO

Summoned

Aleister was dreaming. He was late for class and struggling through a field of sticky molasses. The bell was sounding, and he could see the other pupils heading into the school building, but he could only move in slow motion.

And then just as he was able to pull free from the field of molasses he found himself confronted by a giant bear blocking his way.

'Come with me,' said the bear.

Aleister shook his head. The bear reached out and touched Aleister's shoulder with his paw.

'No,' said Aleister, and then he was awake, or half awake, and the bear was in his dormitory room, shaking his shoulder. But it wasn't a bear exactly; it was a large man. At first Aleister thought it was Mr Rawlins. But it wasn't Mr Rawlins. It was that other gentleman, the brother-in-law – what was his name? Mr Talbot.

'Get up, boy,' said Mr Talbot. 'Why are you sleeping in the middle of the day?'

Aleister was still too much asleep to answer.

'Come on, come on,' said Mr Talbot. 'We have to go.'

'Go?' said Aleister. 'Go where?'

'Pack your things. There's a train to catch. Where's your bag?'

Aleister sat up and rubbed his eyes. He was not quite sure what was going on. 'I don't understand,' he said.

'You're coming with me to Manchester,' said Mr Talbot. 'It's all arranged.'

'But I'm in school. My classes. Horace.'

'Take Horace with you if you like. But what you're getting a chance at now is some experience in the school of life.'

'But ...'

'No time for buts. The carriage is waiting.'

Aleister shook his head. He wanted to ask more questions, but Mr Talbot seemed so certain of things that he just went along. He began to fill one of his bags with clothes. 'How much should I take?' he asked.

'Not much, not much,' said Mr Talbot. 'You won't have to be there long, I don't think. A fortnight perhaps. That's all.'

'Didn't Mr Rawlins say I couldn't go?'

'Don't worry about that.'

Aleister thought perhaps he should argue the point, but he was a bit timid of arguing with an adult. One should respect one's elders, he'd been taught. Obey them. Besides, it might be an adventure: a train ride to Manchester, seeing the grime and soot. He wondered if people's faces turned all sooty there. Mr Talbot's looked clean, but then he was visiting here, and the soot might have fallen off.

He finished stuffing clothes in his bag, hesitated over his Horace and then took *The Count of Monte Cristo* instead.

Outside there was a carriage waiting. Mr Talbot nodded to the driver and hurried Aleister inside. The driver flicked the reins, and the horses began to trot ...

The carriage rattled over an iron bridge. Aleister looked at the railway station looming up in the distance. To his right was the town's old ruined castle. He was really going. Leaving the school, heading to Manchester.

'Did Mr Rawlins say anything about notifying my relations?' he asked.

Mr Talbot had been sitting silent in the carriage as if lost in thought. 'What's that?' he said.

'Mr Rawlins. Notifying my relations. Down at Ludlow.'

'I thought your people were in India.'

'That's my parents,' said Aleister. 'I have an aunt and cousins near Ludlow. I'm supposed to go there for the holidays. I always go there.'

'Well, I'm sure you will again. It's only October after all.'

Aleister nodded, but something made him uneasy. 'You did discuss this with Mr Rawlins, didn't you?'

Mr Talbot turned to look at Aleister, but he seemed to be miles away. Finally, he focused his eyes. 'You are a worrying type of lad, aren't you?'

Aleister paused to consider this, but it seemed a little beside the point. 'I just wanted to know what Mr Rawlins said. You did talk to him, didn't you?'

'Well,' said Mr Talbot – and Aleister felt suddenly very worried.

'Well,' Mr Talbot continued, 'not talked exactly. I left him a note.'

Aleister was horrified. A note – what was a note? 'So he didn't give permission?'

'Oh, I'm sure he will. It's just for a fortnight. I just need you to help me with my – my troubles.'

Aleister felt a bit frightened. He should never have come along with this strange man. What if it was all part of some evil plot? What if he was going to end up imprisoned, like poor Edmond Dantès in *The Count of Monte Cristo*?

The carriage rattled by the ruined castle. Aleister held his breath.

Mr Talbot glanced up at it. 'Interesting old place,' he said. 'Ever been there?'

Aleister could barely squeak out a No. This was it, he thought. Mr Talbot was going to lock him up in the castle and throw away the key. He imagined himself forty years later with a long, tangled, matted beard and a wild look in his eye, padlocked to a bed in a stone cell.

But they rattled on by and nothing happened.

Mr Talbot said little else the rest of the way to the station. He seemed lost in thought, perhaps brooding over his troubles. Aleister wondered what they could be and why Mr Talbot thought he could help with them. He wanted to ask, but didn't know how to begin.

'Mr Talbot,' he said. 'I was wondering ...'

He did not know how to go on. He looked at the tall, greying man beside him and felt completely tongue-tied. He realised Mr Talbot was looking back at him in almost a concerned way.

'Here,' said Mr Talbot, fishing into one of his suit pockets. 'Are you hungry? Try a peppermint.'

Aleister didn't much like peppermint. He preferred almond rock. But he took the mint. It had a sharp, pungent taste. It made him feel relaxed. He sat back in the carriage and waited till they got to the station.

They had to go to two stations, really. There was no direct train to Manchester. They had to change at Crewe. Mr Talbot hurried him off the first train and up over the bridge that crossed the tracks.

'Come on, come on,' he said. 'We mustn't miss the train.'

In fact, they had forty-five minutes to spare, as Aleister, who had read the train schedules, tried to point out. But Mr Talbot was all a-flutter until they reached the waiting room next to the Manchester platform.

'Here we are,' he said. 'Now we can relax' – but he didn't look relaxed. He sat down, then stood up, then checked and rechecked the posted time for the Manchester train, then sat down again and drummed his fingers on his leg.

Suddenly a voice called out. 'Mr Talbot,' it said in a feminine tone.

Aleister looked up. There was a lady with a big, floppy hat and a parasol. With her was a young girl, perhaps Aleister's age, in a frilly dress.

'Mr Talbot,' the lady said, 'how pleasant to meet you here. Are you on your way home?'

Mr Talbot leapt up and lifted his hat politely. 'Mrs Cavendish,' he said, 'what a surprise.' He glanced over at Aleister. 'Permit me to introduce my ... my nephew Aleister.'

Aleister looked surprised. Nephew? He looked at Mr Talbot, who wiggled his eyebrows in an odd way, as if to say, Please go along with this. Aleister stood up and said how do you do.

Mrs Cavendish smiled at him and said, 'And this is my daughter Lydia. You know Lydia, Mr Talbot.'

'Oh, yes, yes,' said Mr Talbot. 'Of course. She's a good friend of Kate's.'

'We were making our way to the ladies' waiting room,' said Mrs Cavendish, 'but now perhaps we shall wait here with you.'

'Oh, please do,' said Mr Talbot. He pulled out a large handkerchief and made a show of dusting off a seat on the bench. He was all smiles, but Aleister had the impression he was just being polite.

Mrs Cavendish gracefully deposited herself on the bench. Lydia remained standing, and Aleister glanced at her. He wasn't sure what he thought about girls, but this one seemed rather pretty.

'So where have you been with young Aleister?' said Mrs Cavendish.

'Oh,' said Mr Talbot, 'Aleister's been at school, but he hasn't really been getting on, so his parents have asked me to see if I can get a place for him as an apprentice clerk.'

Aleister listened to this in astonished horror. Not getting on? That wasn't true at all; he was top of his class. Why did Mr Talbot have to say that? Couldn't he have come up with some other excuse?

'Aleister is quite keen on the insurance business,' Mr Talbot was saying. 'Aren't you, Aleister?'

Aleister looked from Mr Talbot to Mrs Cavendish and then managed to stammer out a Yes.

'Well, that's most commendable,' said Mrs Cavendish. 'Lydia and I are just returning from a visit to my sister's. So beautiful, the country where she lives. Not like our smoky Manchester, I'm afraid.'

'I hear you can't see the hand in front of your face there,' said Aleister, trying to demonstrate that he knew something and wasn't entirely stupid.

'Well, I wouldn't quite say that,' said Mrs Cavendish, laughing, and Aleister felt even worse than before.

He sat in silence the rest of the time they waited for the train. Lydia smiled at him once, but he just blushed. Mr Talbot and Mrs Cavendish chit-chatted about the weather, then fell silent too. Awkwardness descended on the little group. Aleister was happy when the train finally arrived, and they could get out of the waiting room.

The approaching train's whistle blew, and people in the waiting room, and from other rooms Aleister couldn't see, rushed to the platform. The mass of humanity surged past Aleister as he struggled forward, and he felt almost as if he was drowning. But Mr Talbot grabbed him by the hand and pulled him forward, and soon they were in one of the train carriages, along with the Cavendishes.

'Now, isn't this cosy?' said Mrs Cavendish.

It didn't seem particularly cosy to Aleister. Just an ordinary second class railway carriage. As the train pulled out into the Cheshire countryside, he wondered if it would be rude to pull out his book to read. What he really wanted to do was ask Mr Talbot about his 'troubles', whatever they were, but he couldn't do that with the Cavendishes around.

Mrs Cavendish pulled a book out of her bag, and for a moment Aleister thought they would all read.

'What do you have there?' asked Mr Talbot, nodding at the pink volume Mrs Cavendish was holding.

'Something by the wicked Mr Thackeray,' Mrs Cavendish said with a laugh.

'I never read fiction,' said Mr Talbot.

'Oh, it's not fiction,' said Mrs Cavendish. 'These are some essays he wrote. Roundabout Papers he calls them. And would you believe that the very one I'm reading now talks about riding in a railway carriage? It says how easy it would be to murder someone in a first-class carriage.'

'Lucky we're in second class, then,' said Mr Talbot.

Mrs Cavendish ignored this. 'He really is wicked, though,' she said. 'He says that any of us could commit crimes like that and most of us are virtuous only for fear of being found out. What do you think of that, Mr Talbot?'

Mr Talbot was strangely silent.

Mrs Cavendish went on, 'You wouldn't rob or murder just because you knew you could escape detection, would you, Mr Talbot?'

Mrs Cavendish was smiling. Aleister assumed she was simply having a little fun. But Mr Talbot didn't look as if this was fun for him at all. Aleister thought he looked suddenly pale, almost ill.

Mrs Cavendish looked at Mr Talbot expectantly, but for a moment he seemed to have lost the power of speech.

Mrs Cavendish repeated her question, still smiling. 'Are you having to think about it, Mr Talbot? Perhaps you really would murder or rob.'

Finally, Mr Talbot found his tongue. 'Not murder, of course,' he said. 'Murder's immoral, un-Christian. Taking a life. The Ten Commandments.'

'And robbery?' said Mrs Cavendish.

'That too, of course,' said Mr Talbot.

Aleister thought he looked very uncomfortable. Perhaps Mrs Cavendish noticed this too, for she did not pursue the topic.

Instead, she opened her book. 'I think I shall read some more of Mr Thackeray if that's all right with you, Mr Talbot. I think he's going to be talking about stagecoaches now. How lucky we are that we have railways to carry us about the countryside instead of enduring those contraptions.'

'Yes, indeed,' said Mr Talbot.

Mrs Cavendish turned to her book. Mr Talbot looked out the window. Lydia looked at Aleister and smiled. Aleister blushed and picked up his book, escaping into the adventures of the horribly mistreated Edmond Dantès.

CHAPTER THREE

Manchester

Manchester was not exactly what Aleister had expected. He could easily see the hand in front of his face. He could even see the hordes of people bustling to and fro outside the railway station. The city was not black, exactly, though the bricks on the buildings were a curious dark colour. It was more brown, and the air had a certain texture to it, not a healthy-feeling texture. It made Aleister cough.

They shared a horse-drawn cab to the neighbourhood where both Mr Talbot and the Cavendishes lived. The horses' hooves clicked along the cobbled roads as they travelled out of the busy city centre towards a more country-like area, with small parks and houses with tiny bits of lawn in front of them.

They stopped to let the Cavendishes alight first. Mr Talbot helped Mrs Cavendish out of the cab and raised his hat to her as he said good-bye. Lydia jumped down herself. 'Good-bye, Aleister,' she said. Aleister just blushed.

'A bit awkward with the ladies, aren't you?' said Mr Talbot when he got back in the cab.

Aleister said nothing. He suddenly wished he was back in school, where he understood everything and wasn't surrounded by strange things like brown air, men who wanted him to help them with their troubles, and girls. He wondered if Mr Rawlins had missed him by now. Perhaps he was setting off to rescue him this very minute.

Mr Talbot's house was around the corner, behind a low iron fence.

'We'll have to tell Mrs Talbot and Kate something to explain your presence,' said Mr Talbot, opening the gate and leading Aleister down the path to the front door.

'Please,' said Aleister, 'please don't say I didn't get on at school. I get on very well at school. I'm the best pupil Mr Rawlins has.'

Mr Talbot focused his watery-looking eyes on Aleister. 'Of course,' he said. 'Don't worry. I'll think of something.'

He swung open the door. Aleister followed him into a neat little front parlour, a bit over-stuffed with furniture. At first he thought no one was there, but then he noticed a quiet middle-aged woman seated at the window. She looked almost like a piece of furniture herself, because draped over her lap was an enormous quilt flowing out onto the floor like a piece of overgrown upholstery.

The woman looked up from the quilt and said in a mild tone, 'Hello, Arthur. Who have you brought with you?'

She looked at Mr Talbot expectantly, a needle hovering in her hand above the giant quilt. Aleister saw that she was sewing a motto into the middle of the quilt. 'Home Swee – ' it read.

'Ah,' said Mr Talbot, seeming suddenly at a loss for words. 'This is, ah ...'

Aleister looked at him.

'This is Aleister Lister Smith,' said Mr Talbot as if performing a parlour trick. 'He's one of George's pupils.'

'And what is he doing here?' said Mrs Talbot. She spoke very softly, but there was something steely about her manner; Aleister remembered that she might be Mr Rawlins's sister.

'Ah,' said Mr Talbot. 'Well, young Lister Smith here comes from a fine, a noble, a well-placed family in our Indian colony, who, however, by virtue of some unfortunate investments, can no longer afford to keep him in school. So they asked George if he might find a suitable place for him, and George asked me about taking him on at the insurance company. As an apprentice clerk, you know.'

Mrs Talbot peered at her husband over her glasses. It seemed to Aleister that she didn't believe a word her husband had said. And why should she? None of it was true.

'Where will he stay?' she asked.

'Why,' said Mr Talbot, 'I thought, just for a while of course, with us.'

'I see,' said Mrs Talbot and resumed sewing the letter T onto the quilt.

Aleister and Mr Talbot waited for her to continue, as if it was up to her to pronounce on the plan. Aleister shuffled his feet uneasily. He wondered if it was better to be described as poor than stupid.

A voice floated down from the upper floor. 'Papa,' it said, 'is that you?'

Aleister turned in time to see a girl, perhaps a year or two older than him, bound down the stairs.

'Oh,' said the girl, 'who is this?'

'Ah,' said Mr Talbot, turning and smiling. 'Kate.'

Kate ran up to her father and gave him a hug, but she kept an eye on Aleister all the while. Aleister looked at his shoes.

There was silence for a moment, then Mrs Talbot put down her needle, rose from her seat, and spoke. 'I will tell Geraldine to set an extra place for tea,' she said. 'Kate, show young Aleister to the guest room so he can put his things away.'

Kate looked at her mother. For a moment Aleister thought she was going to object, but then she motioned to him to follow her.

Aleister looked at Mr Talbot, who nodded at him to go along, and then he turned to follow Kate. She was already halfway up the stairs.

'Come on,' she said, 'don't dawdle,' and bounded further ahead of him. Aleister watched as her long blonde hair bounced on her neck.

'Here you are,' she said at the top of the stairs, pointing to a snug little room. 'I hope it's not too frilly for you. Usually my cousin Dolly stays here when she visits from Chester.'

Aleister just nodded. It was hard to absorb so many new things at once. He put his bag down on the soft feather bed. It was covered with a quilt with a motto embroidered on it: 'Early to bed,' it said.

'So what are you doing here?' said Kate.

Aleister pondered what to reply. Kate looked at him expectantly. She had piercing blue eyes. Aleister decided he had better stick to the story Mr Talbot had told Mrs Talbot.

'I'm here to become an apprentice clerk,' he said.

'In Father's insurance company?' said Kate.

'Yes,' said Aleister.

'How boring. You don't want to spend the rest of your life in a dusty old office, do you?'

'Well, it's just that ...'

'You look more like a schoolboy than a clerk,' said Kate, eyeing his Shrewsbury blazer. 'Why aren't you in school?'

'Well, I was,' said Aleister.

'How exciting,' said Kate, and her eyes seemed to light up. 'Was it Eton? Harrow? I'd love to go to Eton or Harrow.'

'But those are boys' schools,' Aleister said indignantly.

'Of course, silly, but I'd like to go to one and learn more than they taught us at the silly girls' academy: sewing and piano and deportment. Do you like my deportment?'

She struck a pose, with her head held high and her nose slightly up in the air.

'What does deportment mean?' said Aleister. Could it be her nose, he wondered?

'It's how one carries oneself and behaves,' said Kate. She put on a funny voice as if imitating a teacher. 'A proper young lady has to have an impeccable deportment. No one should be able to say a word against her.'

'Oh,' said Aleister.

Kate laughed. 'It's all incredibly silly. I think it must be much more fun to study at a boys' school and learn real things. What do you learn there?'

'Mostly Latin and Greek,' said Aleister.

Kate looked at him searchingly. 'Well, actually, that doesn't sound much fun either. Have you read Milton?'

Aleister made a face. 'Oh, Milton,' he said.

'What's wrong with Milton?'

'Milton was our punishment piece,' said Aleister. 'If we misbehaved we had to write out lines from *Paradise Lost.*'

'But *Paradise Lost* is such fun,' said Kate.

She smiled and twirled around unexpectedly and went over to the window.

'You can see to the green from here,' she said. 'It's a nice little green, nice to go walking in. Of course, if you're not used to the air here, it may bring on coughing. But we're far enough out of the city that it's not too bad.'

Aleister nodded.

'Did you get to copy the lines about Satan rallying the fallen angels?' Kate asked.

It took a moment for Aleister to realise she was talking about *Paradise Lost* again.

'Maybe,' he said.

'I really enjoyed that part. *What though the field be lost? All is not lost.* Isn't that great?'

'But it's Satan,' he said.

'Oh, yes, of course, but it's still heroic.'

Aleister shook his head.

'I'll let you unpack,' she said. 'You can use the top drawer. And the cupboard.'

And then she was gone.

Aleister shook his head again and began unpacking. The room *was* a bit frilly, especially the frills on the edge of the quilt. Girl stuff, he thought, and wrinkled his nose. He put some clothes in the top drawer of the delicately carved chest of drawers (more girl stuff, he thought) and wondered what was in the other drawers. He ran his hand over the handle of the next drawer, but did not open it. Then he went down to tea.

Tea was a long, solemn time at the dining room table with cakes and rolls presided over by Mrs Talbot. Mr Talbot looked uncomfortable. Aleister assumed he wouldn't normally be there; he'd be at his office. Geraldine the maidservant bustled about, clearing dishes. Kate looked at Aleister a couple of times with what he thought was suppressed amusement.

'Will you be taking Aleister to the office tomorrow, Papa?' Kate asked.

Mr Talbot looked as if he hadn't heard at first; he seemed far away. Then he slowly seemed to gather himself from some distant thought and made a reply. 'Yes, yes,' he said. 'Bright and early. Best to begin at once. And Aleister is anxious to start – aren't you, Aleister?'

Aleister mumbled something.

'Best to start you on the carding desk, I think,' said Mr Talbot. 'Indexing the new policies. Fire and burglary, and losses at sea.'

'No shop talk at the table, Arthur,' said Mrs Talbot, and her husband fell silent.

After tea, Mr Talbot said he and Aleister should go for a walk. 'Just to get some air,' he said. Aleister wondered why he bothered to explain. Mrs Talbot hardly looked up from the chair she had returned to in the parlour.

Outside the house, as evening began to descend, Mr Talbot and Aleister headed towards the green. Aleister could make out the fronts of shops and houses on the other side of it.

Mr Talbot was silent at first, then burst into speech. 'You must be wondering what this is all about,' he said.

'Yes,' said Aleister.

But then Mr Talbot fell silent again, as if musing.

'You can't wear that school blazer to work, you know,' he said at last.

'Pardon me?' said Aleister.

'That blazer,' said Mr Talbot. 'It won't do. We need to get you a black coat. Maybe we can still catch Cookson. The tailor.'

Aleister hesitated. Mr Talbot pulled a pocket watch out of his waistcoat. 'No,' he said, 'it's too late. But you should be all right in your shirtsleeves; the apprentices don't really need jackets. You'll wear the tie, though.'

Aleister nodded uncertainly.

'It's a big place, the insurance company, but don't worry, I'll stick you with Jack Quinn. On the carding desk. It's straightforward work. Shouldn't be hard for a bright lad like you. And you may even enjoy it. I did when I started there. I was an apprentice clerk just like you. Well, I know, you're not really an apprentice. I enjoyed it, though. It was satisfying and simple. Life's too complicated now.'

He stopped talking and walked on in silence. The two of them circled the green. Another middle-aged gentleman hurried by. Mr Talbot absently raised his hat to him. Aleister waited for Mr Talbot to start talking again.

'Life can get very complicated,' Mr Talbot said at last. 'And yet over what? Over the simplest things. Over some urge, some compulsion, some desire. It's hard to explain.'

The dark was falling, and Aleister found it harder to make out Mr Talbot's face.

'Did you ever face some great temptation?' Mr Talbot asked. 'Or even a little one?'

'A temptation?' said Aleister.

'You know, was there ever something you really wanted that you knew you shouldn't have? Or I don't even mean that you wanted it, just that – it's so hard to explain.'

'Sometimes I like to read *The Count of Monte Cristo* when I know I should be studying Horace,' said Aleister.

'Hmm,' said Mr Talbot. 'I'm not sure that's quite the same.

Maybe, though. But you're just a child, really – how could you understand?'

Aleister bristled a little. He was not a child. He was fourteen years old. He was, well, not an adult exactly, but certainly not a child. If Mr Talbot thought he was such a child, why had he asked him to help with his troubles? Perhaps he should tell him to give up the whole thing.

'When we get to the insurance company,' Mr Talbot was saying, 'you'll see a large vault at one end of the main office. We keep our vital records in there, our charters, contracts, certificates of incorporation. That's also where we keep our cash on hand.'

Mr Talbot looked around to see if anyone was in earshot. The green was deserted. Everyone must be getting ready for dinner, Aleister thought.

'I go in the vault regularly,' said Mr Talbot. 'As chief clerk, I often have to check those vital records. I have a key to the drawers where we lock them up. Sometimes there are questions about a contract; the managing director wants to know about some particular clause, and I have one of the junior clerks copy it out. I go in and out of the vault quite freely. I am trusted. The cashier just nods to me.'

Aleister found himself nodding too. But Mr Talbot was looking down at the ground, and couldn't see.

'The cashier just nods to me,' he said. 'If he's even there. Sometimes he's gone, and I'm alone in the vault with the cash. And the files, of course. I'm not in there for the cash. That's the pennies and shillings we've collected from workingmen for their industrial insurance policies. Do you know what industrial insurance is, Aleister?'

Mr Talbot looked up for a moment. Aleister shook his head.

'It's burial insurance, really,' said Mr Talbot. 'It's money put aside to pay for funerals. Pennies, shillings: the men from the cotton factories, they pay this to us to hold, as their premium, and when they die – and they all die horribly young in those horrible factories – we pay for their funerals and give some money to the widows.'

Aleister nodded. He thought he understood.

'We don't make a lot of money on these policies,' Mr Talbot said. 'But we don't pay out a lot either, and in any case it's our sort of service to the community, to the less fortunate. And this money of theirs – I took it.'

Aleister stopped. He wasn't quite sure he had heard right. What did Mr Talbot mean, he 'took it'?

'I don't understand,' said Aleister.

'The cash in the vault,' said Mr Talbot. 'Every day I'd go in and there it was. Those pennies and halfpennies and shillings which our collectors brought in from the factories. All piled up in neat little piles on the counter in the vault behind the cashier. Not very much cash, of course. We don't let it accumulate; we transfer it to the bank every night. But during the day, it comes in, and Cheetham (he's the cashier) piles it up, and there it sits till the end of the day, when our guards take it away.'

A gentleman suddenly materialised out of the dark and hurried by. Mr Talbot fell quickly silent, raised his hat, then looked carefully around.

'Do you think he heard us?'

'I – I don't think so,' said Aleister.

'It's hard even to talk about these things,' said Mr Talbot.

He walked on in silence for a while. Aleister was beginning to become tired. They had circled the green twice now. He was getting hungry too. He wondered what time the Talbots ate dinner.

'Every day I saw the money,' said Mr Talbot, 'and I thought, It's just sitting there. No one's even looking. I could just scoop it up and take it.'

'But that would be stealing.'

'Indeed. That is what I've been trying to say.'

Aleister was silent. He tried to make sense of what Mr Talbot had just told him.

'I know,' said Mr Talbot. 'It is quite shocking. I would not have believed it of myself. I could not believe I had done it. I did not think I was that sort of person. But perhaps that Mr Thackeray was right: any of us would do it, given the chance.'

Aleister thought about this. He did not think he would steal, no matter what the chance or the temptation. He had never had money left in front of him, though.

The two of them walked on in silence.

'You could go to prison,' Aleister said finally.

'I suppose,' said Mr Talbot. 'If caught by the authorities. On the other hand – but first you must understand what it was like. Day after day to see the money there, just lying there, and being trusted to walk on by without touching it. And it was not as if it was very much money – just those pennies and halfpennies. It was just the idea of it being there, available, there for the taking. So one day I just scooped some of it up.'

Aleister shook his head. The whole idea was unbelievable.

'You shake your head,' said Mr Talbot. 'I shake my head myself.'

Aleister did not know what to say.

'If it had been only that one time,' said Mr Talbot, 'it would have been nothing. But ...'

He was silent again for a long time, and then when he spoke, it was almost a surprise.

'It is hard to imagine,' he said, 'how different a thing is after you have done it. There is the thing which you have not done, and you cannot conceive of ever doing it. But then you do it once, and suddenly it is so simple to do it again. The hard thing, in fact, is not to do it again.'

A light twinkled on across the green. Mr Talbot stopped and looked towards it, but he seemed not really to be looking at it; he seemed instead to be in some distant, mystical place, caught up in his own story.

'After that first time,' he said, 'every time I went back to the vault, I scooped up some more pennies. I was nervous, of course, and at first I'd look round very carefully, but eventually it got to become second nature, habit, routine. I went to the vault, swept up some coins, put them in my pocket, and then went about my other tasks.'

Aleister held his breath. He wondered how long this had gone on, wondered what Mr Talbot had done with the money, wondered why no one had caught him, and just wondered in general.

'The pennies and halfpennies began to build up over the weeks,' Mr Talbot went on. 'After a while, they began to turn into a substantial sum, and there came a time when I had to decide what to do: whether I was going to keep this money or use it or perhaps give it back. Mr Cheetham was beginning to shake his head over missing pennies. He was consulting the accountant. They consulted me. This might have been the time to stop, but there is something about momentum and inertia – the scientists talk about it in the natural world ...'

'Newton's laws?' said Aleister.

'Yes, exactly,' said Mr Talbot. 'And someday there will be another Newton to tell us the laws of human nature.'

They walked on. Aleister accidentally kicked a pebble which rolled into the road.

'In the meantime,' said Mr Talbot, 'some bills came in. The tailor or the grocer. I forget which. We'd been putting them off, and suddenly I thought, We can pay them with this money. And that's what I did.'

He paused for a moment, then went on. 'It wasn't as if we needed the money. Or perhaps we did. It was handy certainly. And then of course I had to take more.'

'But why?' said Aleister.

'Yes, why?' said Mr Talbot. 'It lacks logic. But I don't really want to analyse it. I want to – well, what I want is some help. Your help.'

Aleister felt suddenly anxious. Help? What sort of help? Help stealing money from the vault? What had he got himself into? He felt as if he was being dragged into a life of crime, like that boy in the book – stealing handkerchiefs, picking pockets. What was going to happen to him?

Mr Talbot pulled a piece of paper from one of his pockets. 'Look at this,' he said. 'This is what appeared on my desk on Friday, the last time I took some pennies.'

Aleister unfolded the paper, but it was too dark to read what it said.

Mr Talbot frowned and snatched the paper back. 'Here, come with me,' he said, and led the way along the pavement away from the green towards the main road. The lamplighters had been, and the gaslight flickered overhead at the intersection.

Mr Talbot thrust the paper back at Aleister. 'Here,' he said, 'read it now.'

Aleister opened the paper again. It was a piece of stationery from the insurance company. 'Saviour Assurance,' it said at the top as the printed letterhead. Beneath the letterhead there was just a single sentence, printed awkwardly.

'*I seen you take the money,*' it said.

Aleister looked up at Mr Talbot.

'Don't you understand?' said Mr Talbot. 'I'm being black-mailed.'

'Blackmailed?' said Aleister.

'Yes, yes,' said Mr Talbot. 'It's a blackmail note. Undoubt-edly from someone in the office, someone who saw me take the money. What else could it be?'

Aleister shrugged. It seemed somehow wrong for a black-mail note. 'The grammar isn't right,' he said.

'What's that?' said Mr Talbot.

'The grammar in the message,' said Aleister. 'It isn't proper.'

'Yes, yes,' said Mr Talbot, 'but what does that matter?'

'Well, haven't the people in the office been to school?'

'Yes, of course,' said Mr Talbot.

'But no one who's been to school would write a note like that,' said Aleister. Unless perhaps it was someone like Biggs, he thought, who could never get his grammar right.

'Perhaps they were trying to disguise who they were,' said Mr Talbot.

Aleister nodded. He hadn't thought of that.

'It doesn't ask for anything,' said Aleister.

'Yes, that made me wonder,' said Mr Talbot. 'And now I just wait and worry.'

'Perhaps there will be a second note,' said Aleister.

'Yes, perhaps,' said Mr Talbot. 'In any case, what I want to do now – and here is where you come in – what I want to do now is to find out who's behind this. I want you to pay attention and try to learn what you can. Speak to people, listen to them, find things out. Can you do that?'

Aleister hesitated. It wasn't exactly like doing well in school, but perhaps it wasn't too different, really, and he didn't want to lose this opportunity to have an adventure.

'I'm sure I can,' he said.

'Good,' said Mr Talbot.

CHAPTER FOUR

First Day on the Job

The next day Aleister and Mr Talbot took the bus in to work. It was crowded with men in black coats and bowler hats heading to offices in the city centre. Aleister wore an overcoat Mr Talbot had lent him, and had rolled up the sleeves, which were much too long. The coat came down to below his knees, which Aleister thought made him look ridiculous, but Mr Talbot had insisted that he not wear his school blazer. He said they could go and get Aleister a proper black coat at lunchtime.

The bus rattled along cobblestoned roads, the horses clip-clopping in front of it. Aleister's sleeves kept rolling down his arms, and he feared everyone in the bus was silently laughing at him, but he set a stern expression on his face and stared out the window. Mr Talbot sat beside him, not saying a word.

The bus rattled by row after row of similar looking houses, and eventually Aleister stopped seeing them and began to think about what lay before him. He was going to work in an office. He wondered what it would be like. He wasn't sure he was ready to work in an office, though he knew children much younger than he was got sent to the mills and the mines. An office would be different, he hoped; he didn't want to be bent over in an underground mine hauling coal in a cart.

And of course he wasn't really going to work; he was really going to spy, to find out who was blackmailing Mr Talbot. He wondered how he would do that.

Mr Talbot suddenly tapped him on the shoulder.

'It's our stop,' he said, and they clambered down from the bus into a large square. A statue of the Duke of Wellington looked benignly downwards. Aleister found it vaguely comforting, but there was no time to linger. Mr Talbot was dragging him towards one of the grimy yellow brick buildings surrounding the square.

Inside, they climbed a broad staircase and found themselves in a large room, a hall almost, full of tables and desks and chairs. It didn't seem too different from school, Aleister thought. Adults in white shirts and black coats bustled about, sitting down at the tables and, Aleister supposed, starting to work.

'What do you think?' said Mr Talbot, gesturing towards the hall.

'It's very large,' said Aleister.

'Yes,' said Mr Talbot. 'Over a dozen clerks, not to mention underwriters and assessors.'

Aleister looked puzzled.

'They're the ones who write up the insurance policies and judge the claims that come in,' said Mr Talbot. 'And of course at the far end down there is Mr Smithson's office. He's the managing director.'

Aleister looked towards the distant end of the room; the first thing he noticed, actually, was the vault: a large yawning cage, it looked like, with a grill at the front behind which was a white-haired man, presumably the cashier, Mr Cheetham. Aleister glanced up at Mr Talbot, but he was resolutely ignoring the vault. Beside the vault was the big oak door of Mr Smithson's office.

Mr Talbot beamed at Aleister and seemed proud of what lay before them. He was like an officer describing his troops. 'I'm chief clerk,' he said. 'In charge of all the clerks, the juniors and apprentices. Like Jack Quinn over there at the carding desk.'

Aleister looked where Mr Talbot was pointing, at a tall wiry youth perched on a stool and bending over a table. Hearing his name (though Aleister wasn't sure how he could from such a distance), Jack looked up and grinned.

'Let's go over there,' said Mr Talbot.

As they did so, Jack jumped from his stool, still grinning. 'What do we have here?' he said.

'A new apprentice to help you,' said Mr Talbot. 'Name of Lister Smith.'

'How do you do, Lister Smith?' said Jack, holding out his hand.

Aleister shook the proffered hand and looked Jack up and down. Could he be the blackmailer, he wondered? What did blackmailers look like? Jack looked tall and friendly and not too many years older than Aleister.

'Jack here will show you what to do,' said Mr Talbot. 'The carding desk is a vital part of what we do here, isn't it, Jack?'

It didn't look very vital to Aleister. Just a table, not really a desk, with some card trays on it: long narrow black trays stuffed with small cardboard cards standing on their sides on which Aleister could see written various names: Burns, Canfield, Charlton, Dexter, Drake ...

One of the clerks wandered over. He was a slight, dark man carrying a thick document in one hand. He nodded to Mr Talbot, then dropped the document on the carding desk, beside a pile of other documents.

'Another one for you, Quinn,' said the man.

'Thank you, Mr O'Neill,' said Jack.

'There,' said Mr Talbot. 'A newly arrived policy to file. Jack will show you how it's done.'

And with that, Mr Talbot abandoned Aleister to the carding desk and Jack.

'How do you come to Saviour?' said Jack. 'I suppose you're hoping to stay on here as a permanent clerk?'

'Oh,' said Aleister, trying to remember which story he was

supposed to tell, 'I was a pupil under Mr Talbot's brother-in-law at Shrewsbury. He recommended me for a place here.'

'Shrewsbury,' said Jack. 'Never been there. I'm from Salford myself. Just moved to Manchester a few months ago. Not that it was that big a move. Not like coming all the way from Shrewsbury. What's it like in Shrewsbury?'

'There's a castle,' said Aleister. 'But I never went there. Mostly I was in the school. Before that I was in India. My father went out there to work for the Civil Service.'

This last fact did not impress Jack as much as Aleister thought it might. All he said was, 'What's India like?'

'I don't remember much of it, really,' said Aleister. 'My parents sent me back to England to go to school when I was five.'

'And you haven't seen them since?'

'Oh, no, they came for a while when I was eight, but my father didn't much like England. He said it was easier to get on in Calcutta, so they went back. But they said it was important that an English boy get an English education, so I stayed.'

'Must be good to get away from one's father,' Jack said.

'Oh,' said Aleister. He was surprised. This was not the usual reaction he received when he spoke of not seeing his parents for so long. But he had no chance to comment, for Jack was already beginning to tell him the mysteries of the carding desk. Something about indexes, chronological order, alphabetical order – Aleister's head began to swim; he'd rather be doing the fifth declension for Latin class, hard as it was, than this.

He looked around the office. All the rows of clerks at their desks – and one lady clerk, he realised. How odd, and she had a very odd-looking contraption in front of her. He wondered what it was.

'Admiring our Miss Lewisham?' Jack said, making Aleister start.

'Oh, no, no,' said Aleister. 'Sorry.'

'No need to apologise,' said Jack. 'She does brighten up the office, though she's not the type I fancy, if you know what I mean.'

Aleister wasn't sure he knew what Jack meant, but all he said was, 'I didn't know there was such a thing as lady clerks.'

'Well, she's our first,' said Jack. 'Just started this year. You should have heard Mr Talbot go on when Mr Smithson hired her. I was just new myself, having decided it was time to find myself a respectable occupation, and then one day Mr Smithson called us all together and said that as the Saviour Assurance Company had always been at the forefront of progress ...'

In saying this, Jack somehow managed to puff himself up, thrusting his hands under his lapels to look important, as Aleister supposed Mr Smithson must look.

'As Saviour Assurance has always been at the forefront of progress,' Jack continued in his impersonation of Mr Smithson, 'we –' Jack broke off the impersonation for a moment to say, ' "We" is just him, you know.' He went on: 'We have decided to employ lady clerks, or at least one lady clerk to begin with. We are also introducing an extraordinary new machine for producing policies and contracts that look almost printed. Our lady clerk will operate it.'

'That strange-looking machine?' said Aleister.

'Yes,' said Jack. 'A typewriting machine. Going to put all of us clerks out of work, I'm thinking. They won't need us to write things out neatly; it'll all be done by that machine. And then I'll be having to find some other dodge to be getting on with. But that shouldn't be too hard. Would you like to know a secret about Miss Lewisham?'

Jack leaned confidentially forward as he asked the last question. 'Come on with me,' he added. 'You can learn about the carding desk later. Let's go out and have a smoke.'

Aleister was about to say he couldn't, that he didn't smoke, and besides, how could they go out when they were supposed to be working? He would certainly have said all these things if he had been back in Shrewsbury, but things seemed different here. Besides, perhaps Miss Lewisham was the blackmailer, and that's what Jack wanted to tell him.

Aleister followed Jack across the office to a side staircase. 'Going to check on some files in storage,' Jack said to one of the clerks who looked up as they passed. Aleister was surprised to see the clerk wink.

Down the stairs they went and into a small courtyard which seemed to have no exit: surrounding it were several grimy brick buildings. Aleister felt almost as if they were closing in on him.

'This is one of my secret spots,' said Jack. 'When I get tired of the stupid carding desk and being proper and saying "Thank you, Mr O'Neill," I come out here, relax, have a smoke.'

'But don't you get in trouble?' said Aleister.

Jack shrugged. 'Not usually. But if I do, I get over it.'

Aleister considered this novel approach to life. When he got in trouble (not that he often did), it always felt as if he'd never get over it.

Jack reached inside his coat pocket and pulled out a cigar. He bit off the end and spat it on the ground. Aleister looked on in a mixture of admiration and disgust.

'You like cigars?' said Jack. He pulled a box of matches out of his pocket.

'I never – I mean I don't know.'

Jack lit the cigar. 'Here, try a puff,' he said.

Aleister gingerly took the cigar from him and tentatively put it to his mouth. It had a surprisingly pleasant aroma, and he sucked deeply on it, thinking how interesting the smoke patterns looked rising from the tip. Then he burst into a fit of coughing.

Jack laughed and took the cigar from him. 'Takes getting used to,' he said, 'but you look like a natural.'

Aleister was still coughing, and his eyes were watery, but he felt pleased to get a compliment from someone like Jack. Jack obviously knew a lot.

A pigeon cooed overhead, then landed a few feet away. Jack stuck his hand in his pocket and tossed it a few breadcrumbs. The pigeon pecked eagerly at them.

'We better get back,' said Jack.

'But Miss Lewisham,' said Aleister hoarsely, his eyes still watery.

Jack opened the door leading back into the building. 'Oh, Miss Lewisham,' he said. 'Not really a Miss, you know.'

'What do you mean?'

Jack let the door shut again and looked round the courtyard as if someone might be hiding there. 'This is just between you and me,' he said. 'I saw her one day rushing out to meet a young man.'

Aleister shrugged. He didn't see the significance.

Jack went on, 'They got on the bus together, so I got on it too.'

Aleister still didn't see the significance, and began to think they should be getting back inside. The pigeon bobbed its way over to them and cooed. Aleister found it an annoying sound, but Jack ignored it.

'I was afraid Miss Lewisham would see me, but she was so engrossed with her young man that I'm pretty sure she didn't. They got off together and walked to one of those row houses and went in together.'

Aleister perked up at this; that was a bit scandalous. An unmarried woman going into a strange man's house? 'She went inside with him? Oh, but maybe it was her brother.'

'No,' said Jack. 'I asked around. That was no brother. It's her husband.'

'Oh,' said Aleister. 'Well, that's not scandalous – if they're married, I mean.'

Jack shook his head as if Aleister was hopelessly ignorant. 'Of course it's scandalous,' he said. 'She can't be married and work at the insurance company.'

'Why not?' said Aleister.

'I don't know why not; she just can't. Ladies can't work after they're married. Everyone knows that.'

Aleister didn't like the way Jack said this; it made him feel stupid.

'I still don't see why,' he said.

'It doesn't matter why. The important thing is knowing that it's so. Knowing things – that's power. Shakespeare said that.'

Aleister was pretty sure Shakespeare hadn't said that, but he was interested in hearing more from Jack about the things he knew: if anyone knew who the blackmailer was, it was probably Jack. He would have to make sure to spend more time with him to find out more about the people in the office.

Jack opened the door for them to go back inside. The pigeon suddenly flew up, almost clipping Aleister on the head. He ducked out of its way, and the bird flew up the staircase. Jack laughed.

Upstairs they quickly settled in again at the carding desk. Aleister looked around for the pigeon, but couldn't find it. Jack was telling him how to fill out the cards. Aleister dipped his pen in the inkwell.

Suddenly there was a cooing noise overhead. Aleister looked up. There was the pigeon, fluttering high above them, near the vaulted ceiling. The other clerks looked up too. One of them took a piece of balled-up scrap paper and threw it towards the pigeon; it fell well short, but seemed to frighten the bird, which fluttered a bit more wildly, and cooed louder.

Suddenly, except for the cooing, a hush fell over the office. Aleister looked to the far end and saw Mr Talbot with a portly, rounded, older man with a balding head and grey whiskers.

'It's Mr Smithson,' Jack whispered.

Looking up towards the pigeon, Mr Smithson marched determinedly down the centre aisle of the office. Aleister noticed that he was carrying a metallic object in his right hand. A pistol, he suddenly realised.

The pigeon seemed to be hovering directly overhead. Mr Smithson walked over to the carding desk, lifted his pistol, and fired. There was noise and smoke and a flash of light, then a wild flapping of wings.

The next thing Aleister knew, he was under the carding desk. His heart was thumping a mile a minute. He heard a woman's scream, and then a single feather floated down and landed beside him. He waited.

Jack leaned his face down under the desk. 'Have you found a new way to do the carding?' he asked, grinning.

He extended a hand and yanked Aleister to his feet. There was still smoke in the air, and Aleister could see Miss Lewisham at the other end of the office with her hand over her mouth looking terrified. Right in front of him, he suddenly realised, was Mr Smithson, inspecting him.

'Who is this boy?' said Mr Smithson.

Mr Talbot hurried to answer. 'A new apprentice I've just hired,' he said.

'Why has he no coat?'

'We're going to go and get him one today, sir,' said Mr Talbot.

'Hmph,' said Mr Smithson. 'Well, have this mess cleaned up, will you, Mr Talbot?' He pointed to a clump of feathers on the carding desk, then turned and walked away, still carrying his pistol.

'What happened to the pigeon?' said Aleister.

'Mercifully, it escaped,' said a strange voice. Aleister realised that it was the clerk Mr O'Neill standing with them.

'Shooting at an innocent creature like that,' Mr O'Neill continued, shaking his head. 'It's a sin against God's creation.'

Mr O'Neill wandered back to his desk. Aleister noticed a buzz in the air, the sound of the clerks whispering to each other. Miss Lewisham still stood by her typewriter looking horrified.

'I had better see to Miss Lewisham,' said Mr Talbot.

'Quinn, get this mess cleaned up. I'll be back for you soon, Lister Smith, and we'll go and get you a coat.'

Jack scooped up the pigeon feathers and disappeared down the hallway with them. Aleister's heart eventually stopped pounding.

Mr Talbot came back first. 'Let's go right away,' he said. 'To the new department store. We can get you a coat there.'

Outside they walked in silence. The horse-drawn carriages and buses clip-clopped by them.

'Have you found anything out?' said Mr Talbot finally.

Aleister was a bit surprised. The shooting incident had almost made him forget his mission.

'No,' he said. 'Just something about Miss Lewisham.'

'Oh, Miss Lewisham,' Mr Talbot said with a snort. 'Lady clerks. I told Mr Smithson it was a bad idea. She was almost hysterical back there.'

'Well, it was a bit scary,' said Aleister.

Mr Talbot looked at him. 'Irregular perhaps,' he said, as if it had been a completely minor matter.

'Does Mr Smithson always shoot at pigeons?' Aleister asked.

Mr Talbot shrugged. 'We've never had a pigeon before.'

This wasn't exactly what Aleister meant. He tried again. 'Why does he have a pistol?'

'You ask a lot of questions,' said Mr Talbot. 'But I suppose that's what I want you to be doing.'

They stopped to let a carriage cross in front of them. A little boy carrying a broom ran up to them bowing his head and looking eagerly at Mr Talbot. Mr Talbot fished out a halfpenny to give to him, and the boy began industriously sweeping the street where they would have to cross.

'It's all because of the Fenians,' Mr Talbot said.

'The Fenians?'

'Yes, the Fenians. You've heard of the Fenians, haven't you? What do they teach you in that school of yours?'

Aleister said nothing. They had reached a massive seven-storey building. The department store. Mr Talbot pulled open a door, and they went inside.

'The Fenians,' he said, 'are Irish hooligans who set upon innocent people.'

'Why?' said Aleister.

'To free Ireland or some such nonsense. It doesn't matter why. They killed a policeman here a few years back, and were hanged for their crimes. At least some of them were. There are no doubt others. Mr Smithson thinks so.'

'And that's why he keeps a pistol?'

'Exactly. Polishes it himself every day, and sometimes even practises shooting with it. Not in the office, of course – except for today.'

Aleister thought he detected a smile on Mr Talbot's face, but just for a moment. Then he looked serious again, peering down the aisles of the department store.

'All this jumble of merchandise,' he was saying. 'Newfangled nonsense. Things should be kept in their place.'

A shop assistant walked past. Mr Talbot stopped him.

'Where are the coats?' he said. 'We need one for this young gentleman.'

They were shown to a row of coats on a rack. Mr Talbot eyed them distastefully. 'Not even a proper tailor here,' he said, but eventually they found a coat that would fit, more or less.

On the way back, Aleister wondered whether to tell what he had learned about Miss Lewisham. Mr Talbot hadn't seemed too interested, but it might be important. Then again, he didn't see how it could be connected to blackmail – unless someone was blackmailing Miss Lewisham, and that really wasn't the issue. He meditated about this while they walked back to the insurance company.

When they got there, Mr Talbot sent him back to the carding desk. Jack was waiting for him.

'You look smart,' he said.

Aleister blushed.

And then it was on to the intricacies of carding again. Aleister found it strangely fascinating; he enjoyed figuring out how complicated systems worked, and this system seemed quite complicated. Jack laughed when he said so. 'Ah, the wonders of the filing system,' he said. 'Hasn't Mr Talbot given you his little speech?'

Aleister shook his head.

'When I started,' said Jack, 'he told me the whole history of filing. How in his day they just folded up their papers and stuck them in little pigeonholes. "Never to be seen again," he'd say, "never to be seen again".'

Jack made his voice sound just like Mr Talbot's. Aleister was impressed.

'Hey,' said Jack, 'Want to come with us for dinner?'

Dinner, Aleister discovered, was the mid-day meal, which all the clerks ate at one o'clock. He nodded and soon found himself in a group of four or five of the junior clerks and apprentices headed through the streets of Manchester to a little cook-shop.

'Good meat pies there,' said Jack.

The clerks were all talking about the pigeon-shooting. 'Can you believe Mr Smithson?' one of them said. 'A pistol in the office.'

'And where did the pigeon come from?' said another.

'Out of one of Mr Talbot's pigeonholes perhaps,' said a third, to much laughter.

Aleister was amazed by how boisterous they seemed. In the office they were all so restrained and serious.

'And who's this, then?' said a red-haired clerk, indicating Aleister, when they had arrived at the cook-shop.

'It's the new apprentice, Lister Smith,' said Jack.

'He's the one who let the pigeon in,' said a blond-haired youth with a pudgy face.

The clerks all stared at Aleister very seriously, and he felt suddenly guilty, until they burst out laughing again.

'Just having a little fun with you,' said the red-haired clerk. 'Name's Robinson, by the way.' He extended his hand.

Aleister shook it. 'How do you do?' he said.

They all carried their meat pies over to some rickety chairs near the window and someone asked Aleister where he was from.

'India,' Jack said before Aleister could answer. 'He used to hunt tigers while riding on an elephant.'

'Is that true?' said the blond-haired youth, whose name was Palmer. 'What was it like?'

Aleister was too surprised to answer. Jack laughed and said Palmer shouldn't pry. 'He doesn't like to talk about it, you know. He feels sorry for the poor tigers breathing their last after he shot them. Isn't that true, Lister Smith?'

Aleister just looked wide-eyed at Jack, wondering how he could make such things up.

'Then there was the time,' Jack went on, 'when young Lister Smith had just got down from his elephant, not realising a tiger was lurking in the underbrush. The elephant trumpeted a warning and tried to get in the tiger's way – but all he managed to do was step on Lister Smith's foot. That must have hurt. Luckily, the trumpeting scared the tiger, and Lister Smith managed to limp off. You don't still have the limp, do you?'

Aleister shook his head, as if he almost believed the story himself.

'Did the elephant really step on you?' said Palmer.

'Oh, come on,' said Robinson, 'Jack's just pulling our legs.'

'Oh,' said Palmer, and looked annoyed.

'How do you like it here?' said Robinson to Aleister.

'Here?' said Aleister, looking around the cook-shop.

'No, no, I mean at the insurance company,' Robinson said.

'Oh, give him a chance,' said Jack. 'He's only been here a morning.'

Aleister smiled tentatively, but said no more. Instead, he bit into a piece of meat pie. It was spicier than what he was used to. Robinson seemed disappointed at the lack of a reply, but the other clerks hardly paused, and were soon telling jokes Aleister didn't understand and heatedly debating the merits of two racehorses.

'Better watch out,' Robinson said to Aleister. 'Jack will have you betting soon, and you'll lose all your money.'

'Some of us already have,' Palmer muttered.

The others laughed. Robinson leaned over and whispered to Aleister, 'Palmer is always losing money, but he has a rich papa, so it doesn't really matter.'

'What's that?' said Palmer, looking at Robinson.

'Just telling Lister Smith here about your father,' said Robinson.

'Don't talk about my father,' said Palmer, glaring, and there was an uneasy silence at the table.

'Time to be getting back,' one of the clerks said, and the group of them stood up and made their way out to the street.

Robinson walked with Aleister. 'Don't mind Palmer,' he said. 'He's touchy about his father.'

Aleister nodded.

'Are you interested in lectures?' Robinson asked.

'What do you mean?' said Aleister. He thought for a moment that Robinson was going to lecture him right there as they walked.

'You know, talks on interesting subjects,' said Robinson. 'Do you go to those?'

Aleister wondered if he meant school lectures. 'You mean like on Horace or the Battle of Hastings?'

'No, no, nothing like that. Lectures on what it means to be a good clerk. Uplifting talks on how to be a clerk, a Christian, and an Englishman.'

'Oh,' said Aleister.

'It's all about hard work,' said Robinson. 'And of course being polite and respectful.'

Aleister nodded.

'The bishop gave a wonderful speech on that last month,' said Robinson.

'The bishop?'

'Yes. It's reprinted in the latest issue of *The Bee-Hive*.'

'What's *The Bee-Hive*?' said Aleister.

'Oh, I'm not explaining this well at all,' said Robinson.

But there was no time to explain further, because they were back at the office. Aleister followed Jack to the carding desk. Robinson, Palmer, and the others went to their desks further towards the front.

'Was Robinson bending your ear about the YMCA?' asked Jack.

'He was saying something about lectures and the bishop,' said Aleister.

'That's it,' said Jack. 'Christian uplift. A lot of twaddle.'

Aleister was shocked. 'How can you call it twaddle?'

But Jack just smiled and told him to get out his pen.

CHAPTER FIVE

Day Two

At the end of his first day of work, Aleister was so tired he could hardly keep his eyes open on the bus.

'Not used to hard work, I see,' said Mr Talbot, but he smiled as he said this, so Aleister didn't feel too bad. He did wonder, though, how people could do this sort of thing day after day. Riding to work, eight hours in the office, riding home.

'Oh, it's just because it's new to you,' said Kate when he told her this after supper. 'You'll get used to it.'

'I don't think I'll get used to people shooting pigeons over my head,' said Aleister.

Kate laughed. 'No, I suppose not,' she said, 'but I don't suppose that happens every day.'

He slept very soundly that night, and when Mr Talbot knocked on his bedroom door and called out to him, he didn't want to get up at all.

'Aleister,' said Mr Talbot through the door.

Aleister rubbed his eyes and at first was not sure where he was. He thought it was the house monitor at school telling him he was late for class.

He looked around for his Horace book, but couldn't see it. Then he remembered. Oh, he said to himself. He remembered the pigeon-shooting and the clerks, and the first day at work. And the hunt for the blackmailer, of course. He didn't feel he knew anything more about who the blackmailer might be.

Perhaps he should just ask Jack about it directly. Jack seemed to know all sorts of things.

But no, that was probably not a good idea. Mr Talbot wouldn't want more people to know. And what if the blackmailer was Jack himself? But that didn't seem likely; he was too nice, in his slightly rough way.

'Aleister,' Mr Talbot called again through the door.

'Yes,' said Aleister, 'I'm up. I'll be there shortly.'

It all seemed a bit complicated, he thought. Maybe it would be better just to go back to Shrewsbury and Mr Rawlins. He wondered if Mr Rawlins would be trying to get him back.

As he looked around the frilly guest room, he suddenly missed his plain old bed in the residence hall at school. But he washed his face in the washbasin, put on his clothes, and went downstairs to breakfast.

Mr Talbot was there, tapping on the table with what looked like a folded-up letter. He looked annoyed. For a wild moment, Aleister wondered if the blackmailer had written to the house. He looked around. Mrs Talbot was busy over her fried kippers. Geraldine the housemaid hovered at the table. Kate looked up at him and smiled.

'Hurry up, Aleister,' said Mr Talbot. 'We mustn't miss the bus.'

Mr Talbot stood up and slid the letter into one of his inside pockets. Aleister swallowed down a kipper. He somehow would have preferred the lumpy porridge they used to get at school.

As Geraldine cleared the plates away, Kate suddenly spoke up. 'Papa,' she said.

Mr Talbot smiled at her.

'Papa,' Kate repeated, 'I would like to try working at your office.'

Mr Talbot looked in a puzzled way at his daughter, as if not quite understanding. 'What do you mean?' he said.

'I mean working as a clerk like Aleister.'

Aleister ducked his head down. Why did she have to bring him into it?

Mr Talbot's face darkened. 'Aleister is a boy,' he said. 'And he is not a clerk; he is only an apprentice. Our apprentices are boys, and our clerks are men.'

Aleister kept his head down. Oh, don't repeat what he'd said about Miss Lewisham, he thought. But of course that's exactly what Kate did.

'Aleister told me that you have a lady clerk already. A Miss Lewisham.'

Mr Talbot looked ready to explode. 'Is this true?' he said to Aleister. 'Have you been telling my daughter stories about the office?'

Aleister stammered, still swallowing down the last of his kipper. 'I – I told her a bit about my first day,' he said. 'I didn't think there was anything wrong.'

'You didn't think at all,' said Mr Talbot.

Mrs Talbot spoke up. 'Now, now,' she said. 'You can hardly blame Aleister for wanting to talk about his first day. He told me about it too – that nasty Mr Smithson shooting at the pigeon. I had no idea such things went on in your office, Arthur.'

She smiled at Mr Talbot.

'There was no need to upset you with that story,' Mr Talbot said.

'But it didn't upset me,' said Mrs Talbot. 'I found it fascinating. What a troubled man Mr Smithson must be.'

Mr Talbot seemed surprised by this observation and said nothing. There was silence for a moment, and Aleister hoped the storm was blowing over. But then Kate spoke again.

'I should like to try being a lady clerk like Miss Lewisham,' she said. 'Of course, it might be boring, but I can't imagine it being as boring as sitting around here doing nothing but quilting.'

'Kate,' said Mrs Talbot, sounding offended.

But Kate pressed on, ignoring her mother. 'Aleister tells me that Miss Lewisham gets to operate a wonderful new machine. I think that might be interesting.'

Mr Talbot's face had darkened again. Aleister kept a worried eye on him. He feared another explosion of wrath, but instead Mr Talbot spoke very calmly.

'We must leave now, Aleister,' he said. 'Finish your kipper. We have a bus to catch. The ladies will, I am sure, excuse us, and we mustn't keep them from their household duties.'

Outside, Mr Talbot was angrier. 'Don't you ever talk to my wife and daughter about the office,' he said. 'It is not a fit topic for their ears.'

'Yes,' said Aleister.

'And I expect you to be discreet in general. There are things I do not want known. That is the whole reason you are here. Don't forget that.'

'Yes, sir,' said Aleister.

They walked on for a moment in silence, then Mr Talbot pulled a letter out of his pocket. It was the letter he had been holding at the breakfast table.

'Mr Rawlins has written me,' he said. 'He would like you to come home. Apparently, my note did not persuade him.'

He turned the letter over in his hand, rubbing it between his thumb and forefinger as if it were something distasteful.

'I shall write to him,' said Mr Talbot, 'and say that you are perfectly safe under my care. However, if you wish to return, I shall make all the necessary arrangements.'

'Oh,' said Aleister. He suddenly felt confused. He wasn't sure whether he wanted to go or stay.

'I suppose it was a foolish idea to bring you here,' Mr Talbot went on. 'You haven't discovered the blackmailer, have you?'

Aleister shook his head.

'Of course, it has only been one day. Still ...'

Aleister suddenly felt as if he definitely wanted to stay. He didn't like the suggestion that he wasn't good enough to discover the blackmailer.

'Well,' Mr Talbot was saying, 'you needn't decide this instant. We shall go into work, and perhaps you will even make some startling discovery. If not, we can talk about perhaps sending you back tomorrow.'

'I think I should like to stay, actually,' said Aleister. 'If you think I can be useful, I mean.'

Mr Talbot peered at him. 'We shall see,' he said, and then the two of them hurried to catch the bus.

Aleister's second day at work was much less eventful. No pigeons flew over the desks, and Mr Smithson did not fire his pistol. Jack taught him more about carding, and at lunch Aleister went with him and the other young clerks to the cook-shop. Robinson told him more about the YMCA; it turned out *The Bee-Hive* was their newsletter. He even invited Aleister to a lecture.

'About the Christian approach to business,' Robinson said.

'Oh, I don't know,' said Aleister. 'How would I even get there?'

'We could go together after work,' said Robinson, 'and then we could share a cab home.'

'I don't think I can afford a cab,' said Aleister. Robinson looked disappointed.

After lunch Aleister tried to get some information out of Jack.

'You know a lot about the people here, don't you?' he began.

Jack looked at him strangely. 'Why do you ask?' he said.

'Oh, no reason. Just thought you could tell me a bit, so I'd know who's who.'

'Trying to find out all my secrets, are you?' said Jack.

'No, no,' said Aleister, 'it's just interesting is all. Like your story about Miss Lewisham.'

Aleister noticed that for some reason his hand was shaking.

He was no good at finding things out, he decided. Jack would never tell him anything.

But in fact he seemed to have said just the right thing, and Jack smiled and said he was glad Aleister had enjoyed the Miss Lewisham story.

'Do you have any others?' said Aleister.

'Stories about secret marriages, you mean?' said Jack with a grin.

'No, I mean just other interesting stories. Or stories about secrets. They don't have to be about marriages.'

'Ah, so you want to find out other people's secrets,' said Jack. 'I wouldn't have thought it of you, Lister Smith.'

Aleister smiled weakly and hoped Jack would continue.

'Well,' said Jack, 'there's Palmer. He's an interesting case. His father's a big customer of the firm's. Owns some textile company, and they do all their insurance through the Saviour. That's the only reason Palmer got taken on here – as a favour to his father. He's not very bright, you know. His father's visited a couple of times to speak to Mr Smithson, I think to ask that young Palmer be made a permanent clerk, but I don't think either Mr Talbot or Mr Smithson want that. When he finishes his apprenticeship, they'll probably let him go.'

'I see,' said Aleister.

'Robinson you already know all about,' said Jack. 'With all his talk about Christian uplift. But that's not very secret. If you want someone secret, there's Mr Brooks. Do you see him down there?'

Aleister looked where Jack was pointing, at a quiet, dark-haired man bent over one of the desks.

'He's pretty new here and keeps to himself. Says he's from Australia, but I don't know. Sounds Irish to me, and I should know – I'm Irish myself. Maybe he's a secret Fenian.'

'Really?' said Aleister.

'Hard to know for sure,' said Jack. 'And then there's Mr O'Neill – '

But before Jack could say more about Mr O'Neill, a young boy no more than Aleister's age appeared at the carding desk.

'I have some new pens and blotting paper for you,' said the boy.

'Thanks, Billy,' said Jack. 'Do you know our new apprentice? Aleister Lister Smith.'

'How do you do?' said Billy.

Aleister nodded.

'This is Billy Cooper, the office boy,' said Jack.

'You going to bet on the races?' said Billy.

'Oh, I don't know,' Aleister said doubtfully.

'I have a sure winner,' said Billy.

'Billy always has sure winners,' said Jack with a grin. 'Only they never win.'

'That's not true,' said Billy. 'Just last month, there was that horse – what was its name?'

But before Billy could come up with the name, a voice called out, loudly and demandingly. 'Billy,' it said. 'Where's my pens?'

It was Palmer. Billy scurried over to his desk. Aleister watched as Billy handed over some pens and blotting paper. Palmer scowled. Billy looked a bit frightened.

'Palmer's a bit of a bully,' said Jack.

At the end of the day, Robinson came by the carding desk and asked if Aleister had thought about going to the lecture.

'Did you mean this evening?' said Aleister. He had thought he would have more time to decide.

'Yes, look, here's the notice in *The Bee-Hive*.' Robinson opened the newspaper. There was a headline about the evils of drink. Aleister giggled.

'What's so funny?' said Robinson.

'Oh, it's just that in Shrewsbury the Bee-Hive is the name of a pub.'

A strange voice suddenly intervened. 'Trying to win a new recruit, Robinson?' it said.

Robinson and Aleister looked up to see a tall, thin, curly-haired man with a sharp, pointy nose and penetrating eyes.

'Mr Carruthers,' said Robinson.

'And who's this?' said Mr Carruthers, indicating Aleister.

'It's Lister Smith, the new apprentice,' said Robinson. And to Aleister he said, 'This is Mr Carruthers, one of the assessors.'

Aleister nodded and tried to remember what assessors did. Write up policies? No, that was the underwriters. Something about judging claims.

Mr Carruthers was looking Aleister up and down. 'Don't let Robinson mesmerise you with that YMCA mumbo jumbo,' he said. 'Mr Darwin and Professor Huxley have put paid to all those notions.'

'Mr Carruthers,' said Robinson, 'that's very unfair. Just because some modern investigators have suggested that the earth is older than we thought and that men may be descended from, from – '

'From apes,' said Carruthers.

'From apes, if you will,' said Robinson. 'That doesn't mean we can't still learn from Christian teachings and make ourselves better clerks.'

'Lister Smith,' said Mr Carruthers, 'what do you think of all this? Are you a follower of Mr Darwin's, or do you think the universe was created in six days as God's present to Man?'

'I – I'm not sure,' said Aleister.

'You'll have to choose sides,' said Mr Carruthers. 'That's what life is all about. Choosing sides.'

He straightened his coat and headed towards the door.

'Don't listen to him,' said Robinson. 'He just likes to mock. But do come to the lecture this evening.'

And in the end Aleister did. Mr Talbot gave him some money for the cab, though he muttered something about it being a waste of time, and Robinson and Aleister made their way across the square to the nondescript building that housed the YMCA.

Up the steps they went to rooms near the top of the building, where a sign announced that these were the offices of the Young Men's Christian Association. Down a corridor they went, following a few other men who looked like clerks, into a small room with chairs put out for a talk. About half the chairs were full.

'A good turnout,' said Robinson.

A man named Ellis, who was introduced as a successful textile manufacturer, proceeded to address the assembled clerks.

'Hard work is the key,' he said. 'It has been my watchword all my life and served me well. Patience, attentiveness, and hard work – those are the three keys to success.'

The clerks in the audience listened intently. Aleister looked around and tried to understand the proceedings.

'It is never too early to start on this course,' Mr Ellis was saying. 'One is never too young to learn this lesson.'

Aleister suddenly felt as if Mr Ellis was looking right at him. He did feel very young in the room; everyone else in the audience looked much older, though not as old as Mr Ellis himself, whose hair was mostly gone. Just a fringe of white surrounded the top of his head, which glistened with sweat.

'But these three things,' Mr Ellis continued, 'are not enough. They are enough to give you a chance at success – I won't say they will guarantee it, for time and tide happeneth to us all. But if you work hard, pay attention, and wait your turn, you will have a good chance of finding success in the worldly sphere: a good income, a house in the country, a good position.'

Mr Ellis pulled out a handkerchief and mopped his brow. The audience waited attentively.

'But the worldly sphere is not all there is,' said Mr Ellis. 'What profits a man to gain the whole world and lose his soul?

Mankind is a cut above the animals; we do not just struggle for existence. Even if it is true, as some assert, that we have our origins in the animal kingdom, still it is also true that we have evolved, if I may be permitted to use one of the fashionable words of the day. I hope Mr Darwin won't mind.'

The clerks in the audience laughed. Aleister remembered what Mr Carruthers had said. Did one really have to choose sides? Which side should he be on, then? Robinson seemed nice, but he remembered seeing a picture of Darwin, and he'd seemed nice too: like a kindly old father with a newspaper on his lap and some books at his feet. He wondered if his own father looked like that; it had been a long time since he'd seen him.

The clerks were applauding. Mr Ellis had finished. Aleister realised he hadn't been listening to Mr Ellis's conclusion. He hadn't heard what he'd said about what there was beyond the worldly sphere.

The clerks were standing up and milling about, talking and smiling. Aleister thought he recognised one of them.

'Isn't that Mr Brooks?' he said to Robinson.

Robinson looked over at the dark-haired clerk.

'Oh, yes,' he said. 'I often see Mr Brooks here. He's quite interested in Christian matters, I think, though he doesn't stay to talk about them usually.'

And indeed Mr Brooks was now making his way towards the door, not lingering with the other clerks to have tea.

'So did you enjoy the talk?' Robinson said.

'I was surprised he mentioned Darwin,' said Aleister.

'Oh, it was just a joke,' said Robinson.

'You know, Darwin went to my school,' Aleister said. 'I saw it mentioned somewhere.'

'Really?'

'It was a long time ago, of course.'

'I've nothing against Darwin myself,' said Robinson. 'Some people think he's terrible and a threat to Christian morality, but I don't see it that way. He raises issues that are a challenge to our faith, but that's good; we need challenges, don't you think?'

Aleister nodded uncertainly.

'Now let's get some tea before it's all gone,' Robinson said. And he led Aleister over to the tea table.

When they left the hall, it was already dark. Aleister felt suddenly nervous. The city seemed ominous when you couldn't see beyond a few yards. Who might be lurking round the corner?

'It's very dark out,' said Aleister once they were in a cab rolling its way out of the city.

'Yes,' said Robinson. 'Different, isn't it? I like it this way, without the hustle and bustle. But you should see it on Guy Fawkes Night. It will be all lit up then. Bonfires everywhere.'

'Yes,' said Aleister, suddenly thinking that Robinson did not understand him at all. He found himself hoping to be back in Shrewsbury by Guy Fawkes Day. He needed to get back to some place familiar.

CHAPTER SIX

Messages and Visitors

Aleister felt better the next day. The sun was shining, Kate was cheerful at breakfast, and on the way to work Mr Talbot told him he had written to Mr Rawlins suggesting that Aleister stay on just a while longer and assuring him that Aleister was perfectly safe.

At the carding desk Jack asked if he had enjoyed the visit to the YMCA. 'Did Robinson convert you?' he said.

'It wasn't like that,' said Aleister.

'He dragged me off to a speech there one time,' said Jack. 'All about the evils of smoking, especially for the young. How it could lead to all sorts of corruption and immorality. And besides, it might injure my health.'

Aleister remembered their cigar-smoking session in the courtyard on the first day.

'Do I look unhealthy to you?' said Jack.

Aleister looked Jack over and had to concede that no, he looked perfectly healthy.

'Immorality – now that's another matter,' said Jack with a grin.

Aleister looked shocked.

Jack laughed. 'Don't be so earnest, Lister Smith. I'm just joking.'

But Aleister wondered.

At lunch he went with the clerks again. Robinson asked him with a smile if he'd survived the lecture. Palmer muttered something about lectures being silly, then announced that he wasn't really hungry and headed back to the office.

Jack laughed. 'What's he going to do in the office all by himself? Everyone goes for dinner at one.'

One of the other clerks said, 'Maybe his father's here again to demand that his son be made managing director.'

Everyone laughed at that, then got down to eating their meat pies.

Afterwards Jack suggested going out for a smoke.

Robinson frowned. 'You know how I feel about the evils of tobacco, Jack,' he said.

'You talk like a bishop,' said Jack.

'Well,' said Robinson, 'as you very well know, the Bishop of Manchester himself has said this, and I am happy to agree with him.'

'You're not going to agree with our "Bishop", are you, Lister Smith?' said Jack, nodding towards Robinson.

Aleister hesitated. 'I don't know,' he said.

'Well, never mind,' said Jack. 'There's no time now anyway.'

Jack seemed to think the whole thing was a big joke and kept calling Robinson 'the Bishop' all the way back to the office.

'What about drinking, Your Eminence?' he said to Robinson as they entered the building. 'Are you opposed to that too?'

But Robinson never got a chance to answer, and Aleister was surprised to see Jack's laughing expression vanish completely from his face.

A burly middle-aged man with dark black hair, a not very well shaven face, and dishevelled clothes stood in the lobby of the insurance company. His eyes shone very brightly, Aleister thought.

'Jack, my boy,' the dishevelled man said.

'What are you doing here?' said Jack.

'Is that any way to greet your father?' said the man, speaking with a slight Irish accent.

'I'm working now,' said Jack, and proceeded up the stairs.

His father followed him, but seemed a bit unsteady. Aleister wondered why.

Jack fairly leapt up the stairs, his father staggered after him, and the other clerks waited, then followed at a discreet distance.

'Don't you have a few minutes to spare for your old Dad?' said Jack's father, swaying a bit alarmingly at the top of the stairs.

Jack stopped halfway to the carding desk, and came back a few steps. 'Is it just minutes you want,' he said, 'or money for drink?'

'That,' said Jack's father, holding onto a wall now for support, 'that is an insulting insinuation.'

At least Aleister thought that was what he said. It came out sounding a bit slurred. He had never seen anyone drunk before, but it occurred to him that he was seeing a drunk person now.

'Why do you never visit any more?' Jack's father was saying. 'Have you gone and become too good for us, you with your fine clerk's job in this fine establishment?' He looked around the building, but it didn't seem to Aleister that his eyes really focused on anything.

Jack just shrugged and moved away, towards the carding desk. His father followed him and started shouting.

'Look at how this ungrateful son treats his own father,' he said, pointing to Jack.

Jack seemed to wince. Everyone else in the main room turned around to look at the spectacle. Jack's father kept shouting.

'He ignores me, my son does. Never visits. Never brings home the money he owes.' He walked over to the carding desk. 'You owe me money,' he said to Jack in a slightly lower voice.

He reached for some of the papers on the desk. Jack started

to grab them from him, then stopped, as if fearing they would get torn if there was a struggle.

'You waste your time on these papers,' said his father, throwing them up in the air, 'and have no time for me or your poor Mum.'

Jack grabbed at the papers as they flew through the air. His father suddenly collapsed on the floor. Aleister thought he might be crying.

Suddenly Mr Talbot appeared. Some of the other clerks followed behind him, as if eager to see more.

'What's going on here, Jack?' said Mr Talbot.

Jack was still gathering up papers. He stood up quickly and spoke in a flustered voice, not sounding at all like the usual Jack. There even seemed to be a hint of an Irish accent when he spoke.

'It's just my father,' he said. 'Come for a visit.'

Mr Talbot looked down at Jack's father with a hint of disgust.

'This is a place of business,' he said, 'not a place to receive visitors. Besides, your father looks unwell.'

'I'll take care of it, sir,' said Jack.

'Right away,' said Mr Talbot, and left.

Jack tidied up the papers and helped his father to his feet. Most of the clerks began drifting back to their desks, but Palmer lingered and looked on with evident distaste.

'Bloody Irish,' he said. 'Always drunk. Don't know anything about English manners.'

'Watch yourself,' said Jack.

'Why?' said Palmer.

'Someone will get you if you can't keep your thoughts to yourself.'

'Who? You?'

'I didn't say that,' said Jack, and proceeded to help his father out of the main room back towards the staircase. His father looked half asleep.

Palmer shrugged and started to go back to his desk, then noticed Aleister looking at him.

'What are you staring at?' he said.

'Nothing,' said Aleister.

Palmer grunted and walked away.

Aleister found it hard to concentrate the rest of the day. Jack came back to the carding desk, but Aleister didn't know how to ask him what had happened with his father. They just worked silently until five o'clock.

'Right,' said Jack when the clock struck the hour. 'Time to go.'

'Is everything all right?' Aleister finally managed to say.

Jack looked at him and shrugged. 'Palmer's just an ignorant sod,' he said. 'And I'm used to English bigotry and name-calling.'

'I meant about your father,' said Aleister.

'Oh,' said Jack, and seemed suddenly to find it very important to look at one of the contracts on the carding desk. 'He'll be all right,' he said at last. 'I put him on a bus back to Salford. He's not been well lately. Out of work. A cotton worker, you know, but trade has been slack, as he likes to say.'

Aleister nodded. Jack turned again to the contracts on the carding desk, as if wanting Aleister to leave him alone. Aleister put his pen away. Mr Talbot suddenly loomed over him.

'Ready to go, Aleister?' said Mr Talbot.

Aleister nodded, and started to leave with Mr Talbot, then turned back and said, 'See you tomorrow, Jack.' He wished he could say something more to make Jack feel better.

'Come along, Aleister,' said Mr Talbot, 'don't dawdle.'

Aleister hurried after Mr Talbot. Down the stairs, into the street, into the mass of clerks and businessmen heading home. He felt suddenly engulfed.

'I've received another communication,' said Mr Talbot.

Aleister had not really been paying attention. 'Pardon me,' he said.

73

'Another communication,' said Mr Talbot. 'A message. A note.'

'From Mr Rawlins?' said Aleister. He was still not really paying attention. He was thinking about poor Jack and his troubles with his father, and also trying not to get jostled by the stream of clerks hurrying by.

'Not from Mr Rawlins,' said Mr Talbot. 'From our friend, the one who saw me in the vault.'

'Oh,' said Aleister, suddenly understanding. 'Oh. What did he say?'

'I will show you later,' said Mr Talbot.

CHAPTER SEVEN

Waiting

The note didn't say much. Just one line on another piece of insurance company stationery.

'I found it on my desk after lunch,' said Mr Talbot as he and Aleister walked from the bus stop towards the Talbot residence. 'I don't think it was there before, though with all the commotion caused by Jack's father, who knows?'

Aleister was only half listening. He was standing beneath a street lamp rereading the blackmailer's second message. 'Meet me Tuesday night,' it said.

'Meet him where?' said Aleister.

Mr Talbot shrugged. 'I know no more than you,' he said.

They walked on in silence towards the Talbot house.

'He will have to write again,' said Aleister just before they reached the house.

'Yes,' said Mr Talbot, 'and in the meantime we can only wait.'

Aleister nodded, but all through dinner he brooded over the situation. Kate laughed at him afterwards.

'Why so solemn?' she said. 'You look like a miniature preacher, frowning over our sins.'

'I'm not a miniature,' said Aleister.

'No, no, of course not,' said Kate. 'Why, some day you may even be as tall as me.'

And she danced away, laughing.

The next three days were difficult, the Friday and Saturday

at work, just waiting. Jack was more subdued than usual, and none of the clerks seemed in very high spirits. Perhaps it was because of the cold rain that fell and got everyone wet and out of sorts.

Aleister would glance at Mr Talbot whenever he walked past the carding desk, but Mr Talbot always just gave a little shake of his head, as if to say, No, not yet.

So Sunday came and a day off work. No message would come then. In the morning Mr Talbot told Aleister, 'We are going to the morning service. You may join us if you like.'

'At church?' said Aleister.

'Not church,' said Mr Talbot, looking mortally offended. 'Chapel. This is not a Church of England family. If you want that, you should go to the gentry in Fallowfield.'

'Oh,' said Aleister, feeling abashed.

Mr Talbot seemed suddenly apologetic. 'I'm sorry, Aleister,' he said. 'If you would rather attend at an Anglican church, we can arrange that for you.'

'No, no,' said Aleister, 'that's fine.'

And so the family went off to the local Nonconformist chapel. After what Mr Talbot had said, Aleister expected it to look like the tiny chapel at school where morning prayers were said every day, but instead it was an imposing Gothic building that looked more like a castle than a church.

'This is the chapel?' said Aleister.

Mr Talbot looked at him sharply, then sighed. 'The new chapel, yes, though it pretends to be something from the Middle Ages. We used to have a fine, simple chapel, but now we have this, this – '

'Arthur,' said Mrs Talbot, 'hush.'

They entered the building and took seats in one of the middle rows of pews.

'Look,' said Kate in a whisper to Aleister, 'there's Lydia Cavendish all dressed up and looking around to see if anyone's noticed her.'

Aleister looked and saw the girl from the train sitting just a couple of pews ahead of them. He admired her carefully braided hair and frilly dress. Suddenly she caught his eye and smiled at him. He felt embarrassed, and turned away. Kate was looking at him and barely suppressing a laugh.

'I think you're in love with Lydia Cavendish,' she said.

Aleister felt indignant and thought he should make a clever remark to put Kate in her place, but before he could think of one, the service began. The congregation rose and sang 'All the way my Saviour leads me'. It was not a hymn Aleister knew, but he mumbled along out of the hymn book.

The whole service was a bit different. There were lots more hymns than he was used to. 'Tell me not of earthly pleasures' and 'There's a light upon the mountains'. And then the preacher got up before the congregation, looking darkly at everyone from beneath bushy black eyebrows and warning that they were all sinners from birth and doomed to eternal hellfire unless they could somehow acquire grace. Aleister wondered how he was supposed to do that, and he rather wished the preacher wouldn't stare at him the way he seemed to be doing.

The service ended with a pleasant hymn about it being his father's world, but Aleister was still feeling shaken by the disconcerting sermon.

As he walked out of the chapel with Kate, trailing behind Mr and Mrs Talbot, he asked her about it. 'I've never heard a sermon like that,' he said.

'No?' said Kate, hardly paying attention; she was looking at the other members of the congregation as they filed their way out of the building.

'No,' said Aleister. 'All those horrible descriptions of eternal damnation. Is it like that every week? Doesn't it make you feel, I don't know, frightened?'

Kate turned back to look at Aleister. 'Frightened?' she said. 'Oh, Aleister, you take everything so seriously. It's just Reverend Eccles trying to get us to be good.'

Aleister considered this for a moment. 'Does it work?' he said.

But Kate had bounded down the pathway, and did not hear him.

After chapel, there was mid-day Sunday dinner: a silent affair, with Geraldine bringing in the roast beef and potatoes, then disappearing to let the family eat in peace.

All the meals were silent, Aleister reflected, at least compared to the refectory meals at school, with the boys tossing rolls back and forth. But this Sunday dinner was especially so.

Afterwards the family went for a walk on the green, where a number of other families were walking as well. Mr and Mrs Talbot nodded to some of them, and Kate said hello to some of the girls, who seemed more interested in Aleister than in her. Aleister wished they wouldn't stare at him.

Back at the house, the family went into the parlour. Mr Talbot took down a large Bible and settled himself in the large armchair near the fireplace. Geraldine had lit the fire and also came in with some lemonade. Mrs Talbot sat in her smaller armchair and took up some small book to read. Kate sat restlessly across from her, and Aleister sat down too, wondering if he could go and fetch his copy of *The Count of Monte Cristo*. He wondered if they would let him read such a thing on a Sunday.

'That was a powerful sermon from Reverend Eccles today,' Mr Talbot said, looking up from the Bible.

Mrs Talbot looked up too, but only nodded.

'We are all sinners,' said Mr Talbot. 'We can't help ourselves. It is the human state.'

'But we will be redeemed by grace,' said Mrs Talbot.

'Yes, of course,' said Mr Talbot, 'but redemption is out of our hands. We must merely be ready to accept it. There is nothing for us to do but wait.'

'Now, Arthur, you know that isn't what the Reverend meant,' said Mrs Talbot.

'I know that we are fallen and nothing we do can save us.'

'Yes,' said Mrs Talbot, 'but that does not mean we are to do nothing.'

'I can think of nothing else it might mean,' said Mr Talbot and looked gloomily down at his Bible.

Mrs Talbot looked puzzled and seemed almost about to say something, but checked herself.

Aleister found the words of one of the morning's hymns running through his head as Mr Talbot spoke. 'Weary was our heart with waiting,' he remembered the hymn going, 'and the night watch seemed so long.'

He felt weary himself with waiting, and looked around the parlour for something to occupy his mind. His eye lighted on a feathery looking metallic picture attached to the wall. He could barely make out the image of a woman on it.

'Do you like Papa's daguerreotype?' Kate asked, noticing the direction of his gaze. 'It's a picture of Grandmama, taken a long time ago.'

Aleister looked again at the silvery picture. 'What's a daguerreotype?' he said.

'Oh, just the old name for photograph, I think,' said Kate.

'It looks very different from a photograph, though,' said Aleister.

They both looked at it. Aleister admired its fine, spidery lines. He suddenly realised that Mr Talbot was looking at him.

'I can't allow Kate to mislead you,' said Mr Talbot. 'A daguerreotype is not a photograph at all.'

'Oh,' said Aleister.

'Daguerreotypes were invented by Louis Daguerre,' Mr Talbot went on. 'A Frenchman. It is quite curious, really. He invented his daguerreotypes at the very same time that real photographs were being invented here in England by Henry Fox Talbot. A distant relative of ours.'

'But you have a daguerreotype here,' said Aleister.

'Yes, yes,' said Mr Talbot. 'When I was a very young man – hardly a man at all, in fact, hardly older than you – I tended to experiment. Quite excusable in the young, I think. And there is something charmingly delicate about daguerreotypes. So precise and yet so fragile.'

He gazed at the daguerreotype on the wall. 'Of course, they were not practical at all,' said Mr Talbot, 'and so I gave them up.'

Aleister was silent. He felt sorry for the abandoned daguerreotypes.

'But Papa takes real photographs now,' said Kate. 'Some of these on the walls are his.'

Aleister looked around at pictures of Kate and her mother and at what looked like the street in front of the Talbots' house.

'I haven't even done any of those for quite a while,' Mr Talbot said.

'We could do one today,' said Kate.

'It's Sunday,' said Mr Talbot.

'Are we not allowed to take photographs on a Sunday?' said Kate. 'There's just nothing we're allowed to do. It's boring.'

'Sunday is the day to contemplate the Lord's will and His creation,' said Mr Talbot.

Mrs Talbot spoke up. 'I don't think taking a photograph would detract that much from the sanctity of the day, Arthur.'

'And it would be such fun,' said Kate, smiling winningly at her father.

Aleister wasn't sure the idea of fun would win Mr Talbot over, but he had noticed that Kate's smile was very effective with her father.

Mr Talbot hesitated. Kate seemed to get another idea.

'It would also be a good way to record Aleister's stay with us,' she said.

This argument seemed to do the trick. Mr Talbot said he

supposed there would be nothing wrong with a short photographic session out on the green, and before the words were even out of his mouth Kate was racing out of the room, saying she had just the thing for it.

A moment later she came back with a realistic-looking cutlass.

'What on earth is that, dear?' said Mrs Talbot.

'It's a make-believe sword,' said Kate. 'From that play we did at school about pirates.'

'And why do you still have the sword?' said Mrs Talbot.

'Oh,' said Kate, looking suddenly a bit red-faced. 'Well, I just liked it so much that – well, I think they said we could keep our swords. I did like being a pirate.'

'Young lady,' said Mrs Talbot, 'we will have to return that sword immediately. I will not have a thief in the family. Tell her, Arthur.'

Mr Talbot had gone very pale, and didn't seem able to speak at all.

Mrs Talbot looked at her husband expectantly, but still he remained silent.

'Arthur,' said Mrs Talbot, 'are you all right?'

'Oh,' said Mr Talbot, 'yes, I am quite all right. Just surprised. And of course theft cannot be tolerated. We are not that sort of family. But perhaps there has simply been some sort of misunderstanding. Kate did say they told her she could keep the sword.'

'Arthur, you know very well they told her no such thing.'

Mr Talbot seemed to recover at this point and said, 'Yes, of course, you must be right. Kate, you will go with your mother and return the sword tomorrow.'

'Oh, but Papa,' Kate began.

'No, that's an end on it,' said Mr Talbot. 'Now I think you had better go to your room. We won't be taking photographs after all, not with stolen property.'

'But I had such a wonderful tableau in mind,' said Kate.

'Aleister could be rescuing me, like Saint George and the dragon. He would hold the cutlass, and I would be the swooning damsel.'

Kate handed Aleister the cutlass, put her hand to her forehead, and leaned back as if about to faint. 'Oh, save me, Saint George,' she said to Aleister. 'Here,' she added, 'put your arm around my waist. Your left arm. Hold the cutlass in your right and look very stern.'

Aleister did as he was told, but felt completely befuddled. Mr Talbot, he noticed, was beginning to look very angry.

'Kate,' said Mr Talbot, 'there will be no photographs today, certainly none with that stolen sword, and none of this foolish make-believe about Saint George and the dragon.'

'Oh, Papa, you make a very good dragon. Perhaps Aleister should slay you.'

'Kate,' said Mr Talbot, 'go to your room this instant.'

And with this Mr Talbot took the sword from Aleister's hand and sent his daughter out of the parlour. And so there were no photographs that day of Kate and Aleister.

CHAPTER EIGHT

Dreams and Discussions

Monday passed slowly, partly because Aleister was so tired. He hadn't slept well; he'd had bad dreams. He thought perhaps it was because of what had happened about the photograph and afterwards.

Kate had stayed in her room through supper, and there had been a chilly atmosphere in the house. No one said anything, and Aleister felt very uncomfortable.

As soon as he could, he excused himself from the table and went up to his own room. He thought perhaps he would read some of *The Count of Monte Cristo* and escape the unpleasantness around him.

Just before he got to his room, he heard a voice call out to him.

'Psst. Aleister.'

It was Kate calling from her room down the hall. Aleister looked to see if anyone was watching, then cautiously made his way to her door. She opened it a crack.

'Come inside,' she said.

Aleister hesitated.

'Come on,' she said, 'before they see you.'

'I don't know,' said Aleister. 'You're being punished, and besides ...'

'Oh, don't be a nincompoop,' said Kate, and dragged him in.

'There,' she said. 'Sit on the chair.'

He did so, and she sat on her bed. He looked around her room. There was a shelf over her bed with some books on it: an introduction to French and some novels by Thackeray. A black doll with big staring eyes looked at him from one of the pillows.

'Isn't it silly?' she said. 'All this fuss over a little sword.'

'Well, you shouldn't have stolen it,' said Aleister.

'Oh, don't be such a prig,' said Kate. 'You're as bad as Papa.'

Mentioning her father seemed to make her sad, then defiant. She cast down her head, then said, 'I don't think I shall ever speak to Papa again.'

'You don't mean that,' said Aleister.

'You know nothing about it,' she replied with a toss of her head.

Aleister didn't know what to say. He looked down and studied the pattern in the carpet.

'Oh, you're boring,' said Kate, and threw herself face down on her bed.

Aleister thought this would be a good time to leave. He got up and made for the door, eased it open quietly, and went out, taking just a single moment to look back at Kate. She had her head turned away from him and made a point of not turning to look at him. He shrugged and closed the door behind him.

Back in his room, he lay down on his bed and tried to read *The Count of Monte Cristo*, but he wondered if Mr Talbot would somehow find out and reproach him for reading such frivolous material on the Sabbath. He also felt very tired. It had been an exhausting day somehow, after an exhausting week. The words began to swim in front of his eyes. The book fell from his hands, and strange images appeared before him as he drifted off to sleep.

He dreamed he was climbing a long, curving stairway. Robinson was climbing ahead of him and kept turning around and urging him on, but his legs began to feel heavier and heavier. It was as if he would never get to the top.

'Come on,' said Robinson. 'We're going to meet the Bishop.'

The staircase curved, and from around the corner someone suddenly leapt out at Aleister. It was Mr Carruthers.

'Well, Lister Smith,' said Mr Carruthers, chortling, 'have you come to see the Bishop? Who do you think the Bishop is?'

And then he vanished, and Robinson vanished, and Aleister found himself at the top of the staircase, up on the roof of a giant castle. Arrows whizzed overhead. Knights wearing crosses leaned over the parapets.

'We must save the lady,' said one of them. He sounded like Jack. 'The lady, the lady.'

Aleister looked around for the lady, and there she was. It was Miss Lewisham, seated in the middle of the castle roof, working at her typewriter. She was typing so fast, her hands seemed almost to be blazing, and then suddenly the typewriter itself was ablaze.

Miss Lewisham screamed.

'The lady, the lady,' said Jack.

Aleister rushed forward to save her. He had a sword in his right hand, and he put his left arm around Miss Lewisham's waist. The typewriter blazed in front of them. Aleister tried to lead Miss Lewisham away, but she wouldn't leave.

'My typewriter,' she said, 'my typewriter. I need to take a photograph of my typewriter.'

Kate leapt forward, holding a large, awkward camera.

'We can photograph it with this,' she said.

But a giant bird swooped down on them and grabbed the camera from Kate's hand.

'Oh,' said Kate. 'Oh. What will we do now?'

Vainly, Aleister waved his sword at the bird.

'Up on the parapet, Aleister,' said a new voice. 'That's the only way to catch your bird.'

It was Mr Talbot. Aleister hesitated, but Mr Talbot urged him on. Gingerly, Aleister climbed up on the ledge of the parapet. The bird suddenly swooped down at him.

'Kill it, Aleister,' cried out Mr Talbot. 'Kill it.'

Aleister lunged for the bird, and at that moment felt himself falling off the edge of the castle. The bird soared far above him, and Aleister began plummeting towards the ground. Below him he could see a large quilt, and on it, in huge letters, 'God helps those who ...'

But he didn't have time to read the rest of the quilt; he had to do something to save himself. He began to wave his arms, hoping somehow to fly like the giant bird, or at least slow his descent. And it seemed for a moment as if he had indeed slowed down and was perhaps even rising. Perhaps he could fly like a bird; it was his secret talent that no one knew about and no one else had.

But then suddenly a gust of wind threw him off balance. He was plummeting again, right towards the middle of the quilt. He closed his eyes and –

Bang!

He was awake on the floor of the guest room in the Talbots' house, tangled up in the quilt from the bed, with *The Count of Monte Cristo* lying beside him.

He felt groggy for a moment, wondered what time it was, looked out the window and saw only the dark, and decided to go to bed properly. He undressed and washed his face, and climbed between the sheets.

In a moment he was asleep again.

When he awoke in the morning, he felt reasonably refreshed, but by the time he got to work, he was tired again. He must have dreamed more dreams than he remembered.

The work Monday morning dragged. Jack did not seem talkative, and without him to provide entertainment, Aleister found the novelty of the carding desk wearing off. Besides, he could barely keep his eyes open; he almost fell off his stool one time.

'Careful,' said Jack, but then said no more.

At lunch the juniors and apprentices seemed subdued too. One of them started talking about the trade depression. 'They'll be letting us all go,' he said, biting into his Cornish pasty.

'Yes,' said another, 'and they'll be giving all the jobs to lady clerks with their typewriters instead of us.'

'Or to the Germans,' said a third. 'I hear from Arnprior at k that they're hiring dozens of German clerks. Somehow they think Germans are better with their pens than native-born Englishmen.'

Even Robinson seemed gloomy. 'It may be impossible to get on in this city,' he said. 'I saw a circular at the YMCA, though, advertising new opportunities.'

'Where?' said one of the other clerks, a tall, thin youth named Crosbie. He was the one who had complained about the Germans.

'Some place called Manitoba,' said Robinson.

'Where's that?' said Crosbie.

'In Canada,' said Robinson. He seemed to muse for a moment, and played with the food on his plate.

'I've heard of Manitoba,' said Jack. 'It's full of giant buffalo who just lie down at your feet waiting to be slaughtered.'

'Manitoba,' said Palmer with a snort. 'Who wants to go there? The middle of nowhere.'

'Easy for you to say,' said Robinson. 'You don't need a clerk's job. You can always go into your father's business.'

'What do you know about it?' said Palmer. 'What makes you think my father will take me on just like that? Maybe he wants me to make something of myself on my own. Maybe I do myself.'

Palmer seemed suddenly very angry. Aleister could see the veins on his forehead. He was afraid one of them would burst.

No one said anything more the rest of the meal.

Aleister waited hopefully the rest of the day after lunch, looking to Mr Talbot for a sign that another note had come, but there was none. All he could do was keep working at the carding desk. About halfway through the afternoon, Billy Cooper came over to see if they needed more blank cards. They didn't, though.

Billy seemed a bit downcast, not over that, but because he'd lost more money betting on horses. 'It seemed like such a sure thing,' he said. 'Palmer told me about it.'

'Palmer!' said Jack. 'What did you listen to him for? He never knows the winners.'

Billy just shrugged. Aleister looked over towards Palmer's desk, but he wasn't there. He glanced around the office. There he was, in with Mr Carruthers. Aleister watched through the glass. He couldn't hear what was being said, but Palmer looked grim and Mr Carruthers was gesticulating in an agitated way. He wondered what was going on.

Jack was talking to Billy. 'You can go and get us some steel nibs if that will make you feel better,' he said.

'That Palmer,' said Jack to Aleister after Billy left. 'Always causing trouble.'

'He seems to be having an argument with Mr Carruthers,' said Aleister.

Jack looked over at Mr Carruthers' office. 'I've seen them together before,' he said. 'Palmer seems to have something on him.'

'What do you mean "have"?' said Aleister.

'You know,' said Jack. 'He knows something that Mr Carruthers has done that he shouldn't have. Something like that.'

'And he's blackmailing him?' Aleister said excitedly.

Jack looked at him strangely. 'I wouldn't have put it quite that way, but perhaps ...'

'Could he be blackmailing other people too?'

Jack looked at Aleister even more strangely. 'What an extraordinary idea,' he said.

'It's just that –' But Aleister wasn't sure he should confide in Jack.

'What?' said Jack.

'Nothing,' said Aleister. 'This contract here – which name am I supposed to record it under?'

Jack seemed about to ask something more about Palmer and blackmailing, but changed his mind and let the matter drop.

That evening, as he and Mr Talbot walked home from the bus stop, Aleister was all excited over what he had discovered.

'I think it might be Palmer,' he said.

'What?' said Mr Talbot.

'The blackmailer,' said Aleister. 'I think Palmer is the blackmailer.'

'Palmer?' said Mr Talbot.

He stopped. Aleister stopped too. They waited for another gentleman to walk past.

'Palmer?' said Mr Talbot. 'Palmer's an idiot. It couldn't be Palmer.'

'Oh,' said Aleister.

They resumed walking.

'What makes you think it's Palmer?' said Mr Talbot at last.

'I think he's blackmailing Mr Carruthers too.'

'Carruthers!' Mr Talbot stopped again and fell silent, as if thinking. 'What is he blackmailing Carruthers about?'

'I don't know,' said Aleister.

'There was a strange claim he assessed not long ago,' Mr Talbot said musingly. 'A fire? A burglary? I forget now. It was a bit suspicious. But Mr Carruthers has been with us for years. I can't believe that he would falsify a claim or anything like that. You must be mistaken.'

But he was quiet the rest of the evening as if thinking it over, as if he even thought Aleister might be right.

CHAPTER NINE

Guy Fawkes Day

'Why would Palmer want to blackmail anybody?' Mr Talbot said the next day as he and Aleister walked to the bus stop.

Aleister had been thinking about this himself. 'Perhaps he needs the money because of his betting on the horses,' he said.

Mr Talbot shook his head. 'He has a rich father. Why would he need money for his wagers? Besides, how much could he have lost?'

'Perhaps he doesn't want his father to find out,' said Aleister. 'Perhaps he's afraid of being yelled at.'

Mr Talbot glanced over at Aleister as if studying him closely. 'Yelled at?' he said.

'Punished,' said Aleister. 'For losing his money.'

Mr Talbot seemed to consider this, but Aleister was already rushing on with another thought. He was full of thoughts this morning.

'Or maybe it has something to do with him losing his job.'

This comment made Mr Talbot stop short, even though they still had some distance to go to get to the bus stop and if they didn't keep walking, they were liable to miss their bus.

'What do you mean, he might lose his job?' Mr Talbot said. 'How do you know anything about that?'

Aleister felt suddenly guilty, as if he had pried open a secret he shouldn't have. But wasn't he supposed to be prying into things, he thought? He was here to be a spy or a detective.

'I heard talk at the cook-shop,' he said. 'Or maybe it was from Jack.'

'What does Jack know about it?' said Mr Talbot.

'Oh, Jack knows lots of things,' said Aleister. 'At first I thought he might be the blackmailer. But I don't think so any more.'

'Why not?'

'He's too nice,' said Aleister. 'I like him.'

Mr Talbot snorted in disgust. 'What has that got to do with it?'

Aleister was about to respond, but they both suddenly saw the omnibus clattering down the roadway, and broke into a trot to catch it.

The conductor grinned at them. 'Almost missed it, didn't you, governor,' he said to Mr Talbot, 'you and that lad of yours.'

Mr Talbot merely grunted as he paid the fare and led Aleister upstairs to the upper level. The two of them were the only ones brave enough to sit there: it was a windy day, with a threat of rain hanging over them.

At the office there was a hint of excitement in the air. Aleister wondered why. Jack told him it was because of Guy Fawkes Day.

'Guy Fawkes Day?' said Aleister.

'You know,' said Jack, 'the fifth of November. Remember, remember.'

'I know what Guy Fawkes Day is,' said Aleister. 'It's just – '

'You don't know what Guy Fawkes Day is?' said Billy Cooper, who was walking past the carding desk carrying some new blotting paper.

'No,' said Aleister. 'What I said was – '

'But everyone knows what Guy Fawkes Day is,' said Billy. 'Bonfires. Fireworks. A penny for the guy.'

Aleister was beginning to get frustrated. 'Yes,' he said, 'I know all that. It's just – '

But Billy was no longer listening. 'They must be very backward in Shrewsbury,' he said, 'not to know about Guy Fawkes Day.'

'We know all about Guy Fawkes Day,' said Aleister. 'They taught us the whole thing. James the First, blowing up Parliament, gunpowder in the cellar.'

'Gunpowder in the cellar?' said Billy.

'Yes,' said Aleister. 'It was the Gunpowder Plot. That's what you're celebrating.'

Billy shook his head doubtfully. 'It's all about bonfires and fireworks,' he said.

Jack took a couple of nibs from Billy. 'Enough of this, you two,' he said. 'We have work to do.'

Mr Talbot walked past and signalled to Aleister. He looked serious.

Aleister got up to walk with him into the outer hallway. 'What's the matter?' he said.

Mr Talbot showed him a piece of paper. 'I've received a third note,' he said.

Aleister glanced around, then eagerly read the message. 'Meet me at the Medlock Mill,' it said. 'At 7.'

'What's the Medlock Mill?' said Aleister.

'One of the old cotton factories south of here,' said Mr Talbot.

He folded up the note and thought for a moment. 'I wonder,' he said.

'What?' said Aleister.

'Do you really think it's Palmer?' said Mr Talbot.

They both looked into the main hall. Palmer was indistinguishable from the other clerks, bent over a desk, copying an insurance policy.

'I don't know,' said Aleister.

'Could just as easily be your friend Jack,' said Mr Talbot.

'Or anyone. I'd like to know for sure. Or have evidence for later.'

'Evidence?'

'Yes,' said Mr Talbot, and seemed lost in thought. 'We'll talk again after work,' he said finally, waving Aleister back to the carding desk.

The rest of the day Aleister could hardly concentrate. He dropped his pen once and left a big ink blot on one of his cards.

'What's the matter with you?' said Jack.

Aleister mumbled something, and looked Jack up and down. Could Jack be the blackmailer after all? But no, he was sure it was Palmer. Anyway, they would find out tonight.

At lunch the clerks mostly talked about bonfires and fireworks.

'I hope it will be as exciting as last year,' said Crosbie.

Robinson shook his head. 'It's just an excuse for rowdy behaviour and indiscipline,' he said. 'You'd all be better off going home.'

'You're always interfering with people's fun,' Palmer muttered.

'Windows get broken, and people get beaten up,' said Robinson. 'Is that your idea of fun?'

'You're such an old woman,' said Palmer.

Robinson turned to Jack for support, which Aleister at first thought was a strange thing to do.

'You can't enjoy this sort of thing, can you?' he said.

Jack looked at him mildly, raising an eyebrow.

'I mean,' said Robinson, 'all the anti-Catholic nonsense that gets spouted.'

Jack smiled mysteriously. 'When I was younger,' he said, then stopped.

'Yes?' said Robinson.

'One time we got them to stop their nonsense,' said Jack. 'Our gang, their gang. We broke a few heads. They didn't burn their guys that year. Or the Pope.'

Robinson shook his head. 'You're as bad as he is,' he said. 'Do you think violence is the answer to everything?'

'Not everything,' said Jack. 'Some things.'

'That's un-Christian,' said Robinson.

Jack shrugged. Aleister looked at them, astonished.

Crosbie seemed astonished too. 'It's just Guy Fawkes Day, for God's sake,' he said. 'What are you people making such a fuss for?'

'Well, last year,' said Robinson, 'someone even died. A child. The fireworks blew up in his face. It was in all the papers.'

'Why do you have to bring that up?' said Palmer. He looked very red suddenly.

'I'm just saying – '

'Who cares what you were saying?' Palmer said, and got up and stormed out.

'What's the matter with him?' said Crosbie.

'Oh, something's always the matter with Palmer,' Jack said.

Back in the office it seemed as if the day would never end. Aleister could hardly wait for it to be over so that he and Mr Talbot could go and meet the blackmailer. He wondered what it would be like.

He glanced around the room. There was Palmer at his desk, and Robinson and Crosbie at theirs. Miss Lewisham was typing away on her machine. Mr Brooks was just emerging from Mr Smithson's office. And there was Mr Carruthers smirking at Billy the office boy.

He might be meeting one of them at the Medlock Mill that night. He wondered what would happen then. Perhaps he should discuss some plan with Mr Talbot. Perhaps Mr Talbot would come over and talk to him about it.

But Mr Talbot busied himself at the front of the room all afternoon and didn't come over to the carding desk until it was time to go. Then he had a surprise for Aleister.

'I have to go home first to get something,' he said. 'Before we meet the – before the meeting.'

They were standing in front of Saviour Assurance.

'Will we have time?' Aleister said. He didn't think it would be a good idea to be late for the blackmailer.

'I'm not sure,' said Mr Talbot. 'I'll go home myself, and meet you there. If I haven't arrived, explain that I've been delayed.'

'But – ' Aleister thought this was all wrong, though he couldn't quite explain why. 'I can't go alone,' he said. 'I don't know the way.'

'It's just down Oxford Street,' said Mr Talbot. He seemed strangely distracted, as if planning something.

'But I won't know who to look for,' said Aleister.

'Well, neither would I,' said Mr Talbot.

Aleister looked at him helplessly. This seemed all wrong. But Mr Talbot seemed intent on his plan. 'Go and get something to eat, and then show up at seven,' he said. 'I'm sure I'll be there. But I have to leave now.'

It was already getting dark. The sun had set not long before. Mr Talbot started walking off alone.

'But he's expecting you,' said Aleister, 'not me.' He had suddenly realised why the plan was completely wrong. But by this time Mr Talbot was already out of earshot.

Aleister looked around him. Streams of clerks were heading off to omnibuses. He stopped one of them.

'Excuse me, sir,' he said, 'would you happen to have the time?'

The clerk looked annoyed, but pulled out his pocket watch. 'Just gone half five,' he said.

Aleister nodded and thanked him. He had plenty of time, assuming he could find the meeting place. He could go there early to check it out, but he didn't think he'd like the area: too full of beggars and pickpockets. He didn't want to have to wait there.

95

He decided to go to the cook-shop, as Mr Talbot had suggested, even though he wasn't feeling at all hungry.

'Oh, hello, dearie,' said the woman behind the counter when he got there. 'Here by yourself this evening?'

'Yes,' said Aleister.

'Don't usually see you at this time of the day,' said the woman. 'We're just about ready to close up.'

The woman was busy wrapping up pies and putting vegetables away. Aleister started to back out of the shop.

'I suppose I should go, then,' he said.

'Oh, don't run off like that,' said the woman. She smiled broadly.

Aleister saw she was missing a tooth; he had never noticed before. He said nothing and didn't move.

'Are you staying late to watch the fireworks?' the woman said.

'No,' said Aleister. 'I'm meeting someone.'

'Are you?' said the woman. 'On Bonfire Night? All by yourself? Where are your friends?'

'I think they went home,' Aleister said. He didn't like answering all these questions; they made him feel uneasy. 'I have to go now,' he said, and darted out the door.

He decided he would just walk in the city centre for a while before starting off for the meeting place. He tried to remember where it was. The Medlock Mill, the note had said. Down Oxford Street, Mr Talbot had told him.

He walked past the reassuring statue of the Duke of Wellington, then by the big department store, then past some other statues. It was getting truly dark now, and there were fewer and fewer clerks about. In the distance he could see a glow: one of the bonfires, he thought. Perhaps he should start making his way to Medlock Mill.

He found his way to Oxford Street. He began to hear the sounds of fireworks going off and saw a few spinning wheels of light in the distance. The glow from the distant bonfires continued to light the horizon, and he could hear occasional cheers from the crowds that must have gathered near them.

Suddenly a gang of youths turned a corner and seemed to be headed straight towards him. 'Down with Guy Fawkes,' one of them called out. 'No Popery,' said another. 'Rule Britannia,' said a third. Aleister flattened himself against a wall and watched them approach. They were carrying a couple of 'guys' to burn at a bonfire.

Aleister watched them warily and was surprised to see them come to a sudden halt. When he looked behind him, he saw why. A rival gang was approaching. They were carrying clubs instead of guys, and were dressed in green. 'Home rule for Ireland,' one of them shouted.

The two gangs squared off against each other. Aleister thought this would be a good time to get away. He saw an alley and scurried down it. It was dark and dirty. Some creature scurried away in front of him; he tried not to think what it might be.

Behind him he could hear shouts and groans and the sound of clubs striking heads. He thought perhaps he should run. He turned down the next street and sprinted along it. The shouts and noises grew fainter. He felt relieved.

But where was he? He looked around and all he could see was row after row of identical dingy houses crammed together without a blade of grass in front or beside any of them. He wouldn't want to live here, he thought. He didn't even like being here. He should get back to Oxford Street. He wondered if he was late for the meeting. There were no clocks around and no one to ask. His heart was beating fast, he noticed.

He tried to remember which way he had come. Oxford Street should be to his left, surely – or was it to his right? Had he come full circle? He felt a tightness in his chest. What if he was hopelessly lost?

Off to one side were huge mounds of gravel and refuse. He

saw what looked like rats clambering over them. He decided to keep to the other side of the street.

Suddenly a large fireworks explosion lighted up the sky, and he saw a large building with a chimney looming in the distance. Could that be the mill? He headed in that direction, not running now, but with a hurried gait.

The fireworks' glow faded and he found himself in the dark again, but he tried to head towards where the mill had been. It wasn't very far, he thought, but just when it seemed he was getting to it, the street he was on came to an abrupt end. He wondered if he could pick his way between the houses that lay in front of him, but a barking dog made him decide to retrace his steps back to the previous intersection.

It was dark again, and he'd turned around. He wasn't sure quite which way to go. The roads seemed to twist and turn. He wished he knew what time it was.

He finally decided to turn right, then right again, and just as he made the second turn, another fireworks explosion lit up the sky, and he found himself almost stumbling over a young boy sitting at the corner with a dummy beside him, made of rags, with a crudely drawn face on it.

Aleister nearly gasped in astonishment.

'Penny for the guy,' said the boy.

'Oh,' said Aleister, and began to search his pockets.

The boy looked to be only ten, or less, but he had a strange reptilian expression that made Aleister feel nervous.

'I don't seem to have a penny,' said Aleister. 'Only a half-penny. And a shilling.'

'I'll take the shilling,' said the boy.

'I don't think so,' said Aleister doubtfully.

'I'll beat you up, then,' said the boy.

Aleister hesitated. A shilling was all his spending money for the week, but maybe he could get something in return. 'If I give you the shilling,' he said, 'will you tell me the way to Medlock Mill?'

'Course I will,' said the boy. 'But give me the shilling first.'

Aleister handed over the shilling. The boy grabbed it eagerly. His eyes seemed to light up. Then he suddenly jumped to his feet and began to run away.

'Hey,' said Aleister, 'you said you'd tell me the way to the mill.'

The boy had nearly disappeared into the darkness, but he stopped and shouted back, 'Can't miss it, governor. It's just ahead of you. Just past where the street meets the road.'

And then he was gone.

Where the street meets the road, Aleister thought – what did that mean? But he headed in the direction he was going. He did seem to be on a main road now, so perhaps he had found Oxford Street again.

Another gang came marching towards him. They carried a gigantic figure of Guy Fawkes and were chanting the Bonfire Night rhyme:

Remember, remember
The Fifth of November
Gunpowder treason and plot
I see no reason
Why gunpowder treason
Should ever be forgot.

They gestured at Aleister, and Aleister waved back.

'You're going the wrong way,' said one of them. 'The bonfire's down here.'

'I have to meet someone,' said Aleister, and hurried past.

He was at the mill now. Its grimy brick walls loomed before him. The chimney out of which smoke poured during the day was idle. He looked to the left and the right. There were all sorts of nooks and crannies. The blackmailer could be any-where, or nowhere.

'Hey,' said a voice from the darkness, 'what are you doing here?'

Aleister looked up. It was Palmer.

'I'm here to meet you,' said Aleister.

Palmer looked a bit nervous. Agitated.

'What are you talking about?' he said. 'I'm waiting for somebody else.'

'I know,' said Aleister. 'Mr Talbot.'

Palmer shuddered as if someone had passed a sword through him.

'How do you know that?' he said.

'I know everything,' said Aleister. 'The notes, the blackmail, what you saw Mr Talbot do. Everything.'

'You're lying,' said Palmer. 'Where is Talbot?'

'He's coming,' said Aleister. 'He's been delayed.'

A loud explosion of fireworks sounded not far away. Palmer jumped. Aleister felt strangely calm. Exhilarated. It was as if he could be the Count of Monte Cristo now. He would be the hero.

Lights and colours appeared overhead. More fireworks. Palmer's face looked livid and distorted.

'I can't wait here any longer,' he said. 'I could hear you skulking around forever before you finally came forward. Watching me.'

'I just got here,' said Aleister.

'Don't lie to me,' said Palmer. 'What are you doing here anyway? It was supposed to be Talbot. I have to talk to him.'

'He'll be here soon.'

'I can't wait. Tell him I want a job, my job, permanent-like. That's what I want. Not money. I don't need money. It's the job I have to have. I can't go home unless I've got the job.'

And then he vanished into the darkness. Aleister peered after him for a moment, but could not really see. He thought he heard a movement from behind him, but when he turned around he couldn't see anyone there either. Then there was just silence and darkness.

He hesitated for a moment. There were more sounds of fireworks. In the distance he could see the bonfires' glow. He wondered if Mr Talbot was going to show up at all. Could that have been him he had heard in the darkness? Was he the one stalking Palmer? But why would he do that?

Another band of revellers went by shouting out 'Remember, remember' and then breaking into a chorus of 'Rule Britannia'.

Aleister thought he perhaps should retrace his steps and make his way home. But how would he do that, he suddenly wondered? He had no money for a cab: he had given his only shilling to the boy. Perhaps after all he should stay where he was and wait for Mr Talbot.

He heard a cracking sound. More fireworks, he thought at first. But then he heard it again and again. It didn't sound exactly like fireworks, and it came from not far away.

Cautiously, he made his way over to where the sound had seemed to come from. He felt his way along the side of the factory building, then walked out into the darkness beyond.

He stopped. He had no idea which way to go or what he was looking for. He decided to push on in the same direction, walking very gingerly. Even at his slow pace he almost tripped a few seconds later when his toe hit a large soft object.

He knelt down to see what it was. He realised it was a human form. Someone drunk or sleeping, he almost hoped. But they weren't drunk or sleeping. There was blood oozing from their skull; he could feel its stickiness.

It was a dead person, recently dead, and he was pretty sure who it must be, though in the dark it was hard to make out the features. He knelt there for a few seconds, his fingers in the blood.

A huge explosion of fireworks rocked the air. Coloured wheels rotated above, flares soared, rockets glared. There was light enough to see now, and there could be no doubt who the dead man was.

It was Palmer.

CHAPTER TEN

Arrested

Aleister knelt over Palmer's body for quite a while, unable to move. Around him he heard voices eventually. Neighbours who must have heard the shots and who had somehow been able to distinguish them from fireworks. And a policeman. Someone had summoned a policeman who arrived carrying a lantern.

'What's been happening here, lad?' said the policeman. He put a large beefy hand on Aleister's shoulder.

Aleister slowly got up.

'I don't know,' he said. 'I heard something. I didn't know what it was, and then there was Palmer.'

'Palmer?' said the policeman, who had to stop every now and then to keep the crowd away.

'Him,' said Aleister, indicating the body.

'You knew the victim then, did you?' said the policeman.

'Yes,' said Aleister.

A little boy pushed forward from the crowd suddenly. 'It's Guy Fawkes,' he said. 'We've killed Guy Fawkes.' And he danced a little jig.

'Get this child away,' said the policeman.

A sheepish-looking man pulled the boy aside. The policeman returned his attention to Aleister.

'Now,' he said, 'perhaps you had better explain how you came to be standing over the body of your friend.'

'He wasn't my friend,' said Aleister.

'Aha,' said the policeman, pulling out a notebook and

looking for a pencil to write with. 'Not his friend,' he said to himself and wrote something down. 'So what were you, then? Or first of all, who are you? Give me your name.'

'Lister Smith,' said Aleister. 'Aleister Lister Smith.'

'Fancy name for someone wandering in this part of town.'

'I don't live here. I was just meeting Palmer here.'

'Palmer,' said the policeman.

Aleister nodded towards the body.

'Right,' said the policeman. 'So you had an appointment with the victim. Palmer. Did he have a Christian name?'

'Robert, I think,' said Aleister.

'Robert Palmer,' said the policeman. 'Right. So you had an appointment with Mr Palmer.'

'Well, not exactly,' said Aleister.

He was beginning to find this very complicated. He also wondered where Mr Talbot was. Was he still on his way? Had he gone into hiding? He looked at the crowd to see if he was there. More people had gathered. Some of them had brought lanterns. The area was beginning to become almost light. But there was no sign of Mr Talbot.

The policeman adjusted his helmet. 'Well, did you have an appointment with him, or didn't you?'

Aleister sighed. Some things were just too difficult to explain. Where should he begin? In Shrewsbury School, when Mr Talbot first recruited him? Or the day he went to work and first saw Palmer? Should he tell about the blackmail notes? The meeting? But in a way he wasn't even supposed to be at the meeting. It was Mr Talbot's meeting.

'Well?' said the policeman.

'It's very complicated,' said Aleister.

'I think perhaps we'll need to take you down to the station for some further inquiries,' said the policeman. 'But first I had better get some assistance. Stand back.'

A bit confused, Aleister took a step back. The policeman fished in one of his pockets for a large whistle. Aleister hurriedly took a few more steps back. So did some of the people in the crowd.

The policeman gave a mighty blast on the whistle, then another. Aleister put up his hands to cover his ears.

They waited. The sound of the whistle faded into the night air. Some members of the crowd decided it was the better part of valour to depart. Others seemed eager to watch. New people were arriving. There were more lanterns.

Finally, two more policemen could be seen running towards the scene. The first policeman went over to them. There was a brief discussion, then he came back to Aleister.

'I'm going to escort you to the station now,' he said.

He put his hand on Aleister's shoulder again and guided him away from the crowd. The other two policemen took up positions guarding the body. One of them was tall and thin. The other was stocky.

'Hey, what's this?' said the tall one, holding up a piece of paper.

The policeman with Aleister stopped and looked back. So did Aleister. He wondered where the paper had come from. Was it one last message from Palmer?

Which reminded him: where was Palmer's last message? He put his hands in his pockets, but there was nothing there. Mr Talbot had kept it, he decided. He was almost sure of it. He could check his back pocket, but the policeman was already looking at him curiously, and he wasn't sure it was a good idea to let him know about the note, though he wasn't entirely sure why.

Or could that be the last note there, being held up in the flickering light of the lanterns by one of the new policemen?

'What is it?' said the policeman with Aleister.

'Better come see,' said the one holding the paper. 'There's something else here too.'

The first policeman turned around and, bringing Aleister with him, returned to Palmer's body.

The tall policeman showed him the note. The stocky one tried to keep the crowd back.

'What's in that there note?' said someone in the crowd. 'A message from the dead man?'

A few people in the crowd laughed, but others murmured nervously.

Aleister craned his head to try and see the note. He needn't have bothered, because the policeman holding him suddenly turned and thrust it in front of his face.

'Do you know anything about this?' he said.

Aleister looked at the note. It read: 'Remember, remember the Fifth of November.'

He shrugged and said, 'I never saw it before.'

The two policemen conferred.

'It's just the children's rhyme,' said the one holding Aleister.

'But why was it on the body?' said the one who had discovered it.

'Maybe it's a reminder about the meeting,' said the first policeman. He turned to Aleister. 'You sure this isn't some note about your appointment?'

Aleister shrugged again. 'I never saw it before,' he repeated.

The policeman shook his head.

'And look at this,' said the tall one. He pointed at the body. 'There's a fireworks cracker on his chest.'

The policeman with Aleister stared at the body. So did Aleister.

'The cracker didn't kill him, did it?' the policeman said.

'No, no,' said the tall one. 'There are gunshot wounds. You can see two, maybe three of them. But whoever shot him must have put the cracker on him afterwards.'

'Any sign of the gun, by the way?' said the first policeman.

'We'll have to look,' said the tall policeman.

The first policeman grunted and began leading Aleister off.

Suddenly there was a commotion at the other side of the crowd.

'Let me through, let me through,' an agitated voice was saying.

The crowd parted, a bit reluctantly.

'Who's there?' said the policeman holding Aleister.

He let go of Aleister and reached for his truncheon. The stocky policeman held his lantern in the direction of the voice, and into view, stumbling a bit, almost tripping over a tripod and some camera equipment that he was carrying, came Mr Talbot.

'What's going on?' he said.

'I might ask you the same question, sir,' said the first policeman.

Mr Talbot paused a moment to take in the scene: the policeman holding Aleister, the two other policemen guarding Palmer's body, the crowd ebbing and flowing like ocean waves. In the distance, the bonfires created an eerie light. There was the occasional sound of exploding fireworks.

'What is going on?' he said again.

'There's been a murder, sir,' said the policeman. 'Perhaps you know something about it.'

'Why should I know something about it?' said Mr Talbot.

He attempted to draw himself up into a dignified pose to better express his indignation at the suggestion, but the effect was somewhat spoiled by his losing his grip on the tripod, which clattered to the ground. Then, in endeavouring to pick it up, he stumbled again and had to be caught by the policeman.

'May I ask why you are carrying all this equipment, sir?' the policeman said.

'I ... I – I don't see that I have to explain myself,' said Mr Talbot. 'Cannot a gentleman venture out of an evening in the hopes of taking some photographs?'

'In the dark, sir?'

'I have the latest magnesium ribbon from Salford,' said Mr

Talbot. 'Guaranteed to produce clear pictures even on the darkest night.'

'Is that so?' said the policeman.

'I should have thought the police department would know about such things,' said Mr Talbot.

He pulled out a piece of ribbon to show the policeman. The policeman examined it with interest. 'Perhaps,' he said, 'you could demonstrate.'

'What do you mean?' said Mr Talbot.

'There's a body here needs photographing,' said the policeman, and he led Mr Talbot towards the spot where Palmer lay.

'Oh, my God,' said Mr Talbot. 'It's Palmer.'

'So you know the victim too, sir,' said the policeman.

Mr Talbot said nothing.

The policeman went on, 'I am thinking I should take you down to the station along with the lad here.'

'You're arresting Aleister?' Mr Talbot said.

'So you know the lad, do you, sir? Were the two of you acting in concert?'

'This is absurd,' said Mr Talbot. 'I am a respectable member of the insurance profession. I work for the Saviour Assurance Company and live in Didsbury.'

'Didsbury?' said the policeman. 'You're a long way from home, sir.'

'I have listened to just about enough of these scurrilous insinuations,' said Mr Talbot.

The policeman shrugged slightly. 'I am afraid I shall have to ask you to accompany me to the station,' he said. 'But first, if you really can take photographs in the dark, we should be much obliged to have one of the victim.'

Mr Talbot hesitated. Aleister wondered what he would do. He wasn't really going to let them be arrested, was he? How could things have come to this?

Finally, Mr Talbot spoke. 'If it will help the police in the performance of their duties,' he said, 'of course I will take the photograph.'

'Very good, sir,' said the policeman. 'You can set up wherever is convenient.'

'First I need to get my tent,' said Mr Talbot. 'It's in the cab.' He gestured back behind him.

'Ah,' said the policeman, 'you have brought a cab. Very convenient. You have thought of everything. I shall accompany you there, and the lad can stay with my colleagues.'

Aleister watched as Mr Talbot and the policeman made their way back through the crowd. He tried to make sense of what had just happened. Why had Mr Talbot brought his camera? He remembered him saying something about getting evidence; had he wanted a photograph of Palmer to prove that he was the blackmailer? How would that have helped?

And now they were going to be taken off to the police station. He reviewed the events of the evening in his mind. Could he have done something differently? It all seemed so inevitable, looking back on it – and if he were the policeman, he'd probably arrest him too: a boy found kneeling over the corpse. He shook his head.

'You look very serious,' said the tall policeman.

'Oh,' said Aleister.

'Did you kill him, or was it your father did the deed?'

'He's not my father,' said Aleister.

'No?'

'No, he's ...' But how was he going to explain his relationship to Mr Talbot? The brother-in-law of his schoolmaster in Shrewsbury? The whole thing seemed so incredible, he thought they might as well convict him now. Would they hang him, he wondered? He couldn't help feeling his neck. But they didn't hang fourteen-year-olds any more, did they? Maybe they would send him to Australia – but no, they didn't do that any more either, he was pretty sure.

He gasped slightly. It suddenly struck him. He really was

going to end up like Edmond Dantès in *The Count of Monte Cristo*, falsely imprisoned for a crime he didn't commit.

'Come on, lad,' said the tall policeman, 'it's not as bad as that, is it?'

Aleister realised that tears were running down his cheek. Everything seemed like such a mess. Things had been much easier back in Shrewsbury when all there was to worry about were a few bullies and Mr Rawlins sarcastically suggesting you didn't understand the first thing about Latin poetry.

Mr Talbot came back with his tent. He fussed with it and with a holder for his magnesium ribbon and with the tripod and the camera. Aleister could hardly watch. There was a sudden bright light as the ribbon lit up. Then Mr Talbot was fussing in the tent, developing the photograph.

And then they were being bundled into the cab and driven to the police station.

CHAPTER ELEVEN

In the Police Station

'Fairfield Street, that's where we're going, sir.'

The first policeman was replying to Mr Talbot, who had asked about their destination. Aleister hardly paid attention, just looked out the window. He felt numb.

As the cab clattered along, he noticed a strange pair of street signs right next to each other, plastered on a wall. 'Oxford Road,' said one. 'Oxford Street,' said the other.

The road meeting the street, he thought in a barely interested way; well, that was the answer to that mystery. It hardly seemed to matter now.

He began to wonder who had killed Palmer. It occurred to him that if the real culprit could be discovered, then he and Mr Talbot would be let go – unless, of course, Mr Talbot was the culprit. Could he have shot Palmer first and then come back to the scene lugging all that camera equipment? It seemed unlikely.

The cab stopped on Fairfield Street in front of the police station. Aleister stepped out and felt dwarfed before the stone building. The policeman led them inside past a screaming woman and two youths with bleeding heads.

A policeman inside the station looked at Aleister and Mr Talbot. 'More Guy Fawkes revellers?' he asked.

'Murder suspects,' said the policeman escorting Aleister and Mr Talbot.

The new policeman looked interested, but his attention was

diverted by one of the bleeding youths, who was struggling with the two constables holding him.

'Let me go,' said the youth, 'let me go. Why have you arrested me, you stupid coppers? I'm the one who got beat.'

'All in good time,' said one of the constables, 'all in good time. We'll let the magistrate sort things out.'

'Bugger the magistrate,' said the youth.

'You'd do well to keep a civil tongue in your head,' said the constable.

The youth fell silent. Aleister wondered if he and Mr Talbot would also be seeing the magistrate. He looked around the grimy front room of the station; on benches against the walls were sullen, defiant, angry, sad, grinning suspects. Guy Fawkes celebrators, pickpockets, burglars. He shuddered a bit.

'This way,' said the policeman who'd brought them in.

He led them past an imposing high desk at which a stern sergeant sat. A woman in rags suddenly rushed towards the desk, screaming and scratching herself.

'They're crawling all over me,' she said. 'Crawling all over me.'

She pulled at her hair, then banged her arms on the desk. A constable came and took her away.

Aleister was glad to be taken from there and down a corridor. He and Mr Talbot found themselves in a small room lit by soft yellow gaslight. Behind a desk a friendly looking man with a small moustache sat glancing through a notebook. He gestured to them to sit down. The policeman who had brought them went over and whispered something to the man, who nodded. The policeman left.

'I am Inspector Brown,' the man behind the desk said.

Aleister shifted uneasily. It was like being called before the headmaster. Not that he ever had been. Would they be flogged? Or just given a stern talking to? He wasn't sure which would be worse.

But the inspector was being quite friendly. 'Would you like a cup of tea?' he said to Mr Talbot.

Mr Talbot just shook his head.

'How about you?' the inspector said to Aleister.

Aleister shook his head too.

'I understand you know something about a murder,' said the inspector.

'We know nothing about it,' said Mr Talbot. Aleister thought he looked sullen.

'The constable tells me you were on the scene,' said the inspector. 'Or at least the boy was. And the two of you knew the victim.'

'What of that?' said Mr Talbot.

'Murder is a very serious crime,' said the inspector. 'If you can help us in any way ...'

'We know nothing about it,' said Mr Talbot.

'Perhaps you can tell me something about the victim,' said the inspector. 'His name perhaps.'

'It was Palmer,' said Aleister.

'Don't say anything, Aleister,' said Mr Talbot. 'We don't have to tell them anything.'

The inspector nodded. 'The gentleman is quite right,' he said, 'and I should caution you that anything you do tell me can be used in court in any proceedings against you.'

'Proceedings against us,' said Mr Talbot indignantly. 'What sort of proceedings against us do you envisage?'

'None at this time, sir,' said the inspector. 'We are just trying to determine what happened to this unfortunate Mr Palmer.'

'Unfortunate?' said Mr Talbot. 'Ha.'

'You don't consider the victim to have been unfortunate?'

Mr Talbot shrugged. 'He is beyond misfortunes now,' he said. 'But I sit here in a police station. That's unfortunate.'

'Yes, sir,' said the inspector, and seemed about to say something, but Mr Talbot had suddenly become talkative.

'I sit here in a police station deprived of my liberty,' he said. 'There's misfortune.' He shook his head. 'And deprived of my photographic equipment,' he added in a low mutter.

'What's that, sir?' said the inspector.

'I said you have not only deprived me of my liberty, but you have taken away my camera.'

'You were carrying a camera when the constable brought you in?' said the inspector.

'A camera, a tripod, a developing tent, my new magnesium ribbon holder, a roll of magnesium ribbon, some photographic plates ...'

The inspector sat back in wonder. 'And why were you carrying all this material, sir?'

Mr Talbot was silent.

The inspector stroked his moustache. 'Very curious,' he said.

'I should like it all back,' said Mr Talbot.

'Of course, sir,' said the inspector. 'The constable will have put it aside for safekeeping. But it is very curious.' He looked at Aleister. 'Don't you think so?'

Aleister hesitated. 'Perhaps,' he said.

Mr Talbot glared at Aleister. 'There's nothing curious about it,' he said. 'I was planning to take some photographs. I wasn't planning to murder anyone.'

'Murder is not always planned,' said the inspector.

'What do you mean by that?' said Mr Talbot.

'It was just an observation,' said the inspector.

'Well, I didn't murder anyone,' said Mr Talbot, 'with or without a plan. I was just out to take photographs.'

'Of what, sir?' said the inspector.

'Of – of ...'

'Of the fireworks,' said Aleister helpfully.

The inspector turned to Aleister. 'You were involved in this photographic expedition?' he asked. 'Are you the gentleman's assistant?'

'Not a photographic assistant,' Aleister said hesitantly.

'Look here,' said Mr Talbot, suddenly galvanised into action, apparently in order to protect Aleister. 'Leave the boy alone. I'll tell you all you need to know.'

'Very good, sir,' said the inspector. He picked up a pencil and his notebook.

'My name is Arthur Talbot,' said Mr Talbot. 'I live at 123 Moore Street with my wife and daughter. I am chief clerk at the Saviour Assurance Company. Young Aleister here – Aleister Lister Smith – is, is ...'

Mr Talbot seemed to falter over how to describe Aleister. How many stories, true and not so true, must he have been revolving in his head? Aleister decided he had better speak up.

'I work at the insurance company too,' he said. 'I am an apprentice clerk.'

'I see,' said the inspector. 'And the two of you were out on insurance business tonight?'

'No, of course not,' said Mr Talbot.

'Ah,' said the inspector.

'I was out photographing, as I told you,' said Mr Talbot.

'And the boy?'

Aleister and Mr Talbot looked at each other. It was so difficult to explain. Besides, there were things that were better left unexplained.

The inspector leaned back in his chair.

'The constable told me,' he said, 'that not only was the boy found kneeling over the body, but it was also not by accident that he was there; there was an appointment. Is this true?'

Aleister and Mr Talbot looked at each other again, and hesitated. The inspector looked at them and waited.

There was a knock at the door.

'Yes?' said the inspector.

The first policeman leaned his head in. 'Just thought I should let you know, sir, that we've recovered the weapon.'

'Ah,' said the inspector, his eyes lighting up. 'Where is it?'

The constable entered carrying a pistol and placed it on the inspector's desk. Aleister and Mr Talbot leaned forward to look at it. Mr Talbot gave a sudden intake of breath. The inspector looked up at him sharply.

'Is something the matter, sir?' he said.

Mr Talbot shook his head.

The inspector turned towards the constable. 'Where did you find it?'

'Not far from the scene, sir,' said the constable. 'Down an alleyway.'

The inspector nodded and picked up the pistol.

'Fine piece of work,' he said, handling the gun, but keeping one eye on Mr Talbot. 'Wouldn't you say so, sir?'

'I don't know anything about guns,' said Mr Talbot.

'Have you seen this one before?' said the inspector.

He brought the pistol close to Mr Talbot. Mr Talbot shrank away from it.

'Initials carved in the handle,' said the inspector. 'H-S. Know whose those might be?'

Mr Talbot said nothing.

The inspector suddenly stood up.

'I think we've got all that we're going to get for now, from the gentleman and his young friend,' he said to the constable. 'Perhaps they can tell us more tomorrow.'

'Can we go, then?' said Mr Talbot, rising.

The inspector shook his head. 'No,' he said, 'I think we shall offer you our hospitality for the night. Take them to the cells, constable.'

Mr Talbot looked aghast. 'Look here,' he said, 'you can't do this. I have a wife and daughter to get back to. And you have no reason to, to – detain us.'

The inspector surveyed Mr Talbot mildly, then said: 'The constable will provide you with paper so you can write a note home.' And then he left.

The constable escorted Aleister and Mr Talbot down

116

another corridor, then opened a sturdy oak door and ushered the two of them inside.

'I'll bring you some paper and a pen, sir,' he said through the door. Then he was gone too.

Aleister looked around. It wasn't as horrible as he might have imagined. It looked in fact not much different from an ordinary room, a sparsely furnished bedroom, containing two beds, each against a wall. There was a writing table in the middle and a couple of chairs, and a washbasin and a pitcher. Only the bars on the tiny window suggested that this was not just an austere room in a private home.

Mr Talbot sat down on one of the chairs. It seemed to Aleister that he almost collapsed into it, like an accordion that someone had sat on.

He sat there wearily for a moment, then looked up at Aleister. 'I am being punished for my sins,' he said.

Aleister shifted uneasily.

'Let this be a lesson to you,' said Mr Talbot. 'It should certainly be a lesson to me. Temptation was placed in my path, and I did not resist it. No, I yielded to it. And now I am paying for it.'

He stared mournfully in Aleister's direction, but without really focusing on him.

'Am I paying for it too?' said Aleister a bit hesitantly.

Mr Talbot looked up at him, not comprehending for a moment.

'What's that?' he said. 'Oh, I see. No, there's no reason you should pay. You never took any money from the vault. I will tell them you had nothing to do with it.'

'With the stealing?'

'Yes.'

'But I don't think they've arrested us for stealing.'

'God moves in mysterious ways,' said Mr Talbot. 'I will explain everything and accept my punishment. It is only just.'

Aleister was about to say something, but changed his mind. Mr Talbot seemed in a strange world all his own.

There was a knock at the door. It was the policeman with paper and pens.

'I must write to dear Agnes,' said Mr Talbot. 'But how ever will she understand this?'

He scrawled a few lines on a sheet, folded it over, handed it to the policeman, then collapsed again on his chair.

'I shall tell them about the theft and the blackmail,' he said at last, after the policeman had gone.

'Is that wise?' said Aleister.

'Wise, wise, what is wise?' said Mr Talbot. 'I am no judge. I am a sinner. A thief. I will tell them everything and let them judge. That will purge my soul, and God may then forgive me.'

'But, but ...' Aleister knew this was a bad idea, but found it hard to explain why.

'You must not deter me from my duty,' said Mr Talbot.

'But if you tell them about the blackmail,' said Aleister, finally finding the words to explain, 'they will think you killed Palmer.'

'Let them think what they like,' said Mr Talbot. 'I am tired of lies and deception.'

'They will think I helped you kill him,' said Aleister, a bit desperately. 'And I was the one they found with blood on my hands.'

Mr Talbot considered this for a moment. 'Did you kill him?' he said.

Aleister was too surprised to reply.

'I only asked you to speak to him,' said Mr Talbot, 'not kill him.'

'I did speak to him,' said Aleister, 'and I didn't kill him.'

'Oh,' said Mr Talbot. 'Well, that's good. What did he say?'

'Something about wanting to keep his job.'

'I see,' said Mr Talbot.

They both fell silent.

'Who did kill him?' said Aleister at last.

'How should I know?' said Mr Talbot. 'Though it's strange ...'

'What is?' said Aleister.

'The gun,' said Mr Talbot.

'Yes?'

'I'm pretty sure I recognised it,' said Mr Talbot. 'But it doesn't make any sense.'

'What do you mean?' said Aleister. He wished Mr Talbot would snap out of his daydream or whatever it was. This strange mood of his was almost scarier than anything else.

'It's Mr Smithson's pistol,' said Mr Talbot. 'I'm almost sure of it. It even had his initials on the handle. H-S. Harold Smithson.'

'Oh,' said Aleister. 'Did Mr Smithson kill Palmer?'

'Don't be absurd,' said Mr Talbot.

They fell silent again. Aleister walked over to the barred window. The moon was shining, and he could make out the outlines of a little courtyard below them. He wished he had *The Count of Monte Cristo* with him. Something to occupy his mind and take him away from this awful nightmare.

Though on second thought *The Count of Monte Cristo* might be a bad choice. Too much like what he was going through. Some other book, then. Even his Latin schoolbook. Anything to save him from thinking about his situation.

Then again, perhaps it would be a good idea to think about it. Maybe he could figure out some solution. He remembered something Palmer had said. He'd accused him of skulking around before coming forward to speak. There must have been someone else skulking around. Someone who had followed Palmer perhaps. Or been waiting for him. Or just waiting for anybody. It might have been an accident that Palmer was the victim.

Except if it was Mr Smithson's pistol, then it wasn't an

accident. Someone had followed Palmer with Mr Smithson's gun and shot him. Someone who wanted Palmer dead. Did Mr Smithson want him dead? He wanted him gone, it seemed, dismissed, let go – but dead? Perhaps Palmer's father was making it difficult to get rid of Palmer, and this was the only way.

Still, it was hard to imagine Mr Smithson skulking in the night.

There was another knock on the cell door. The policeman came in, and with him was Mrs Talbot. And Kate.

CHAPTER TWELVE

Telling All

The policeman excused himself, and Kate ran to her father.

'Papa,' she said, throwing her arms around Mr Talbot, 'what has happened? What are you doing here?'

'It's all just a misunderstanding,' Mr Talbot said. Then turning to Mrs Talbot, he added, 'You shouldn't have brought her here. This is no place for a girl.'

'It's no place for anyone respectable,' said Mrs Talbot. 'I never expected to be here myself. And I certainly never expected to hear that a husband of mine had been incarcerated in the local jail.'

Mr Talbot hung his head.

'And somehow you've involved the boy too,' said his wife, indicating Aleister.

'They say you murdered someone,' Kate said to Aleister. 'Is it true?'

'No,' said Aleister.

'Were you defending some lady's honour?' said Kate. 'Or fending off ruffians?'

Mrs Talbot spoke: 'Kate, don't talk nonsense. You heard your father. It is all a misunderstanding.'

'Yes,' said Mr Talbot, 'no one has killed anyone.'

'Someone killed someone,' Mrs Talbot said, correcting him.

'Yes, of course,' said Mr Talbot. 'Someone killed poor Palmer from the office. I only meant ...'

He let the sentence trail off.

Mrs Talbot cast her eye over the cell. 'You and Aleister are sharing this room?' she said.

'I don't know,' said Mr Talbot. 'They put us in here.'

'I will speak to a lawyer in the morning,' said Mrs Talbot. 'And I've already written to George.'

'George!' said Mr Talbot.

It took Aleister a moment to realise they were talking about Mr Rawlins.

'I think we can use his help,' said Mrs Talbot.

Mr Talbot began: 'I really don't think – '

'Never mind,' said Mrs Talbot, 'it's done. Now we have to decide what to do about Aleister's parents.'

'What about Aleister's parents?' said Mr Talbot.

'Shall we notify them that their son is in jail?' said Mrs Talbot.

'Oh, don't do that,' said Aleister.

The adults ignored him.

'They really should be informed,' said Mrs Talbot.

'I suppose,' said Mr Talbot doubtfully.

'On the other hand, it would take weeks by letter.'

'You could send them a telegram,' Kate said brightly.

'To India?' said Mrs Talbot.

'Oh, yes,' said Kate, 'I've been reading all about it. They have a cable underneath the Red Sea now. Everything's connected.'

'Even so,' said Mrs Talbot doubtfully.

'It breaks down all the time, I hear,' said Mr Talbot, shaking his head mournfully. 'Everything does, you know. And it would be very expensive.'

'Besides,' said Mrs Talbot, 'what would they do when they heard the news? Even if they dropped everything to come here, it would take them weeks, and by that time all this might be cleared up. Better to let things take their course and inform them afterwards.'

Aleister thought this might be best, though he wished they

might consult him about it. But Mrs Talbot seemed to consider the matter settled and was pressing on with new concerns.

'I still do not know what has been happening,' she said to her husband. 'I'd like you to explain it all. But not with the children present.'

She moved to the door and banged on it. A moment later, it opened and the policeman stuck his head round.

'Yes, ma'am,' he said.

Mrs Talbot replied: 'I wish to speak to my husband alone. Can you remove the young people for a while?'

'Actually,' said the policeman, 'the inspector was telling me he wanted the young gentleman in his own cell in any case, so I'll conduct him there now. The young lady can wait with me in the front room.'

'Oh, no,' said Kate. 'I'd rather go with Aleister.'

Mrs Talbot nodded at the policeman. 'Let her go with him,' she said. 'It couldn't be any worse than the front room.'

'Begging your pardon, ma'am,' said the policeman. 'We do what we can to keep things civil out there, but there's no helping things when we have to bring in the sort of riff-raff we do. Not meaning yourself, sir,' he added hurriedly to Mr Talbot. 'But I shall do what you say, ma'am,' he said to Mrs Talbot.

So Kate followed Aleister and the policeman down yet another corridor in what was beginning to feel like a maze, until they reached a smaller cell in a corner.

'Here you go, young fella,' said the policeman. 'I hope you find it comfortable. I'll come back in half an hour for your lady friend. It's always nice when chaps have a lady friend to visit them.'

He winked at Aleister, who didn't quite understand what he was suggesting, but thought it couldn't be very pleasant, so he just ignored him.

Kate waited impatiently while the policeman took his leave, then almost pounced on Aleister.

'Tell me what's going on,' she said. 'A policeman came to the house and said you and Papa were being held at the police station over some murder, and I couldn't believe it.'

'I hardly believe it myself,' said Aleister.

Now that he was away from Mr Talbot and the policemen, the horror of the situation was beginning to sink in. He was in jail. The police thought he had committed a murder. He didn't see how he would convince them otherwise. After all, he'd been found with Palmer's blood on his hands, and he'd had an appointment with Palmer, or Mr Talbot had. It was an impossible situation.

He suddenly realised that Kate was waving her hand in front of his face.

'Halloo,' she said. 'Aleister. Are you there?'

'Oh,' he said. 'Sorry. I was thinking.'

'Just tell me what happened,' she said. 'Who was killed?'

'One of the clerks from the office,' said Aleister. 'Palmer. Nobody liked him.'

Kate nodded sagely and took a seat in the middle of the cell. There were chairs and a table in this cell too. Only one narrow bed, though. Aleister sat down on a chair across from Kate.

'Why didn't anyone like him?' said Kate.

Aleister struggled to organise his thoughts. 'I don't know,' he said. 'He was gruff and unpleasant. He bullied Billy Cooper.'

'Billy Cooper?'

'The office boy.'

'So did Billy Cooper kill him?' said Kate.

'I don't know,' said Aleister. 'I don't know anything.'

'And why were you there?'

'It's a long story,' said Aleister.

'And Papa. He was there too.'

'Yes.'

'I don't understand.'

Aleister hesitated. Mr Talbot had warned him not to say

anything about the blackmail to anyone, especially Kate and Mrs Talbot, or even to talk about the office to them. But things were different now. Probably Mr Talbot was telling his wife the whole thing. It was probably all right to tell Kate. But he hesitated.

'Come on, Aleister,' said Kate. 'Explain things.'

And so he did. He explained how her father had come and snatched him away from school and plunked him down in the middle of the insurance company to help track down the blackmailer. He explained how her father had taken money from the company vault – she let out a little gasp at that part – and how someone (Palmer, they now knew) had seen this and sent threatening notes about it.

He explained about the meeting at the cotton mill and how he had seen Palmer and how Palmer had said he wanted to keep his job. And then he described the sound of the gunshots and how he had found the body and how the policeman had found him. And how her father had shown up late, carrying his camera equipment.

When he had finished, Kate was silent a long time.

'I can't believe Papa could have taken money like that,' she said at last.

Aleister just nodded.

'Do you believe it?' she said.

'He told me himself,' said Aleister.

Kate nodded and looked very serious.

'The police will think Papa wanted Palmer killed because of the blackmail,' she said.

Aleister nodded again.

'But he didn't kill Palmer, did he?'

Aleister shook his head. 'I don't think so,' he said. 'He showed up too late.'

'Just like Papa,' said Kate. 'But maybe the police will say Papa got you to kill Palmer.'

Aleister shrugged. 'It's possible.'

Kate looked at Aleister closely.

'That's not what happened, is it?' she said.

Aleister shook his head, but said nothing. Maybe it was what had happened. His head was beginning to spin and he could hardly think straight any more. Maybe he had killed Palmer and couldn't remember it.

But Kate was shaking her head too.

'No,' she said, 'I know you couldn't kill anyone. Nor could Papa. It must have been someone else. We'll just have to find out who.'

Aleister nodded, but suddenly felt very tired.

'You'll have to tell me who you think did it,' said Kate.

'But I don't know,' said Aleister. 'How should I know? I'm really very tired, Kate, and think I need to lie down.'

'You can't lie down; we have to figure this out. You don't want to go to prison for life, do you? Or to one of those reformatories. And they could hang Papa for this. No, no, we have to figure it out.'

'Maybe later,' he said. 'I can't think straight now.'

'Just tell me who else might have done it,' said Kate. 'Like Billy Cooper. You said he didn't like Palmer.'

'Just because someone didn't like him doesn't mean they killed him,' said Aleister.

Kate stopped to think about this.

'I suppose that's true,' she said, 'but where else can we begin? It's a bit like plunging into darkest Africa, isn't it? We're like Stanley trying to find Livingstone. It might seem impossible or frightening, but the thing is to begin.'

'I don't know how I can begin at all,' said Aleister, 'locked up in here.'

'Well,' said Kate, 'I will go and find things out and come back and tell you about them.'

'Will they let you come here again?'

'If they won't, I'll write, and you can write back. They'll let you write letters, won't they?'

'I think so,' said Aleister. 'Your father wrote a letter to you.'

'Good,' said Kate, and so it was agreed.

The policeman came and took Kate away and Aleister waited in his new cell and looked out the barred window at the darkened courtyard, and eventually threw himself down on the narrow bed to try and sleep.

But he couldn't sleep. All he could do was think of Palmer's body lying on the ground and his sticky blood on his hands, and the fireworks going off, and the bonfires burning.

CHAPTER THIRTEEN

A Letter

The next two days were a blur for Aleister. A fussy old man who said he was the lawyer the Talbots had hired told him he looked like an upstanding respectable boy and no jury would convict him.

The policeman brought him some food that he could hardly taste and also a change of clothes the Talbots had sent.

Once a day he was allowed into the courtyard to walk around for exercise. The first time, he had the yard to himself. But on the second day there were others there too. Other detainees, Aleister supposed. Boys no older than himself who grinned and looked dangerous, a sad man wearing rags, and one sharply dressed gentleman who kept checking his fingernails. No sign of Mr Talbot, though.

Perhaps they were keeping them apart, Aleister thought, so they couldn't arrange their stories.

The only time he saw Mr Talbot was on the morning of the first day, when a constable came and took him to a special little room with a high bench, behind which a magistrate looked down on him and Mr Talbot.

The inspector was there too, explaining why he thought Aleister and Mr Talbot should be held for trial. The magistrate listened seriously, said something that Aleister determined meant he agreed with the inspector, and then left. The constable took Aleister back to his cell. Another constable led Mr Talbot away.

On the evening of the second day, Aleister had a visitor. The policeman opened the door, and in walked Mrs Talbot carrying some packages.

'For you, Aleister,' she said. 'I've brought some more clothes and some food, and your book.'

She placed his copy of *The Count of Monte Cristo* on the table. Aleister looked at it with distaste. He was tired of it.

'And there's someone else here to see you,' she said.

Aleister looked up in time to see a big bear-like figure enter the room.

'Mr Rawlins,' he said.

'Yes, lad, indeed. It is I,' said Mr Rawlins. 'I understand you've been reading that cheap adventure trash' – he gestured at *The Count of Monte Cristo* – 'instead of studying your Horace.'

Mr Rawlins looked at him sternly for a moment, then smiled. At least, Aleister assumed it was a smile. He did not remember Mr Rawlins smiling much.

'Just a little humour to lighten things up, Lister Smith,' Mr Rawlins said. 'Don't worry about Horace. Our only concern is to get you out of here.'

'I didn't do it, Mr Rawlins,' said Aleister. 'I didn't kill Palmer. I only went to meet him, and I talked to him, and then he was dead. Someone shot him, but it wasn't me.'

Mr Rawlins patted him on the head. 'Don't you worry,' he said. 'We'll get to the bottom of this. I've already spoken to the inspector, and tomorrow I'm going to speak to Mr Smithson.'

'Mr Smithson?'

'Yes,' said Mr Rawlins, 'at the insurance company. He's agreed to see me. Indeed, he's agreed to let me speak to anyone at the company. The police don't seem inclined to investigate any further, but I shall pursue my own inquiries.'

'But, but,' said Aleister, 'you don't know anyone there. How will you know who to ask?'

'I'm quite experienced at ferreting out wrongdoers, Lister

Smith,' said Mr Rawlins, 'but now that you mention it, if you can give me some advance information about the employees at the firm, that might be useful.'

So Aleister told his schoolmaster about Jack and Miss Lewisham, and Robinson, Crosbie, and Billy Cooper. And Mr Carruthers and Mr Brooks, and anyone else he could think of from the Saviour Assurance Company.

The next day, in the evening, he received a note. It came on pretty pink paper and was addressed to Master Aleister Lister Smith. When he opened it up, he saw it was from Kate. She had written it that afternoon.

Dear Aleister (it said),

What an exciting day this has been. In the morning, Uncle George announced that he was going in to Papa's work to ask questions about the murder. I said I would go with him. He said of course not, but I hung on his arm and pleaded, and said I could help, and eventually he gave in, especially when Mama said she would go too.

First we rode on that awful omnibus, crowded with clerks, with the horses clip-clopping most annoyingly. Then we walked across Piccadilly to the very ugly building where the insurance company is. I never realised Papa worked in such an ugly building. It seems so unnecessary. Of course, the soot doesn't help. Perhaps it would look better if they cleaned it.

Inside, we met Mr Smithson, who is very fat. He and Uncle George closed themselves up in Mr Smithson's office, and Uncle George said Mama and I should go shopping or something and come back later. Of course we did no such thing.

I said to Mama, We can play detective too. She was not sure we should, but I told her we could talk to the clerks and maybe they'd tell us something useful.

I remembered you telling me how you worked with Jack at the carding desk, so we went there. Jack is very handsome –

why didn't you tell me? And he told us all sorts of interesting stories.

He said how shocked everyone had been, of course, by the murder of Palmer and the arrest of you and Papa. He said he didn't think you could have killed anyone, or Papa either. It's all everyone's been talking about the last two days, he said. I asked him who he thought had killed Palmer, but he just looked at me searchingly and didn't answer.

He told me that Mr O'Neill's been put in charge as chief clerk in Papa's place, temporarily. What a lot of Irish work at your insurance company. I was surprised. I thought they all lived in hovels in Ancoats or Salford. Of course, Jack's father lives in Salford. He told me about him and how Palmer insulted him. Do you think Jack's father killed Palmer? Or maybe Jack did to avenge the insult. Wouldn't that be romantic?

We met Billy Cooper, the office boy, who kept running all over the place with blotting paper and ink. Did you kill Palmer, I asked him?

Oh, no, Miss, he said, I was at home with my parents. Do you think we should check? I can't imagine him really staying home on Bonfire Night.

Another clerk, I think his name was Crosbie, came and spoke to us. Mama said later it was because he liked the way I look. There are advantages to being a girl, I see. Maybe I should become a lady detective; I could easily get the men to talk to me. What do you think?

Crosbie had his own theories about the murder. He said them in a very low voice too, as if he was afraid someone would hear. It was the Germans, he said. It seems he thinks there are German clerks trying to get all your jobs, and they killed Palmer to create an opening. What do you think? It sounded a little odd to me. Besides, I didn't see any Germans, only Irish.

I noticed one clerk – Mr Brooks, Jack said it was – hovering in the background all the time, looking very mysterious. I immediately decided he must be the murderer, but when I told Jack, he just laughed. Women's intuition, he said in a mocking voice. I liked him less then. I said to him, Maybe it was you, then; you look like the murdering type. But he just laughed again. I've decided now I don't like him at all.

After that, I wandered around the office a bit. I spoke to Miss Lewisham, your lady clerk. That typewriter looks very interesting. I asked her what she thought about the murder. She said she hardly knew Palmer, but he'd seemed like an unpleasant gentleman, so she wasn't entirely surprised he'd met a violent end.

I don't suppose she could have been involved. Though why not? A woman can commit murder just as well as a man. But not that way perhaps, not skulking through the streets and firing a pistol. Putting arsenic in the tea, that's the way I would do it. Pistols are so dirty.

Every once in a while someone would go into Mr Smithson's office. Uncle George said later they were interviewing people there to try to find out more about the murder, but he didn't say very much about what they found out. He did tell me about the pistol, though. Apparently, it was stolen right out of its case in Mr Smithson's office, though he didn't notice it was gone till the next day.

At least, that's what Mr Smithson says. Do you think he's lying? He could have used his own pistol and made up a story about it being stolen.

In the end, I'm afraid I'm not sure about anything. But do write back and tell me what you think.

Yours faithfully,
Kate

Aleister shook his head over the letter. He was pleased to have received it, but it didn't seem to advance things very much. If only he could get out of jail, and help. Though what could he do? Where would they start? Could there be anything to the Irish aspect, he wondered? Palmer had been very anti-Irish, or at least had seemed so that day when Jack's father was there.

He read the letter again. For some reason he didn't like the part where Kate said Jack was handsome. Or the part about Crosbie liking the way she looked. It made him feel depressed. Of course, he was depressed already, locked up in this tiny cell. He walked over to his window and looked out on the empty courtyard. Then he lay down on his bed and went to sleep.

CHAPTER FOURTEEN

On the Loose

The next day the sun was shining. Little rays of it cast striped shadows through the bars into the cell. Aleister was up early and wandered restlessly around the enclosed space. He picked up *The Count of Monte Cristo*, then put it down again. He thought about asking for a pen and paper to answer Kate, but he didn't want to be writing; he wanted to be doing.

He gobbled down the breakfast the policeman brought, then sat and thought. For some reason, Mr O'Neill came to mind. It was all this talk about the Irish. Mr O'Neill was Irish too. He suddenly felt that it was urgent to talk to him. There was something about him, something about the way he'd reacted when Mr Smithson shot at the pigeon. Something ...

An hour later the policeman came by to lead him outside for his exercise in the courtyard. There were people there again. The sharply dressed gentleman was gone, but there were several new youths, some of them looking a little the worse for wear.

'Friday night scuttling,' someone whispered in his ear.

Aleister jumped. It was one of the new prisoners, a boy not much older than he was.

'Gang fighters,' the boy said, gesturing towards the beaten-up youths. 'They go out on Friday nights and pick fights with each other.'

'Why?' said Aleister.

The other boy shrugged. 'Look,' he said, 'they're going at it again.'

And indeed two of the youths had gone from exchanging words to reaching for each other's throats. A couple of other prisoners went to join them, and soon there was a brawl going on at the far side of the courtyard.

'Oh,' said Aleister, half nervous and half intrigued.

Two constables came racing across the yard, truncheons held high. A couple more came out of the police station to join them. There were shouts and cries, and the sound of a wooden truncheon hitting a skull.

'This way,' said the boy talking to Aleister.

He gestured towards the police station, and headed towards it. Aleister followed him. Inside, a horde of constables rushed past them to get to the disturbance out in the courtyard. They ignored Aleister and the other boy.

Aleister wondered if the boy was leading them back to their cells, but the corridor they went down did not look familiar. He did not recognise it until they suddenly emerged into the front reception area where he had been the first night.

There was a sergeant at the main desk and one other constable in the room overseeing a suspect, but neither of them paid any attention to Aleister and his new friend.

'Come on,' said the boy.

Not completely understanding, Aleister followed the boy out of the front room, down the station stairs, through the big front doors and onto the street. They were free.

Aleister blinked in the sunshine. He was just beginning to grasp the significance of what had happened. He was out of jail. Free. Released from captivity. He felt a moment's elation – but only a moment's. He wasn't really supposed to be free; he hadn't been cleared; he wasn't out legitimately. No one could really blame him, though, could they? He'd just been following the other boy, not even really thinking, just obeying, and suddenly they were outside. It was all a bit of an accident. Perhaps he should just walk back into the police station and turn himself in. Explain that he got confused during the melee, and tried to escape it however he could. Perhaps he shouldn't use the word escape, though.

He looked around for his companion, but he was gone, melted into the crowds. He looked back at the police station. If he went back inside, how would he find out who had killed Palmer? And if he didn't find out, then he and Mr Talbot could be locked up forever, or worse. The police had decided they were guilty, and that was without even knowing about the blackmail. If they found out about that ...

No, he had to get away. He noticed a constable come to the top of the station steps and scan the crowd. He had to get away now. He turned his back on the station, and headed along the street, losing himself among the people walking past. It was easy.

He began walking aimlessly in the city centre. It occurred to him that he had no place to stay. He could hardly head back to the Talbots' place. Mrs Talbot and Mr Rawlins wouldn't harbour him; they'd tell him to go back to jail, turn himself in. For the first time he felt like a criminal.

The sun climbed high in the sky. It was almost mid-day. This being Saturday, the clerks at Saviour Assurance would be getting off work soon to go home. Perhaps he could ask one of them to help him. Jack perhaps. Jack would even find it exciting, helping someone who'd escaped from jail. He wondered where Jack lived. Somewhere not far from the city centre, he thought, because he remembered Jack saying he walked to work. It might be interesting to stay with him.

But even as he thought this, he felt an overwhelming wave of guilt sweep over him. He couldn't stay with Jack and be a criminal on the loose. It was wrong. He had to go back to the police station.

Slowly, he made his way back through the streets that led

to the station. With every step he took he thought he could feel people's eyes on him. He thought they could all tell he was a prison-breaker. He kept his head down and hurried along.

When he neared the station, he paused to see what was going on. Was there a search party of constables preparing to look for him? But he saw no such gathering, and cautiously made his way up the front steps and into the reception area.

He had barely entered it when he was surprised to see Mrs Talbot and Mr Rawlins. They seemed surprised to see him too.

'Aleister,' said Mrs Talbot, 'have they let you go already?'

Aleister did not quite understand what she meant, and it did not seem the time to ask, because Mrs Talbot, who had always seemed so strong, suddenly dissolved into tears. Mr Rawlins helped her to one of the benches next to the wall.

'Oh, George, George,' she said to Mr Rawlins, 'why did he do it?'

Mr Rawlins patted her arm.

'What did who do?' Aleister said.

'Mr Talbot has made a full confession,' said Mr Rawlins.

'About the stealing?' said Aleister.

'About everything,' said Mr Rawlins. 'He said he was being blackmailed by Palmer over the theft of money from the vault, and that he killed Palmer to keep him quiet.'

At these words, Mrs Talbot burst into sobs again.

'But that's not right,' said Aleister. 'He didn't kill Palmer.'

'No?' said Mr Rawlins. 'Then who did?'

'I don't know,' said Aleister. 'I just don't think it could have been Mr Talbot.'

'Oh, it couldn't have been Arthur, could it have?' said Mrs Talbot. 'I could barely believe that he took money from the company vault, but murder ...'

Mr Rawlins looked thoughtful. 'Why would he confess to something he didn't do?' he said.

Aleister shrugged. He had a horrible suspicion that Mr Talbot had done what he had to protect him, Aleister.

'What did he say about me?' Aleister said.

Mr Rawlins looked at him closely.

'He said you had nothing to do with it. He kept saying that over and over again, but at first nothing more. Then when pressed he told a story about how he got there first and killed Palmer, then waited till you showed up, letting you discover the body and end up with blood on your hands.'

Aleister nodded. Mrs Talbot let out a stifled cry.

'It's not true, is it?' she said.

'I don't think so,' said Aleister.

'Oh, my God,' said Mrs Talbot, 'what is to become of us?'

Mr Rawlins patted her arm again.

'Was it just a story?' he said to Aleister.

Aleister nodded, but before he could say anything more, a constable came up to them.

'There you are,' he said to Aleister. 'We've been looking all over for you to let you loose, but it seemed you had got loose already.'

'I – I hid after the fight in the courtyard,' said Aleister.

'Where?' said the constable, looking at him sharply.

'I don't know exactly,' said Aleister. 'I just wandered for a while, then found myself here.'

The constable frowned. 'Well, I suppose it doesn't matter,' he said, 'since we're releasing you anyway now that Mr Talbot's confessed. Strange, though.'

Aleister went home with Mrs Talbot and Mr Rawlins. He felt a confused mass of emotions. Relief, guilt, worry. He couldn't let Mr Talbot be hanged for something he didn't do, especially if he was doing it to keep Aleister from the same fate. He should never have complained the way he did to Mr Talbot. He should have been braver, or more clever. Well, he could be clever now.

'We have to find the real murderer,' he said to Mr Rawlins as they rode home in a cab.

Mr Rawlins motioned him to be quiet. 'Later,' he said in

a hushed voice, and nodded towards Mrs Talbot, who was lying back with her eyes closed.

Aleister lay back himself and tried to think.

CHAPTER FIFTEEN

Beginning Again

When he got back to the Talbots' house, Aleister found he had lost his room to Mr Rawlins.

'We've moved your things to the study,' Mr Rawlins said, and Aleister found himself relegated to a corner of the room where Mr Talbot used to go to read. There were books of Milton in the heavy wooden bookcase that occupied one wall, along with a whole series of volumes labelled *The Decline and Fall of the Roman Empire*.

But Aleister paid little attention to the books. He was tired of books. He was tired in general. He wanted to lie down and sleep, but it took a while before Mr Rawlins and the maid Geraldine could arrange to wheel a little bed into place for him. It required a lot of moving of furniture, and even then Aleister felt crowded, with chairs and desks and bookcases all around him. He felt ousted too, pushed aside, as if Mr Rawlins was taking over and turning him into a schoolboy again.

Well, it didn't matter, Aleister thought. He would live in the crowded study and solve the murder from there.

But not today. He needed sleep now more than anything else. He lay down on the bed and fell into oblivion.

In the morning, he felt better. It was Sunday, but the family didn't go to chapel. Mrs Talbot stayed in her room. She was not ready to go out in public, Mr Rawlins said.

Outside, the rare November sunshine from the day before

had vanished, leaving Manchester shrouded in its customary grey clouds. Aleister wandered around the house feeling empty and unsure how to occupy his time. Kate stayed in her room too for the morning, and when she finally emerged, it looked like she had been crying.

Aleister cast his head down, unsure what to say to her. To his surprise, she suddenly ran to him and began hitting him in the chest.

'It's all your fault,' she said. 'Everything was fine before you came here. Why'd you have to come and destroy everything?'

'But – but ...'

Aleister could hardly think what to say. He tried to pull away, but Kate held onto him for a moment, then pulled herself away, threw herself down on a couch and started sobbing.

Aleister stood there uneasily, not knowing whether to go or stay.

'I'm sorry, Aleister,' Kate said, drying her tears after a few moments. 'I'm just upset. Papa's in jail, and maybe they will hang him, and it's just too horrible.'

Aleister nodded.

'Maybe it would be better,' Kate said, 'if we tried to think of something to do for him.'

'Yes,' said Aleister, glad that the crying seemed to be over. He sat down across from her.

'You don't think Papa really killed that nasty Palmer, do you?' Kate said.

Aleister shook his head.

'Why would he say he did, then?' she said.

'I'm afraid he may have been trying to protect me,' said Aleister.

'You mean you killed Palmer?' she said.

'No, no,' said Aleister, 'but I was worried it would look that way, and your father must have – I don't know. It was good of him to protect me.'

141

Kate shook her head. 'Silly Papa,' she said. 'We shall have to save him.'

Aleister nodded.

'Do you have a plan?' Kate asked.

'A plan?' said Aleister.

'Mama says the lawyer may get the judge to be lenient. Or they could ask the Home Secretary for a commutation, but that would still mean Papa would go to prison.'

Aleister wasn't entirely sure what a commutation was, but just nodded.

'I don't want Papa to go to prison,' Kate said decisively.

'No,' said Aleister.

'We will just have to prove him innocent despite his confession.'

Aleister nodded.

'We have to find some clue,' Kate went on, 'something to help us prove he didn't do it, something to show that someone else did it.'

'Yes,' said Aleister, 'and I've been thinking about Mr O'Neill.'

'I think it might be Billy Cooper,' said Kate.

'Why?' said Aleister.

'Do you really think he went home on Bonfire Night the way he said? I don't.'

Aleister shrugged. 'I still think it might have been Mr O'Neill,' he said. 'But there's something else.'

Kate looked at him expectantly.

'Yes?' she said.

'I've been wondering about what the police found on Palmer's body that night.'

'What was that?'

'A cracker – you know, a fireworks type cracker – and a note saying "Remember, remember the Fifth of November".'

Kate thought about this for a moment.

'That's strange,' she said. 'Is it some sort of message?'

'I think so,' said Aleister, 'but what does it mean?'

Kate shook her head. 'I have no idea,' she said. 'But what I think we should do is talk to the clerks at work again.'

And so, on Monday, Aleister took Kate in to work, or at least to the cook-shop where the clerks usually had their midday meal.

There was Jack at their usual table, with Robinson, Crosbie, and, unusually, Billy Cooper.

'Lister Smith,' Jack said in surprise. 'Didn't think you'd be showing up again.'

'Hello, Jack,' said Aleister.

'And young Kate, I think it was,' said Jack, beaming at her.

Kate beamed back. Aleister frowned for a moment.

'I thought you were in jail,' said Crosbie.

'They let me go,' said Aleister.

'Good thing,' said Crosbie. 'They should be looking for those Germans.'

Aleister repressed a smile. 'The police aren't looking for anyone,' he said. 'They think Mr Talbot did it. But Kate and I are sure he didn't.'

'Who do you think did?' said Billy Cooper.

Aleister looked at him; he seemed scared, and ready to shrink into invisibility. It reminded Aleister of boys trying not to be called on in Mr Rawlins's class.

Kate spoke up. 'We don't know,' she said, 'but we're trying to find out.'

'Aha,' said Jack, 'and you think perhaps it was one of us.'

'No, no,' said Aleister.

'Of course you do,' said Jack. 'And it would be only natural. After all, we all hated Palmer.'

'I didn't hate him,' said Robinson.

'No, no, Christian charity and all that,' said Jack. 'Of course. But he gave you a hard time about being a killjoy over Guy Fawkes Day. You couldn't have liked that.'

'I certainly didn't kill him for it. I wouldn't kill anybody.'

'Oh, I don't know,' said Jack. 'Anyone could kill in the right circumstances.'

'I don't know about that,' said Robinson.

'Anyway,' said Aleister, 'the question isn't killing in general; it's who killed Palmer on Guy Fawkes Night.'

'Very good, Lister Smith,' said Jack. 'Get to the heart of the matter. I suppose you want to know where we all were that night.'

'I was at the YMCA,' said Robinson. 'In their reading room.'

'Oh, Robinson,' said Jack.

'It's true,' said Robinson. 'You can ask the secretary there.'

'I was at the bonfires with my mates,' said Crosbie.

'I was with my mates too,' said Jack.

'You weren't in that gang of Home Rulers, were you?' said Aleister. 'I saw them about to get into a fight.'

Jack laughed. 'I can think of better things to do than get into fights about Home Rule. Politics is not for me.'

Crosbie stood up. 'Time to get back,' he said.

'Wait,' said Jack. 'Billy hasn't told us where he was.'

Billy looked more frightened than ever.

Kate said, 'Billy told me he went home to his parents.'

Billy nodded.

'But I thought we'd go ask them just to be sure,' she added.

'No, no,' said Billy, 'don't do that.'

'Why not?' said Kate.

'You mustn't,' Billy said.

And he suddenly bolted out of the shop.

The others looked at each other.

'What's that all about?' said Jack.

'We better check,' said Kate, and headed out the door after Billy.

The others followed. It was raining, a light steady drizzle that made the city look grey. Aleister watched as Kate and the others hurried back towards the insurance company, as if that's where Billy would have gone. He saw them go past a tiny alleyway, and wondered.

When he got to the alleyway, he stopped and looked down it. There, huddled against a brick wall, was Billy.

'There you are,' said Aleister.

Billy looked up, but said nothing. Aleister thought he'd been crying, but it might just have been the rain.

He squatted down beside Billy. It was wet, and he didn't much like ruining his clothes, but it seemed the best way to get Billy to talk to him, and it suddenly seemed that Billy might have something important to say.

Billy watched Aleister settle in beside him. Neither of them said anything for a moment, then Billy finally spoke. 'Don't go talking to my parents,' he said.

Aleister nodded, and said, 'Why not?'

'I wasn't really at home that evening,' said Billy, 'and they think I was working late at the office, so if you go asking them questions ...'

'Where were you?' said Aleister.

Billy suddenly looked sullen. 'I didn't kill Palmer, if that's what you're getting at.'

'No, no,' said Aleister, 'though he did bully you a lot.'

Billy shrugged. 'That didn't bother me,' he said. He had a faraway look in his eye. 'I liked Palmer. He was good to me. He gave me tips on the horses.'

'They always lost, I thought.'

'That wasn't his fault,' said Billy. 'And he said he might let me into his gang.'

'Palmer had a gang?' said Aleister, with interest.

'Yes,' said Billy. 'That's who I was with that night. Palmer said to go and meet them, and he'd come along later to join in the celebrations. We were going to go with him to one of the bonfires, but he never showed up.' Billy sounded extraordinarily sad. He added, 'You mustn't tell my parents any of this.'

'No, no, of course not,' said Aleister. 'But can you tell me where I could meet some of the other gang members?'

'Well,' said Billy doubtfully, 'they meet most nights out near Granby Row to play pitch-and-toss.'

'Can we go see them tonight?' said Aleister.

'I – I suppose,' said Billy. 'But why?'

'It might be a way to find out more about Palmer, and then figure out who might have killed him.'

'But the gang was all out at Granby Row,' said Billy. 'None of them could have killed him.'

'No, I suppose not,' said Aleister. 'Still ...' He had a sudden idea. 'Is anyone else from the office in the gang?'

'Oh, no,' said Billy. 'Palmer said to keep it quiet from the office. It was a secret. Not the sort of thing the office clerks would understand, he said. It's not a gang of clerks, you know.'

'No, no,' said Aleister.

'More errand boys and butchers' boys and such-like.'

Aleister nodded and stood up. 'Come on,' he said. 'Let's go back to the office.'

Billy stood up slowly. His face still looked wet, from tears or rain, but he seemed a little more composed now, and he followed Aleister back towards the office.

When they were almost there, they encountered Kate and Jack.

'You found him,' said Kate.

Aleister nodded. 'Billy told me something interesting,' he said.

Kate and Jack looked at him expectantly.

'Palmer had a gang,' said Aleister.

Kate and Jack looked puzzled.

'A gang,' said Aleister. 'We should check it out.'

'Why?' said Jack.

'Because it might tell us something,' said Aleister.

'But Aleister,' said Kate, 'I thought it had to be someone from the office, because they used Mr Smithson's gun.'

Aleister sighed. 'Yes,' he said. 'I suppose you're right. But ...'

He shrugged. Kate was right. What did it matter about the gang? None of them could have got hold of the pistol. And yet it just seemed like a good idea to speak to them. He couldn't explain it; he just knew it was something they should do.

'I still think we should speak to the gang,' he said. 'Billy can take us to them. He was going to join them.'

Billy looked a little frightened again. 'You're not all going to come, are you?' he said. 'They might not like that. They might get angry.'

'No, you're right,' said Aleister. 'I'll go. Kate should go home.'

'Well, you want me along, I think,' said Jack.

'No,' said Aleister, 'it might be better if I go myself. With Billy, of course.'

Jack shrugged. 'Suit yourself,' he said, and headed into the insurance building.

Kate said, 'I don't want to just go home. There must be something I can do.'

Aleister thought for a moment. The answer seemed obvious, but for some reason he didn't want to say it. Finally, he brought himself to.

'Speak to Jack some more,' he said. 'Find out what he was doing on Guy Fawkes Night.'

'But he told us,' said Kate.

'Well, get him to prove it,' said Aleister.

Kate looked at him strangely. 'All right,' she said. 'I will.'

CHAPTER SIXTEEN

Investigating

After work, Aleister went with Billy to Granby Row. It was dark, and Aleister could barely make out the outlines of the back-to-back houses. There were no trees or grass. In the distance, he could hear children shouting. Playing games or getting into mischief.

'How much further?' he said to Billy.

'Not too far,' said Billy.

'Did Palmer live around here?' Aleister asked dubiously.

Billy shook his head. 'No, he just came here to be with the gang, I think.'

'Odd,' said Aleister.

They turned a corner. Aleister was about to ask why Palmer would come to a neighbourhood he didn't live in when his nose was assaulted by a truly noxious smell.

'What is that?' he said to Billy.

Billy looked puzzled for a moment.

'Oh, it's just the river,' he said. 'You get used to it.'

'The river?' said Aleister.

'Or what people dump into the river,' said Billy. 'Palmer always used to say, "You don't want to go swimming in that river." '

'No,' said Aleister.

'I think Palmer used to live near here,' said Billy. 'He told me once that his family kept moving when he was young. To better places. But he started out here.'

Aleister nodded. They walked on. He could hear sounds close up now, and when they turned the next corner they came upon a group of boys peering at the pavement.

'They're all heads,' said one of the boys triumphantly as he scooped up a collection of halfpennies.

'No, they weren't,' said another. 'Give them back.'

'You accusing me of cheating?'

'They weren't all heads.'

A bigger boy intervened. 'Toss 'em again,' he said, 'and this time let us all see them when they land.'

The first boy looked like he was going to protest, then changed his mind and tossed the coins.

Aleister and Billy watched for a moment, till someone noticed them.

'It's Billy,' said one of the smallest boys.

The other boys looked at them. Aleister felt slightly uneasy.

'Who's that with you?' said one of the boys, addressing Billy.

'A friend of mine,' said Billy.

'Don't know that we want any new members,' another boy said.

'I knew Palmer,' Aleister said.

There was silence. The big boy who had intervened in the dispute came over and looked Aleister in the eye.

'Who are you?' he said.

'I worked with Palmer,' said Aleister, 'and I was with him when he died.'

He thought he could hear a gasp or two from the younger gang members.

'What were you doing with him, then?' said the big boy.

'I was meeting him at the Medlock Mill,' said Aleister. 'Then someone shot him.'

The big boy nodded. 'We heard about it.'

'We heard they got the man that killed him,' said another boy.

'They've got the wrong man,' said Aleister.

'I heard they had a boy in jail too,' said the big boy, looking at Aleister significantly.

'I was in jail, but they let me go,' said Aleister. 'I didn't kill Palmer, and neither did the man they're still holding. I'm trying to find out who did.'

The big boy looked at Aleister closely. He seemed the angry type, Aleister thought, and not very clean.

'How are you going to do that?' said the boy.

Aleister shrugged. 'I'm not entirely sure,' he said. 'I thought perhaps you might have some ideas.'

The boy opened his mouth and laughed at the suggestion. Aleister noticed that he was missing a tooth.

'How would we know who killed him?' said the boy.

'I thought – since you knew him ...'

Aleister felt suddenly uncertain, but he forced himself to go on.

'I thought you might know who wanted him killed,' he said.

The boy snorted in disgust, turned his back on Aleister, and began to walk away.

'Wait,' said Aleister. 'Can't you tell me anything?'

The boy turned around and walked part of the way back.

'You don't belong here,' he said. 'You come from somewhere posh. Palmer told us about blokes like you.'

'I'm just trying to find out what happened,' said Aleister.

'Why do you care what happened?' said the boy. 'What do you care about Palmer? We cared about Palmer. We were his mates. You just worked with him.'

He walked away again. Aleister watched him helplessly.

'Billy,' he said, 'can't you do something?'

Billy shrugged. 'I'm not even really a member of the gang yet,' he said. 'I don't think they'd listen to me.'

Aleister shook his head.

'I have a feeling they could tell me something,' he said.

He watched as the boys resumed their game. They pitched their coins, then raced to see where they had fallen.

Aleister wanted to go and talk to them again. He was sure they could tell him something. But they did not seem very friendly, and when Billy tugged on his sleeve to go away, he went.

Billy hurried off in one direction and Aleister trudged away in another. He didn't think there were any buses at this hour, and he had no money for a cab, so he walked. Along the treeless streets south of the city centre he went, then down one of the main thoroughfares leading to the inner suburbs.

Street after street, mile after mile. It was quiet tonight and not raining any more. No one was about – not like on Guy Fawkes Night. No bonfires in the distance. No fireworks. No children begging for pennies for their guys. And no gunshots.

Aleister shivered a little, remembering that night. It was less than a week ago, but things had changed so much. And less than a month ago he had been safe in school, far from Manchester and gangs and murders. He sighed.

He was nearly at the Talbots' house now, walking past the green. A carriage rattled by: a cab. He watched it go, and to his surprise it stopped in front of the Talbots' house. To his even greater surprise, Kate stepped out of it and went inside.

Aleister hurried to catch up with her, but by the time he reached the house, she was already inside. He fumbled for the key he had been given, all the while hearing movement from inside and then some uncharacteristically raised voices.

He finally opened the door and walked into the parlour. Mrs Talbot was there, and Mr Rawlins and Kate.

'How could you go off gallivanting like that?' Mrs Talbot was saying to Kate. 'I was worried half out of my mind.'

'I was perfectly safe,' said Kate. 'I was with Jack Quinn from Papa's office.'

'A respectable girl does not spend time alone with men

from her father's office,' said Mrs Talbot. 'Where did you go with him?'

'He took me to his local pub,' said Kate.

'Oh my God,' said Mrs Talbot.

At this point, the three of them noticed Aleister.

'And you,' said Mrs Talbot, 'where have you been?'

Aleister hesitated. He didn't like the antagonistic atmosphere in the room.

'I was investigating Palmer's murder,' he said. 'Talking to his gang.'

'His gang?' said Mrs Talbot. 'Lord help us. As if I don't have troubles enough, now the two of you are off, off – '

'Off trying to prove Papa didn't commit murder,' said Kate defiantly.

'Don't interrupt me,' said Mrs Talbot. 'And don't get any ridiculous notions into your head about investigating the murder.'

'What would you have me do?' said Kate. 'Stay at home and cry like you while Papa goes to the gallows?'

'Kate,' said Mrs Talbot, 'go to your room this instant. I have never heard such insolence.'

Kate was already halfway to the stairs, as if she knew she had gone too far.

'And as for you,' said Mrs Talbot turning to Aleister, 'I think you should go to your room too.'

Aleister considered saying he no longer had a room, but thought better of it. He did say: 'I was only trying to find out if someone other than Mr Talbot committed the murder.'

Mr Rawlins spoke up: 'You should leave all that to your elders, Aleister. We know best.'

Aleister nodded, but inside he was thinking that they didn't know best at all. However, now did not seem the time to discuss this or the murder, so he headed off to the study and got ready for bed.

CHAPTER SEVENTEEN

A Visitor

Everyone was calmer the next day, sitting in the parlour after breakfast, but when Kate talked of doing some more investigating, her mother was firm.

'No more of that, Kate,' she said. 'I don't want you getting into trouble too.'

'But Mother ...'

'That's final, Kate,' said Mrs Talbot. 'Your uncle and I are preparing an appeal to the Home Secretary, in case that is needed, and our lawyer will be arguing for leniency in court.'

'You don't think Papa did it, do you?' said Kate.

Mrs Talbot shook her head slightly. 'I don't know what to think,' she said. 'It is hard to believe that your father could ever have indulged in violence. And yet he confessed to it.'

'Oh, he just did that to protect Aleister,' said Kate.

'To protect Aleister?' said Mrs Talbot. 'What do you mean? Aleister, what does she mean?'

Aleister shifted uneasily.

'I think he didn't want me to get in trouble for the murder,' he said, 'so he confessed to it himself.'

Mrs Talbot stared at Aleister.

'I think,' said Aleister, hurrying on, 'that he felt responsible for bringing me into all this, and wanted to make sure I didn't suffer because of what he'd done.'

'What do you mean?' Mrs Talbot said. 'Are you saying he did commit the murder?'

'No, no, not that,' said Aleister.

'Then what?' said Mrs Talbot.

Aleister felt even more uneasy, and mumbled a reply:

'I mean taking the money from the vault,' he said. 'He wanted to pay for that, I mean be punished for that, and I asked if I would have to pay for it too, and he must have – he must have decided – I mean ...'

Mrs Talbot looked both angry and tearful.

'So it's your fault,' she said. 'If not for you, he wouldn't be in this mess at all.'

Mr Rawlins spoke up. 'Now, now, Agnes,' he said. 'It's no use looking to blame someone. Besides, Arthur began all the problems by taking the money in the first place. And it was his idea to send Aleister alone to meet that Palmer person so that he could fetch his camera. A damn fool idea, I think.'

'You never liked Arthur,' said Mrs Talbot to Mr Rawlins, a tear forming in her eye. 'You've never liked him, and now you are prepared to see him go to his death.'

'Agnes,' said Mr Rawlins, 'you know that's not true. I will do everything in my power to save your husband.'

To save his impecunious brother-in-law, Aleister thought, remembering the first thing Mr Rawlins had told him about Mr Talbot. He thought Mrs Talbot was right: Mr Rawlins didn't like Mr Talbot. He wasn't sure he liked him himself, but now he felt guilty about getting him into trouble. It was important to save him.

'I really don't think Mr Talbot killed Palmer,' he said. 'I don't see how he could have been there in time and then have shown up with his camera equipment afterwards. Someone else was lurking in the darkness. The question is who.'

The others were silent for a moment.

'It's a good question, Lister Smith,' said Mr Rawlins, acting as if they were back in the Shrewsbury classroom. 'It's a good question, but what is the answer?'

Aleister shrugged. The answer seemed further away than ever.

Mrs Talbot picked aimlessly at the quilt she had on her lap. Geraldine the maid bustled in.

'Mrs Cavendish is here, ma'am,' she said.

'Mrs Cavendish?' said Mrs Talbot. 'What does she want? Tell her I am not at home. Tell her – '

But it was too late for Geraldine to tell her anything, for Mrs Cavendish had already bustled into the parlour.

'Mrs Talbot,' she said, coming over to her with the most sympathetic expression on her face and looking as if she wanted to take Mrs Talbot's hand, only Mrs Talbot's hands were busy beneath the quilt.

'Mrs Talbot,' said Mrs Cavendish again, 'how terribly dreadful for you. I have just heard the news. Your poor husband locked up in jail. Who ever would have thought he could have committed murder?'

Mrs Talbot winced slightly and managed a nod.

'If there's anything I can do,' said Mrs Cavendish.

She looked around the room as if checking her audience, and seemed slightly disappointed to see only one other adult there, not counting the maid (who soon left in any case). But noticing Aleister seemed to remind her of something.

'You're Mr Talbot's nephew, aren't you?' she said, smiling in what Aleister felt was a most unpleasant way.

'Something like that,' Aleister mumbled.

'I remember you from the train,' she said. 'And isn't it an extraordinary coincidence that I should have been reading that interesting essay by Mr Thackeray about murderers, and now your uncle is – that is, well, I mean I'm sure he couldn't really have ...'

Mrs Cavendish trailed off, having caught Mrs Talbot's eye. Mrs Talbot was positively glaring at her.

'Of course, I don't mean to say ...' said Mrs Cavendish. 'That is, I may have heard the news all wrong, and I'm sure if

155

Mr Talbot murdered somebody, he had very good reasons for doing so.'

Mrs Talbot put down her quilt and got to her feet.

'It was very good of you to pay a visit, Mrs Cavendish,' she said, 'but as you can imagine, this is a difficult time for all of us, and what we now are most in need of is a little time to ourselves.'

'Oh, of course,' said Mrs Cavendish.

She began to retreat towards the door, but suddenly seemed curious about Mr Rawlins.

'I don't believe I've had the pleasure,' she said, nodding to him.

'Mrs Talbot's brother,' said Mr Rawlins.

'Ah,' said Mrs Cavendish.

'Mr Rawlins,' he added.

'Charmed,' said Mrs Cavendish, holding out her hand for Mr Rawlins to take. 'And now I shall leave you to your ... your privacy,' she added, and went out.

Aleister held his breath. He didn't know whether Mrs Talbot would burst into tears or angry exclamations. But before she could do either, Mr Rawlins burst out laughing.

'What a silly woman,' he said between laughs.

Mrs Talbot seemed to smile despite herself. She patted at her eyes with a handkerchief, and then seemed quite calm.

'I think we must do something,' she said, standing up. 'It is no good sitting here feeling tearful or bickering. We must act.'

She looked at Aleister.

'If Aleister is right,' she said, 'we ought to be devoting all our efforts to finding out the true murderer. Only if that fails should we worry about leniency and appeals for mercy.'

Kate bounced out of her chair, looking happy and animated.

'So I can go investigating again?' she said.

Mrs Talbot looked at her carefully.

'I think,' she said, 'that if you exercise due caution and do nothing unbecoming to a respectable young lady, then perhaps that would be a good idea.'

'Oh, Mama,' said Kate, and ran and hugged her.

'The thing to do,' said Mr Rawlins, 'is to be systematic, to determine who else could have committed this heinous deed.'

He looked at Aleister. They all looked at Aleister.

Aleister said, 'Well, we can rule out Billy Cooper. It looks like he was with Palmer's gang at the time of the murder. I really think the gang may have some useful information for us, but they didn't seem to want to talk to me.'

'I think we should speak to Palmer's father,' said Kate.

'Oh?' said Mr Rawlins.

'Jack told me that Palmer didn't get along with his father.'

'But the pistol,' said Mr Rawlins. 'How would he have got hold of Mr Smithson's pistol?'

'Oh,' said Kate, sounding a bit deflated. 'I don't know.'

Aleister spoke up. 'It might not be a bad idea to speak to Mr Palmer, though,' he said. 'We have been too narrowly looking at who could have done this. We need to find more out about Palmer in general.'

'I don't see how that can possibly help us,' said Mrs Talbot. 'What does it matter who Palmer was? The question is who the murderer was.'

'Aleister may have a point, though,' said Mr Rawlins. 'A student must explore all avenues. You never know what stray fact may provide the answer to a problem.'

Mrs Talbot looked unconvinced. 'I think we should concentrate on the actual suspects,' she said. 'Who are they?'

Again everyone looked at Aleister.

'Well,' he said, 'there are the other junior clerks and apprentices at work. Robinson, Crosbie. Robinson says he was at the YMCA. Crosbie says he was with his mates celebrating Guy Fawkes Night. We could check.'

'But you don't think it's them, do you?' said Mrs Talbot.

Aleister shrugged. 'There's Jack,' he said, looking at Kate.

'It wasn't Jack,' said Kate, sounding very certain and looking less happy.

'How do you know, dear?' said Mrs Talbot.

'He showed me where he was that night,' said Kate, looking suddenly expressionless, 'and his – his companions vouched for him.'

Aleister looked at Kate strangely for a moment, but felt somehow pleased, though he didn't know why.

'Well, if you say so, dear,' said Mrs Talbot. 'Who else is there?'

'There are the more senior clerks and assessors,' said Aleister. 'Mr Brooks, Mr O'Neill – I wondered before about Mr O'Neill. And Mr Carruthers.'

'Mr Carruthers is an interesting possibility,' said Mr Rawlins. 'Arthur told me there was something improper going on concerning him.'

Aleister nodded. 'Yes. Mr Talbot told me about a suspicious claim that he assessed. And Jack said something that made me think Palmer was blackmailing him. Maybe Palmer was blackmailing lots of people. Maybe there were lots of people with reason to kill him.'

'And what about Miss Lewisham?' said Kate.

'What about her?' said Mr Rawlins.

'Perhaps she had a reason to kill Palmer,' said Kate.

Aleister suddenly remembered the secret Jack had told him about Miss Lewisham. About her not really being a Miss. About her secret husband. Could Palmer have found it out too? Was he blackmailing her? Had she killed him as a result? Followed him in the dark, shot him with Mr Smithson's pistol? He shook his head. It seemed unlikely. And what could Palmer have hoped to gain by blackmailing Miss Lewisham? If he was blackmailing people with influence to keep him on in his position as clerk, Miss Lewisham hardly seemed the person to bother with.

'Aleister,' said Kate. 'Are you daydreaming?'

'Oh,' said Aleister. 'Just thinking about Miss Lewisham. I don't think she would have had a reason to kill Palmer, but we can try to find out where she was that night, I suppose.'

'I think,' said Mr Rawlins, 'that I will go into the office and speak again to some of the people involved. I especially want to find out about Mr Carruthers.'

'And we can go and speak to Palmer's father,' said Kate.

Mrs Talbot looked hesitant.

'Oh, please, Mama,' said Kate. 'I want to help Papa.'

'All right,' said Mrs Talbot, 'but I shall go with you.'

CHAPTER EIGHTEEN

A Wonderful Discovery

It didn't take long to get ready, and soon the four of them were
headed off, all crowded into a cab. It was decided that Mr
Rawlins would go into the city centre to make inquiries at the
office, while the others were dropped off to seek out information at the Palmer family's house in one of the other suburbs.

The Palmer house was larger than the Talbots', and more
ornate. Mr Palmer must have done well for himself, Aleister
thought.

They knocked at the door, and a maid dressed all in black
answered it. Mrs Talbot asked if they could see Mr or Mrs
Palmer. The maid shook her head and said the whole household
was in mourning.

'Young Mr Robert died just a week ago,' she said.

'Yes, I know,' said Mrs Talbot, and explained who they
were.

The maid shook her head again, but said she would check.
Mrs Talbot, Kate, and Aleister waited outside in the light rain
that began to fall. The maid soon returned, and said that Mrs
Talbot could go in, but the children would have to remain
outside.

Aleister began to object. 'Will you know what to ask?' he
said to Mrs Talbot.

Mrs Talbot looked imperiously down at him.

'I think I have a good enough grasp of the situation,' she
said in an icy tone, and followed the maid into the house.

Aleister and Kate huddled in the doorway as the drizzle became more steady.

'I don't know,' said Aleister, shaking his head. 'Will she ask the right questions?'

'Oh, Mama is quite clever,' said Kate. 'She could have done all sorts of things with her life if only women were allowed to.'

Aleister nodded. 'I hope you're right,' he said.

They waited in front of the Palmers' door for several minutes. Aleister looked up and down the street. It was filled with leafy trees and looked a cut above the Talbots' neighbourhood. A carriage clip-clopped past them, but otherwise no one else appeared.

'So what happened with Jack?' Aleister said.

'I don't want to talk about it,' said Kate, turning her head away.

'He didn't do anything improper, did he?'

Kate frowned at him. 'Don't be an idiot,' she said.

'Then why won't you talk about it?'

'Because, because – oh, just because.'

Kate started walking away from the house, as if she couldn't stand talking with Aleister any longer.

'Wait,' said Aleister, hurrying after her.

Kate looked back at him, but did not slow down. Aleister broke into a trot to catch up.

'Why are you walking so fast?' he said.

'If you can't keep up,' said Kate, 'perhaps you should go back and wait at the door.'

Aleister huffed and puffed a bit. It was hard to talk and trot at the same time.

'I just wanted to know if you were sure Jack couldn't have been at the murder scene,' he said.

Kate was quiet for a moment, and Aleister wondered if she had heard him. Maybe she just didn't like the question. But he needed to know the answer. He started to ask again, but she interrupted him.

'I am sure he wasn't at the murder scene,' she said. 'Are you satisfied?'

'It would be nice to know how you know,' said Aleister. 'Are you just taking his word for it?'

Kate stopped suddenly, and turned to face him.

'No,' she said. 'I am not just taking his word. I went with him to that pub of his: the Wandering Pilgrim, I think it's called. Some ridiculous name like that. And full of very vulgar people getting intoxicated on cheap beer. Quite revolting.'

For a moment Aleister thought Kate looked like her mother.

'And these vulgar people,' said Aleister. 'They vouched for Jack?'

'Yes,' said Kate. 'One in particular. Someone named Lizzie. Horrid name. "Oh, yes, dearie," she said. "Me and Jack were together the whole time, if you know what I mean." And then she positively leered at me with her heavily made-up eyes and painted lips. It was disgusting.'

Aleister nodded. 'Maybe we should get back,' he said.

Kate nodded back at him, and the two of them returned to the house. There was no sign of Mrs Talbot, and the rain was falling harder. They were both quiet, trying to keep dry in front of the door, which suddenly opened.

They turned around, expecting to see Mrs Talbot, but instead it was the maid.

'I'm not sure how much longer the lady will be visiting,' she said, 'and it's raining rather hard, so I thought you might like to stop in the front parlour.'

She held the door open, and Kate and Aleister went inside.

'Thank you so much,' said Aleister, casting his eye over the very cluttered room, full of over-stuffed chairs, tables, mirrors, photographs, and bric-a-brac.

'It was horrible what happened to Mr Robert,' said the maid.

'Yes,' said Aleister.

'That horrible Guy Fawkes Night,' the maid said. 'I told Mr Robert that he shouldn't go out on it. Especially after what happened last year.'

'What happened last year?' Kate asked.

'Oh, it was terrible,' said the maid. 'Somebody died. A young boy. He had just become one of Mr Robert's friends.'

'He was in Palmer's – Mr Robert's gang?' said Aleister.

'Gang?' said the maid.

'Group, friends, mates,' said Aleister.

'Yes,' said the maid.

'How interesting,' said Aleister.

'It was very sad,' said the maid, seeming to find Aleister's reaction different from what she had expected. She began to withdraw from the room.

'Wait,' said Aleister. 'Do you remember this boy's name?'

'No,' said the maid. 'I don't think so. It was in the paper, though. I will direct the lady here when she is done.'

And she was gone.

'The paper,' said Aleister. 'His name was in the paper.'

Kate shrugged. 'So?'

'Don't you find it odd?' Aleister said. 'Somebody Palmer knew – a member of his gang – died last year on Guy Fawkes Night, and this year Palmer himself dies.'

'Is someone trying to kill off his gang?' Kate asked.

'I don't know,' said Aleister, 'but maybe we can find something out by checking up on the boy who died last year.'

'How can we do that?' said Kate.

'The maid said it was in the newspaper,' said Aleister. 'And now that I think of it, someone said that at work too.'

'Someone at work knew that a boy from Palmer's gang died last year?' Kate asked.

'No, no,' said Aleister. 'It was Robinson. He'd just read about a child dying. He didn't know it was in Palmer's gang.

But come to think of it, Palmer got very upset. I didn't know why then, but it makes more sense now.'

'Someone in his gang died,' said Kate. 'He was upset, so out of vengeance he went and – '

She stopped and shook her head. 'But he was the one who got killed.'

'Yes,' said Aleister, 'it doesn't exactly make sense.'

'Still, it might be helpful to read what it said in the paper,' Kate said.

'Yes,' said Aleister, 'but where can we find last year's newspaper?'

Kate thought about this. 'I remember Papa one time ...' she began.

'Yes?' said Aleister.

'He said he thought he might go to the newspaper office to see what had been written about the Queen's visit to Manchester when she came here years ago.'

'And was he able to see?' said Aleister.

'Oh, he never actually went,' said Kate, 'but perhaps we should.'

She suddenly leapt up.

'Where are you going?' said Aleister.

'To the newspaper office,' said Kate.

'But your mother ...'

Kate was already in the hallway.

'We can't wait all day here,' she said. 'There's a murder to solve.'

She dashed down the hall, then quickly came back.

'We can leave a note on this,' she said.

She handed Aleister an ornate, flowery card.

'This is a calling card,' said Aleister, looking it over, 'from Sir William Dalrymple. I can't write on this. Besides, I have no pen.'

'Oh, what good are you?' said Kate in frustration. 'I'll have to look for the maid.'

But before she could, Mrs Talbot arrived.

'Come along with me, children,' she said.

Aleister was very anxious to learn what she had discovered, but waited patiently until they were outside.

'What a colossal waste of time,' said Mrs Talbot as they stood outside the Palmers' door preparing to head down the street.

The rain had let up, and Mrs Talbot suggested they walk for a while until they could find a cab to take them home. Kate had other ideas, however.

'Aleister and I made a wonderful discovery,' she said. 'A friend of Palmer's died last year.'

'Yes?' said Mrs Talbot. 'And the significance of that would be what exactly?'

She seemed in a bad mood, and for that matter it suddenly seemed to Aleister that the death of someone in Palmer's gang might have no significance whatsoever.

'I mean,' said Kate, 'that this friend of his also died on Guy Fawkes Day, only the year before.'

'Yes,' said Aleister, 'in a fireworks accident, I think it was. It was in the newspaper.'

Mrs Talbot still did not seem to see the significance.

'We think it might all be connected,' said Kate, 'and we want to go to the newspaper office to check it out.'

'Well, I'm not sure about that,' said Mrs Talbot. 'Where is the newspaper office anyway?'

'I think it's in Cross Street,' said Aleister, 'not far from the Saviour.'

Mrs Talbot considered this for a moment.

'That would also not be far from the police station,' she said. 'I am thinking I would like to visit Mr Talbot, and then we could all join Mr Rawlins at the insurance company afterwards.'

And so they all took a cab to the newspaper office, where

Kate and Aleister got out, and Mrs Talbot rode on to Fairfield Street.

On the way to the newspaper office, Mrs Talbot told what had happened at the Palmers.

'Mrs Palmer wouldn't see me,' she said. 'She was still too overwrought. But Mr Palmer, the father, allowed me a few minutes in his study. At first he didn't want to speak to me either; he said he had nothing to say to the wife of the man who had killed his son. But eventually I convinced him that there was a good chance Mr Talbot had not killed his son and that if he were helpful to me, the true murderer might be discovered.'

'And what did he tell you?' Aleister said eagerly as the cab rattled along the suburban streets.

'Very little, I'm afraid,' said Mrs Talbot. 'He didn't even know that his son led a gang. Or he pretended not to know. "When we lived near Granby Row," he said, "young Robert of course played with the neighbour lads. Perhaps that was a sort of gang. I must say, I didn't like the character of that neighbourhood. But after we moved away, he put all that behind him." '

'Did he say anything about Palmer at work?' said Aleister.

'Only that he couldn't imagine anyone from there wanting him dead, and couldn't understand why – why Mr Talbot might have killed him. I told him Mr Talbot did no such thing and he apologised, but I must say – ' She broke off for a moment before continuing. 'This has been very hard on me, children.'

Aleister nodded. 'But did he talk about Palmer's difficulties at work? I heard he was about to be dismissed.'

'Mr Palmer said nothing about that,' said Mrs Talbot. 'Only that his son was working at the insurance company, and he had hopes of him rising to a high position there.'

'He's lying,' said Aleister, almost surprising himself with his own vehemence. 'Why, Jack told me that Palmer's father had to pay a visit to Mr Smithson to ask that they keep Palmer on.'

166

'Well, he said nothing about that,' said Mrs Talbot. 'He said he did not know of any enemies his son might have had, that his son had been a hard-working young man destined for a good career, and now he had been cut down before he could even embark on it.'

Aleister shook his head. 'That doesn't help us at all.'

'No,' said Mrs Talbot, 'not really. Of course, he was just putting a good face on things, and who wouldn't, with their son dead. Still, I don't think he really knew much more that could have helped us. Though he was in deepest mourning clothes, and still at home from work, it seemed to me he hardly even knew his son.'

Aleister nodded, and thought of his own father in India. Kate seemed lost in thoughts of her own. And the rest of the ride passed in silence.

CHAPTER NINETEEN

Old Newspapers

Aleister and Kate got out at the newspaper office, letting Mrs Talbot continue on to the police station. The newspaper office was in a large, imposing building in the heart of the city centre. Aleister and Kate hesitated for a moment before climbing its broad stairs and entering its entrance hall.

A porter there asked them their business. He was old and thin and disapproving. 'What do you want here?' he said in an unfriendly voice.

Aleister felt unprepared for the question and had no answer ready. He thought perhaps he should ask for the appropriate department of the newspaper, but which one would that be? Kate, however, jumped right in.

'We want to find out about the boy who died last year,' she said.

'What boy?' said the porter. 'Lots of boys die every day.'

Aleister thought he was sneering at them. Kate, however, was undaunted.

'We don't know his name,' she said. 'That's what we want to find out. He died on Guy Fawkes Day. Not this year, but last.'

'You should probably go to the police,' said the porter. His lip curled, and he seemed irritated, as if they were demanding too much of him.

'We were told it was in the paper,' said Aleister. 'We want to look it up in the old papers. Do you keep those?'

The porter looked at Aleister with scorn. 'Do you think we just throw them out? They're records of our times.' He cleared his throat and pointed vaguely. 'Go up the stairs and into the big hall on the left. You'll find the bound volumes there.'

Aleister and Kate hurried up the stairs, glad to get away from the fierce guardian at the gate.

'What's a bound volume?' said Aleister.

Kate shook her head as if to say she didn't know, but it soon became clear what they were. Large books, huge books, with heavy covers were lined up on a counter encircling the hall. 'For public consultation' said a sign on one wall, and a few members of the public were indeed looking through some of the big books, gingerly turning the pages of old newspapers that were found inside.

Aleister went over to one wall. Each volume there had a date embossed on its cover: 1868, 1869, 1870. He found the volume for the right year, and hesitated in front of it.

'Well, open it up,' Kate said impatiently.

'It seems so odd,' said Aleister. 'Looking at old newspapers. It's like looking back into time. It gives me the shivers.'

'Oh, don't be silly,' said Kate, and flung open the cover.

There were the headlines from January of the previous year. The war in France, the Prussians advancing. Floods now forgotten. Fires, murders, speeches in Parliament. Shipping news, the previous year's advertisements. News about the Queen.

'Oh, my,' said Aleister, feeling slightly overwhelmed by the rush of past events. 'Look at all this.'

'Never mind that,' said Kate. 'Let's look at the paper for November the fifth. We have to find out about that boy.'

Aleister nodded, recovering himself, and said, 'November the sixth, actually. It would have to be the next day's paper.'

'Right,' said Kate.

But they looked all through the paper for November the sixth, through the advertisements on the front page and the

169

editorials at the back, through the news stories and the small print, and there was no story of a Guy Fawkes Day accident.

'Perhaps it's the wrong newspaper,' said Kate. 'Perhaps it's the *Guardian* we should be checking. I wonder where their office is.'

'No, no,' said Aleister. 'It's not their sort of story. It must be this newspaper. Let me think.'

He flipped some of the pages over, looking back to the fifth, though he knew that was too early, then suddenly realised something and flipped ahead to the seventh.

'It must be on November the seventh,' he said. 'It happened too late on the fifth to even get into the next day's paper. We have to check November the seventh.'

And there indeed it was, under the headline 'Terrible Tragedy on Guy Fawkes Night'.

'Look,' said Aleister.

They both read the article.

'A horrible accident took place in the Granby Row on Guy Fawkes Night,' the article read. 'A bucket of fireworks went off in the face of a young boy who was trying to light it, causing horrible injuries.'

'So he didn't die,' said Kate.

'Wait,' said Aleister, 'read on.'

The article continued:

'Unfortunately, though some bystanders, including a passing medical man, did what they could for the child, he died in agonies within the hour.

'We have not often raised our voices in favour of government intervention into industry and commerce, nor advocated meddling with the freedoms of our people, but surely a nation that can regulate the hours of work in factories can find some way to ensure the safety of the crackers, squibs, and rockets our young people like to set off on festive occasions.'

Kate craned her neck to see over Aleister's shoulder.

'Are they going to give us his name?' she said.

'Yes,' said Aleister. 'Here it is. Jimmy Doyle. Odd name, really.'

'What's odd about it?' said Kate.

'Well, it's Irish,' said Aleister. 'I didn't think the Irish celebrated Guy Fawkes Day.'

Kate shrugged. 'The thing we have to do is find him,' she said.

Aleister looked at her strangely.

'I mean find his family,' she said, 'or someone who can tell us more about what happened.'

'But will that lead us anywhere?' said Aleister. 'I think your mother might be right. This boy died in an accident; what's that to do with someone killing Palmer?'

'Maybe someone didn't think it was an accident,' said Kate. 'Maybe they blamed Palmer. What did that note say again?'

'The note on the body?' said Aleister.

'Yes, the note, the note,' Kate said impatiently.

'It was just the first lines of the rhyme,' said Aleister. 'Remember, remember the fifth of November.'

'Sounds like revenge to me,' said Kate.

Aleister nodded. 'Could be,' he said. 'And with that fireworks cracker left on him too ...'

'Let's go back to the insurance company and talk it over with Mama and Uncle George,' said Kate.

Aleister nodded, and they made their way out of the big hall, down the stairs, past the fierce porter, and into the street.

It was raining again. As they passed an umbrella stand, Kate suggested they hire an umbrella, but Aleister had no money on him.

'You need to be better prepared,' Kate said.

Aleister shrugged. He wanted to protest that he wasn't used to having to worry about money for umbrellas, but thought that might just prove her point.

When they got to the insurance company, not too terribly wet, they made their way up to the main hall and were ushered into Mr Smithson's office. Mr Rawlins was there, sitting across from Mr Smithson, who looked somehow small behind his large desk. Aleister looked around the room and noticed a case sitting on a table by the window. The pistol case, he supposed. Empty now.

Mr Smithson beamed at Kate and Aleister. 'Did you have a good outing, children?' he said.

Kate wrinkled her nose, and Aleister was afraid she'd say something rude, but she held her tongue.

Mr Smithson carried on. 'Mr Rawlins and I have been having an interesting conversation,' he said. 'Not entirely productive, I'm afraid, but I still hope something can be done for poor Mr Talbot. Mr Talbot was an excellent chief clerk, and I would hate to see anything happen to him.'

Something about Mr Smithson's speech didn't ring true to Aleister: perhaps it was only the notion that Mr Smithson cared about Mr Talbot. Or was there something more sinister going on?

Mr Rawlins was speaking. 'Mr Smithson has informed me,' he said, 'that Mr Carruthers has been relieved of his duties owing to some questionable activities of his that the late Mr Palmer may very well have known about.'

This was interesting, Aleister thought.

'Unfortunately,' Mr Rawlins went on, 'it seems that on the evening in question Mr Carruthers was at a dinner party with five other people who can vouch for his whereabouts.'

'Oh,' said Aleister.

'It is disappointing,' said Mr Rawlins, 'at least from our point of view.'

'Yes,' said Aleister.

He felt caught up in the disappointment, almost forgetting about the new idea he and Kate had come up with. Meanwhile Mr Rawlins was going on.

'There are other possibilities, though,' Mr Rawlins said. 'There's that Mr O'Neill you were mentioning. And Mr

Brooks. Mr Smithson pointed out something interesting about Mr Brooks.'

Aleister looked at Mr Smithson, who beamed even more broadly in response, as if he were Father Christmas or an American Santa Claus bringing a present.

'Mr Brooks is from Australia,' said Mr Smithson.

Aleister suddenly remembered Jack saying something about that.

'Yes,' said Mr Rawlins, 'Australia, where we used to send all the convicts. For all we know, he's committed murder before.'

'Do you think so?' said Aleister.

'Of course he had excellent references,' said Mr Smithson, 'and they said nothing about criminal activity. But there are all sorts of forgeries in circulation nowadays, it being so hard to get a position, and impossible without testimonials.'

He nodded to himself as if he had completely forgotten the murder and was caught up in the vicissitudes of the economic trade cycle and the difficulties of finding positions.

'This is all silly,' Kate said. 'Who cares if he's from Australia? Where was he on Guy Fawkes Night? Maybe someone should find that out. Meanwhile Aleister and I have come up with another idea entirely.'

Mr Smithson turned his attention to Kate, and smiled at her good-naturedly.

'Perhaps you should leave these things to us,' he said.

Kate ignored him and spoke to her uncle. 'We were at the Palmers' house,' she said, 'and their maid told us that a member of Palmer's gang died a year ago in an accident on Guy Fawkes Day that year.'

'Mr Palmer had a – a gang?' said Mr Smithson.

Kate ignored this too. 'Aleister and I have just been to the newspaper office in Cross Street, and we found out the name of the boy who died last year.'

173

Mr Rawlins nodded, taking a moment to absorb this information.

Kate hurried on. 'Now we want to find the boy's family.'

'How will you do that?' said Mr Rawlins.

For the first time Kate hesitated. 'I'm not sure,' she said. 'In the post office directory?'

'What's the boy's name?' said Mr Rawlins.

'Doyle,' said Aleister, feeling a little left out of the conversation. After all, he was the one doing the investigating, wasn't he? Why should Kate get all the glory? 'Jimmy Doyle,' he repeated.

Mr Rawlins shook his head. 'Do you know how many Doyles there are likely to be in the directory? It would take forever to track them all down.'

Everyone was silent for a moment. Finally, Kate spoke up.

'Then the thing to do,' she said, 'is to speak to Palmer's gang. They'll know something about the boy, and about his family too, I should think.'

Mr Rawlins shook his head more decisively. 'You're not surely thinking of visiting those – those gang members yourself, Kate. I would not hear of it. Your mother would certainly not hear of it.'

Kate seemed about to protest, but said nothing for a moment; then she turned to Aleister. 'It will have to be you, then,' she said to him. 'You'll have to find the gang again.'

Aleister looked at her in surprise. He wasn't sure he was ready to encounter the gang again. They certainly hadn't been very friendly the first time. But as soon as she said it, he knew she was right. Mr Rawlins said something about going himself, but Kate told him the gang would never speak to someone like him; it had to be a boy like Aleister. Aleister nodded.

'I don't know about this gang business,' said Mr Smithson. 'I can't believe that one of my employees was involved in a gang. This is a respectable enterprise, you know. If I had known, I would have dismissed him on the spot. As it is, we were going to be letting him go.'

'Why is that?' said Mr Rawlins.

'Well,' said Mr Smithson, 'not to speak ill of the dead, and of course it is horrible what happened to him, but he really wasn't suitable clerk material. Mr Talbot told me he wrote an execrable hand and misspelled words and was generally unpleasant in the office. His father came to see me about it, but we were still going to dismiss him. We'd only hired him as an apprentice in the first place because of his father. The son is not always like the father, you know.'

Aleister wondered for an instant what Palmer's father was like, but his main concern now was with revisiting Palmer's gang. He took a step towards the door.

'May I be excused?' he said. 'I should really talk to Billy Cooper to arrange to see the gang again.'

The others nodded at him, and he left the imposing confines of Mr Smithson's office to find Billy.

CHAPTER TWENTY

Gangland

Billy was reluctant to take Aleister back to the gang.

'I don't think they really want me there,' he said. 'They're never going to let me join.'

'But this is important, Billy,' Aleister said, and eventually he was able to convince him.

After work, the two of them set off again for the dark streets around Granby Row. Aleister thought he heard an owl hooting, or maybe it was only a boy imitating an owl. As they made their way through the narrow streets, he thought the people were staring at them. He probably looked out of place, he thought: too dressed up.

Some of the people here were wearing rags, he noted, just like in his old picture books. Poor people, impecunious, he thought. Much worse off than Mr Talbot – except they weren't in jail for murder.

They turned a corner, and there was the gang. Just sitting there this time, not playing pitch-and-toss.

One of them looked up and saw Billy and Aleister. 'Whatcha want?' he said.

'Are you in charge?' said Aleister.

The boy who had spoken – it was indeed the boy who had seemed in charge the previous time – ignored Aleister and spoke to Billy.

'No use you coming around,' he said. 'We've decided against having you in.'

Billy nodded and started to back away.

'Wait,' said Aleister to the boy who seemed in charge.

'I wasn't talking to you,' the boy said.

He flicked a pebble into the gutter and watched it roll down the street.

'No, wait,' said Aleister. 'This is important. This is about Palmer.'

The boy in charge stood up. 'I told you I wasn't going to speak to you about Palmer.'

'Well, then,' said Aleister, 'how about speaking to me about Jimmy Doyle?'

Aleister thought he could sense the gang members looking at him more closely. The boy in charge stood up slowly and came over to him.

'What's your name?' he said to Aleister.

'Aleister Lister Smith,' said Aleister.

'What kind of a hoity-toity name is that?' said the boy – and suddenly, without warning, he aimed a punch right at Aleister's stomach.

Aleister doubled over in pain.

Billy cried out, 'What'd you do that for, Tommy?' But Tommy just gave Billy a shove and walked back towards the other boys.

'Come on,' he said to them. 'I don't like this neighbourhood any more. Too many Nosey Parkers here.'

He moved off in the direction away from Aleister and Billy, and the rest of the gang got up and moved with him – all except one little boy, who lingered behind, as if just a little slow to follow along, but then more as if he was hoping to stay behind inconspicuously.

When the rest of the gang disappeared out of sight, the little boy made his way over to Aleister and Billy. Aleister was holding his stomach.

'You all right?' said the boy.

It was an effort to speak, but Aleister gasped out a Yes.

'You shouldn't ought to mess with Tommy,' said the boy. 'He's a good type, but still upset about us losing Palmer.'

Aleister nodded. He was still recovering.

'I heard you asking about Jimmy Doyle,' said the boy.

Aleister nodded again. 'Yes,' he said, 'did you know him?'

The boy nodded.

'This is Freddie,' said Billy. 'The youngest boy in the gang.'

'I'm nine years old,' said Freddie. 'Not so young. Just two years younger than Jimmy.'

'Tell me about Jimmy,' said Aleister.

'Jimmy was my friend,' said Freddie. 'I met him on the street. He was Irish.'

'Go on,' said Aleister.

'Jimmy wanted to join the gang, but he didn't know if he could,' said Freddie. 'Because he was Irish, you know.'

Aleister turned to Billy. 'Do you know anything about this?'

'It was all before my time,' said Billy, shaking his head.

Freddie was eager to continue his story. 'Jimmy wasn't obvious Irish,' he said. 'He didn't have no accent or nothing. But we knew from his name, of course.'

'How did he die?' said Aleister.

Freddie screwed his face up, remembering. 'It was horrible,' he said. 'On Guy Fawkes Night, you know. Last year, not this one. And we had crackers and squibs and stuff, and Jimmy wanted to take part with us, even though somebody called him a stupid Catholic just like Guy Fawkes hisself.'

Aleister nodded. Freddie seemed pleased to have such an attentive audience.

'It was Palmer who did it, really,' said Freddie.

'Did what?' said Aleister.

'Palmer pushed him,' said Freddie.

'Shoved him?' said Aleister.

'No, no,' said Freddie. 'I mean pushed him, encouraged him. Told him that if he ever wanted to be real English, he should light the fireworks.'

'He didn't want to light them?' said Aleister.

'Jimmy wasn't so good with things like that,' said Freddie.

'I thought you said he wanted to be part of things.'

'He did,' said Freddie. 'Only he didn't want to light the bucket – we had them all in a bucket. He was scared, I think.'

'But Palmer made him do it?'

'Yeah,' said Freddie. 'He did. And then it blew up in Jimmy's face. It was awful, just awful. And sometimes I think it was my fault. I told him about the gang.'

Aleister realised that perhaps Freddie needed some reassuring. 'It wasn't your fault,' he said.

'He was bleeding and lying there,' said Freddie. 'It was awful.'

Aleister felt a bit at a loss for words. Freddie looked like he was going to cry. Aleister couldn't think what to say to comfort him.

'You shouldn't blame yourself,' he said at last. 'It was Palmer's fault, really.'

Freddie looked at him. 'But he was in the gang 'cause of me,' he said.

'It was Palmer who pushed him to light the fireworks,' said Aleister. 'You said so yourself. I'd blame Palmer.'

Freddie looked doubtful.

'Maybe other people blamed him too,' said Aleister. 'Maybe other people in the gang. Did Tommy blame him? Did Tommy want to be leader? Maybe he wanted to get rid of Palmer, so he could take over himself.'

'No,' said Freddie. 'No, no, no.' He was very emphatic. 'Tommy loved Palmer.'

Aleister shrugged. 'Friends fall out sometimes.'

'But Tommy was with me and the gang that night,' said Freddie.

'Well, that's a good point,' said Aleister.

'And none of us blamed Palmer,' said Freddie. 'Palmer was our leader.'

'All right,' said Aleister.

He tried to think what to say next, but he didn't have to. Freddie spoke up first.

'There was someone who blamed Palmer,' he said.

'Really?' said Aleister. 'Who?'

'Not anyone in the gang,' said Freddie. 'We wouldn't blame him or – or kill him.'

'No,' said Aleister.

'But Jimmy's father was upset with him,' said Freddie.

'Aha,' said Aleister. 'Of course. That makes sense. Did he come and speak to Palmer?'

'No,' said Freddie. 'He spoke to me. He didn't really know about the gang too much, but he knew I was Jimmy's friend, and he asked me to tell him what happened.'

'So you told him about Palmer pushing Jimmy?'

'Yes, and he got very mad, and asked me all about Palmer.'

'That's very interesting,' said Aleister.

'He wanted to know where Palmer worked, and things like that,' said Freddie.

'Did you tell him?' said Aleister.

'I didn't really know where Palmer worked,' said Freddie, 'but one night I let Jimmy's father come along with me to see the gang.'

'So he did meet Palmer.'

'No,' said Freddie, 'when we got there, he said he didn't want to meet him, just see him. So we watched from beside a building, and then he went away. He seemed sad at the end, not mad any more.'

Aleister thought about all this.

'Can you take me to see him?' he said.

'Jimmy's father?' said Freddie.

'Yes,' said Aleister.

180

'I heard he went away,' said Freddie, 'but I can take you to see his wife.'

'That'd be good,' said Aleister.

So Billy and Freddie and Aleister headed off for the house of Jimmy Doyle.

CHAPTER TWENTY-ONE

Looking for Mr Doyle

As Aleister, Billy, and Freddie made their way through the narrow, dirty streets near Granby Row, Aleister began to think they looked almost like a gang themselves. A small gang, and a bit younger than most, but still a gang. It gave him pleasure for a moment, because he felt that he was leading this little collection, but then he began to think it might create the wrong impression when they visited Mrs Doyle.

Maybe it would be better if it was just him and Freddie, he thought. But how could he tell Billy not to come along without getting him angry or upset? All the pleasure of leading the gang vanished, and suddenly he thought that being in charge involved far too many difficulties.

Luckily, Billy himself decided he didn't want to visit the Doyle house.

'It's getting late,' he said, 'and I should be getting home.'

'Yes,' said Aleister, 'three's probably too many of us anyway' – but as soon as he said it, he realised he shouldn't have. Billy looked unhappy. Aleister remembered that Tommy from the gang had just told Billy he couldn't join them either. There was no need to tell Billy he wasn't wanted on the Doyle visit.

It bothered Aleister the rest of the way to the house, and so he hadn't thought of anything to say when they got to the door.

Freddie looked at him when they got there, at the door of a small nondescript house jammed in among dozens of identical looking small houses. It seemed that Freddie expected Aleister to do the knocking, so he did.

A middle-aged woman came to the door and opened it just part of the way to see who was there. She looked unfriendly.

'Yes?' she said.

'Mrs Doyle?' said Aleister, though Freddie was pulling at his sleeve and saying it wasn't Mrs Doyle.

'I ain't Mrs Doyle,' said the woman. 'You've got the wrong house.'

Aleister looked at Freddie in some bewilderment.

'Didn't Mrs Doyle use to live here?' said Freddie.

'I don't know who used to live here,' said the woman. 'Why should I care about that? I moved in six months ago, and that's all I know.'

She was closing the door in their face.

'Do you know where Mrs Doyle might have gone?' said Aleister.

'I'm telling you I don't know any Mrs Doyle,' said the woman. 'Now get off my doorstep and leave me alone.'

She closed the door on them.

'What do we do now?' said Aleister.

'We could try the neighbours,' said Freddie.

Aleister was doubtful about this idea, but they began knocking on doors. Some people just shooed them away; others weren't home or pretended not to be. But some talked to them.

'Poor Mrs Doyle,' said one, another middle-aged woman, but with a kind expression on her face. 'Losing first her child, then her husband.'

'How'd she lose her husband?' said Aleister.

'Oh, he just ran off,' the woman said. 'Went a bit strange, if you know what I mean. And who could blame him, with his son dying like that. But it left Mrs Doyle in an awful fix. No son, no husband. I think she went to live with relations in Liverpool.'

'And Mr Doyle?' said Aleister.

'Don't know where he went,' said the woman. 'Just disappeared. What a shame it all was, too. He'd just got a promotion at the bank he was working at.'

'Oh?' said Aleister. 'Where was that?'

He wasn't sure how this information would help, but he decided the best thing might be just to follow where things led, and he found out that Mr Doyle had been working at the local branch of one of the big banks.

This was all that the friendly woman could tell him. When he asked again where Mr Doyle might have gone, she said maybe he had moved to Liverpool too.

'I saw him one time in the street,' she said. 'He looked all distraught, upset, and he said something about wanting to get away. So maybe he left Manchester. Maybe he went to Liverpool too. Or America. Lots of Irish go there, you know.'

Aleister thanked her and thought about her information as he and Freddie made their way back through the streets. Freddie soon darted off to go home, and Aleister found a cab at a cab stand and rode off to the Talbots. This time Mr Rawlins had given him cab fare.

When he got to the Talbots, everyone was up, waiting for him in the parlour.

'Well,' said Kate, looking excited, 'what did you find out?'

Aleister realised that he'd found quite a bit out and remembered being excited himself about it, but now it all seemed to have led to a dead end. Or a missing end. Where was Mr Doyle? Was he really in Liverpool? If so, it was pointless to look for him because he couldn't have committed the murder.

'Oh, I'm sure he's not in Liverpool,' said Kate. 'That's where Mrs Doyle went, you said. No, Mr Doyle went stalking Palmer like a hunter tracking a lion. Did you hunt lions in India, Aleister?'

'That's Africa,' said Aleister.

'Well, we have to become hunters now,' said Kate. 'Mr Doyle hunted Palmer. Now we have to hunt him.'

184

'But how?' said Aleister.

Kate was silent. Mr Rawlins spoke.

'It might be useful,' he said, 'to go to his place of work.'

'But I think he must have left there,' said Aleister. 'That woman said he had disappeared. I'm sure she meant from work too.'

'Let's not be too hasty in our conclusions, Lister Smith,' said Mr Rawlins, slipping into his schoolmaster's tone. 'And even if he has left, his employer may know where he has gone.'

And so the next morning Aleister and Mr Rawlins headed off to the bank branch where Mr Doyle had worked.

It was a large stone building, with lions carved in front of it. Hunting lions, Aleister thought, just like Kate had said. He followed Mr Rawlins into the building.

Mr Rawlins, in his schoolmaster's way, was able to get the clerks at the front to introduce them to the bank manager who occupied the back office. A Mr Henry.

'How do you do?' said Mr Henry, standing up as they came into his office. 'What can I do for you?' 'It's about one of your employees,' said Mr Rawlins. 'A Mr Doyle. I don't think we know his Christian name.' He looked at Aleister, who shook his head.

'Oh,' said Mr Henry. 'Poor Mr Doyle.' He shook his head too.

'Why?' said Aleister eagerly. 'What happened to him?'

'Who is this?' said Mr Henry, looking down at Aleister, and Mr Rawlins explained briefly who they both were.

'Ah,' said Mr Henry. 'I see' – though Aleister thought that if someone didn't already know the story, what Mr Rawlins had said would seem quite confusing. Aleister was the pupil of the brother-in-law of the man accused of killing the young man who might have been responsible for the death of the son of Mr Doyle.

'I see,' said Mr Henry. 'And you want to find Mr Doyle for what reason?'

185

Aleister worried that if Mr Henry liked Mr Doyle as he seemed to, he might not want to help them. After all, they were hoping to find Mr Doyle guilty of Palmer's murder so that Mr Talbot could go free. And if Mr Talbot went free, it would be Mr Doyle who would go to prison – or worse.

But Mr Henry seemed quite willing to talk about Mr Doyle.

'Edward Doyle,' he said. 'A good man. A very good man. And an excellent worker. Started at the bottom here and had just been promoted to chief clerk under me. Very promising career ahead of him. Branch manager at least. But then of course ...'

He trailed off.

'Why do you want to know about him?' he said.

'We thought he might be able to shed some light on the unfortunate incident with young Palmer,' said Mr Rawlins.

'Indeed,' said Mr Henry. 'You don't think he had anything to do with it, do you?'

'We don't know,' said Mr Rawlins. 'We hoped you might tell us something that would let us find out.'

Mr Henry stroked his chin.

'It was a terrible thing, you know,' he said. 'Terrible. His boy dying like that. He never recovered. I made him take some time off, but even when he came back, he just wandered about looking lost.'

He paused, as if remembering.

'So he no longer works here?' Mr Rawlins said.

'No,' said Mr Henry. 'He came to me one day and said he couldn't concentrate on his work any more; he said he'd lost all sense of purpose and meaning. I told him that was perfectly normal and that he'd get over it, but he didn't want to listen. He told me he had to leave and get away and be something else. I remember that; I didn't quite understand it: Be something else, he said.'

'What is it he wanted to be?' said Aleister.

186

'I don't know,' said Mr Henry. 'I don't think he knew himself.'

'When was it that he left?' said Mr Rawlins.

'Oh, not long after the incident,' said Mr Henry. 'He didn't stay with us much longer. December perhaps. It was certainly before Christmas.'

'And you never saw him again?' said Mr Rawlins.

'He did come round one more time, just before Christmas,' said Mr Henry. 'And he looked terrible. He hadn't shaved, and his clothes seemed dirty. He asked if I could lend him some money. Of course, I was happy to, and asked if he wanted to come back here to work, but he just kept his head down, not looking me in the eye, and said he was finished with that sort of thing, but if I could just see my way to giving him a few pounds to tide him over, he'd be most grateful.'

'And that's the last time you saw him?' said Mr Rawlins.

'Yes, just before Christmas,' said Mr Henry.

'He's not at his old house,' said Mr Rawlins. 'Would you happen to know where he is staying?'

And Mr Henry did know, or knew approximately. 'When he came to see me,' he said, 'he mentioned a lodging house in Ancoats. I got him to write down the address for me.'

And so Aleister and Mr Rawlins made their way into the poor suburb of Ancoats, east of the city centre, where the less well off factory workers lived, along with those who had no work and scrabbled for money on the streets, entertaining the passers-by with pet mice or dogs, or selling fish or fruit, or picking pockets.

Aleister found it a bit exotic walking down streets named Bengal, Naples, and Portugal, but the streets themselves didn't seem exotic, just sad and tawdry, full of rundown houses and people in rags.

Aleister worried that Mr Rawlins would be upset at having

187

to come to such a nasty neighbourhood, but he seemed almost cheerful.

'Reminds me of Paris in '48,' he said. 'Went out one day and found myself in the middle of a revolution. The people were setting up barricades and carrying banners. Then the soldiers arrived and, without warning, began firing. A bullet whistled right past my head. Those were the days.'

Aleister did not quite see what the attraction was of having a bullet whistle by one's head, but he said nothing, and they continued on their way past sad-looking beggars and frightening-looking street-sellers.

The lodging house they wanted was on Silk Street. It seemed one of the worst streets in the neighbourhood. For one thing, the smell was worse; also, a beggar sat in the middle of the road picking at his sores. Aleister shuddered to look at him. As they walked past, the beggar caught his eye and said, 'A few pennies, governor, to help me buy some ointment for my scabs.'

Aleister looked the other way, but Mr Rawlins dropped a penny in the man's hat.

When they got to the lodging house, Mr Rawlins peered inside into the gloom. Aleister hung back, behind him, but looked in too. He saw what seemed like a dozen people squeezed into a large room, with beds made of straw against the walls. Some of them looked up at Mr Rawlins, and their eyes lighted up.

'A few pennies, governor?' they said, holding out their hands.

Mr Rawlins fished in his pockets for some more copper coins.

'I'm looking for a man named Doyle,' he said as he handed the money over.

'Doyle, Doyle,' said one of the chattering beggars, as if repeating some crazed incantation.

'I can be Doyle if you like,' said another, holding out his hand for more change.

Mr Rawlins shook his head. 'Is the landlady around?' he said. But this question made the beggars shrink away in fright.

'No, no,' they said. 'She beats us.'

Mr Rawlins shook his head again and looked around the room. Aleister looked too. He caught sight of a scurrying creature that he hoped wasn't a rat. In a corner, one lodger sat by himself holding a book, bowing, and muttering as if in prayer. The prospect of finding Mr Doyle did not seem very hopeful.

Aleister wandered over to the lodger in the corner. To his surprise, the book that the lodger was bowing over was not a Bible, but a cheap, tattered edition of something called *Self-Help.*

'Doyle gave it to me,' the lodger said without looking up.

'The book?' said Aleister.

The lodger bobbed his head up and down. 'Changed his life, he told me. Changed his life.'

'Where is he now?' said Aleister.

'Perseverance, that's the key,' said the lodger, as if not hearing Aleister's question. 'Lives of great men all remind us. Hard work, industry, perseverance. And purpose, of course. Doyle found his purpose.'

'What purpose was that?' said Aleister, but the lodger seemed to disconnect from their conversation and lost himself in his tattered book.

Mr Rawlins came over to see what Aleister was up to.

'This man says he knew Doyle,' said Aleister. 'He says Doyle gave him that book.'

'Really?' said Mr Rawlins, and he fished out a coin to give to the meditating lodger.

But the lodger would not take it. 'No, no,' he said. 'No help from without, only help from within. Self-help.'

'Very well, my good man,' said Mr Rawlins. 'But I will take your help if you can give it: where is Mr Doyle?'

The lodger shook his head. 'Gone away,' he said, 'gone away. To fulfil his purpose. Gone away.'

Aleister had a sudden inspiration. 'Who gave the book to Mr Doyle?' he said.

A faraway look came into the lodger's eye. 'Wilson,' he said. 'Mr Wilson gave it t' him.'

'Who is Mr Wilson?' said Mr Rawlins.

But that was all they could get out of the lodger.

Mr Rawlins turned to face the room. 'Anybody know a man named Wilson?' he bellowed, as if he were looking for someone in his class to translate a difficult passage from Horace.

A murmur went through the room.

'We don't want him here,' said one of the lodgers. 'He took our money, he did.'

'Is that so?' said Mr Rawlins. 'And how did he do that?' Aleister thought that Mr Rawlins was really getting into his schoolmaster's role again.

The lodgers were suddenly silent, as if feeling guilty or ashamed.

'Well,' said Mr Rawlins loudly to Aleister, 'I suppose we'll just have to find out for ourselves. Sounds like a case of thievery, to my mind. Something the police might be interested in. Perhaps we should have them round.'

And with that he put on his hat and headed for the door.

As he had no doubt expected, however, he had not taken more than a few steps before one of the lodgers called out, 'You can find him down by the tobacconist's shop.'

And so Aleister and Mr Rawlins made their way back to the street and headed for the little shop around the corner. When they got there, they asked the shop assistant for Mr Wilson, and the assistant, with a bit of a sour face, nodded towards a man standing outside.

'Come to throw your money away too?' the assistant asked. 'You look like you should know better.' And he ducked behind his counter, shaking his head.

Back outside the shop, Aleister and Mr Rawlins approached the man on the corner. He had a cheery expression on his face and a huge moustache that didn't quite suit him.

'Hello there, gents,' he said. 'Come to make a little wager? I can give you good odds on Idle Fancy in the third race.'

'We're not here for wagering,' said Mr Rawlins.

'No, no, of course not,' said the man. 'An upstanding gentleman like you, with his son, out for a stroll. Though you might have picked a more salubrious neighbourhood. Which of course might lead you to ask why I don't pick a better neighbourhood myself. Well, it's the customers, you know. You have to go where the customers are. If I stood on a corner in Withington, no one would come up to me, except perhaps a copper telling me to move along – or to come along, which would be even worse, you understand. Not that I'm complaining. Complaining is for the unsuccessful, and I'm quite successful in my line of work. Not that it's come easy, of course, but nothing in this world ever does. Nor should it, for it is all part of God's plan to make us work harder, and by hard work we shall enter the Kingdom of Heaven.'

Aleister listened open-mouthed to what by the end almost seemed like a sermon, something he found odd coming from the mouth of a – a bookmaker, he thought the term was.

Mr Rawlins was speaking. 'This is all very interesting,' he said. 'But we are actually here in search of a man named Doyle, and we were told that you might know him. That is, if you are a man named Wilson.'

'Wilson's my name, all right,' said the man. 'And I've known quite a few Doyles in my time.'

He was about to say more – Aleister had the impression that Mr Wilson always liked to say more – but his attention was diverted by the appearance of a skulking little man just a few feet away.

'Excuse me, gents,' said Mr Wilson. 'A customer, I think. Have to keep at it, you know, so unless you want to put down a few bob yourself ...'

He let his words trail off and went to conduct his business with the skulking little man. Mr Rawlins watched him for a moment, then went up to him again when the customer had gone.

'Changed your mind, have you?' said Mr Wilson. 'A couple of bob on Idle Fancy? Or if you'd like to consult the *Chronicle* and make your own choice, they sell them inside.' He indicated the tobacconist's shop.

Mr Rawlins ignored the suggestion. 'This Doyle's first name was Edward,' he said. 'That's what the manager at the bank he worked at told us.'

'Ah,' said Mr Wilson, 'a bank clerk. Don't deal with many of those, as a rule. But you'd be surprised at the nature of the clientele I get. I wouldn't be surprised if there were some sons of lords seeking me out from time to time because they know they can get good odds from Bob Wilson.'

'This Edward Doyle ceased to be a clerk,' said Mr Rawlins, 'and was living in a lodging house around the corner.'

'You gave him a book,' said Aleister. 'About self-help.'

'Oh,' said Mr Wilson, 'Eddie Doyle. Why didn't you say so? Didn't know he'd been a bank clerk. Well, I knew he'd been some sort of clerk. Maybe he did tell me he worked in a bank once. You hear so many stories in my line of work that it's hard to keep them straight.'

'Can you tell us where he is?' said Mr Rawlins, a bit impatiently.

'Well, that's hard to say,' said Mr Wilson. 'If I racked my brains a bit, it might come to me. Or it might not. Perhaps if you were to come up with some money for a wager, I might have time to think. Not that I guarantee anything, of course.

Can't make guarantees in my line of work. No such thing as a sure thing, that's what I always tells the customers. I can give out tips and the like, word I've heard, but you never know how a horse is going to feel of a morning. And if a horse don't feel right, well, then, it just won't run right. Not like a man. That's the difference between us and the other creatures. A man can wake up feeling poorly and still know he has his duty to do, and he'll do it. But a horse – well, that's another matter.'

Mr Rawlins looked more impatient than ever, but he dug two shillings out of his pocket and handed them over.

'Here you are,' he said, 'two on Idle Fancy or whatever the beast's name is. In fact, never mind about putting it on the horse, just keep the money and tell us where we can find Mr Doyle.'

But Mr Wilson was already filling out a little slip and handing it to Mr Rawlins.

'An agreement's an agreement,' he said. 'I offered you a wager, and you must have your betting slip and a chance to win. I'm an honourable man, you know.'

Reluctantly, Mr Rawlins took the slip. Aleister wondered if they might win a lot of money with it.

'Now, my good man,' said Mr Rawlins, 'Mr Doyle's whereabouts.'

'Ah,' said Mr Wilson, putting away Mr Rawlins's two shillings in an unusual-looking sort of purse that he immediately whisked beneath his coat. 'That's hard to say. Hard to say.'

'You don't mean to say you want more money for the information,' said Mr Rawlins, with a note of irritation creeping into his voice.

'Sir,' said Mr Wilson, 'nothing of the sort. I resent the implication. I am not an extortionist. I merely state the fact that it is hard to say where Eddie Doyle has got to.'

'Well,' said Mr Rawlins, 'where did you last see him?'

'That would have been here,' said Mr Wilson. 'In this neighbourhood.'

'Why did you give him that book?' said Aleister. 'He gave it to someone else in the lodging house.'

'Did he now?' said Mr Wilson. 'Well, I'm not sure that was wise. The book is not for everyone. A wonderful book, though. By Mr Samuel Smiles. Have you read it, sir?' This last question he addressed to Mr Rawlins.

'I am familiar with it,' Mr Rawlins said, sounding almost insulted by the question.

Aleister felt insulted on Mr Rawlins's behalf. Of course his schoolmaster would be familiar with the book.

Mr Wilson was going on. 'It is a quite marvellous book,' he said. 'It changed my life. Changed my life.'

'That's what the lodger said Mr Doyle told him,' said Aleister.

'I don't doubt it,' said Mr Wilson. 'That book is the key to everything.'

He reached inside his coat and pulled out another copy of it.

'Here,' he said, handing it towards Aleister, 'I will give you one if you like.'

Mr Rawlins reached out and pushed the book away. Aleister felt mildly disappointed. It would be interesting to read a book that was the key to everything, he thought.

'It's very kind of you,' said Mr Rawlins, 'but what we're really looking for is information about Mr Doyle.'

Mr Wilson put the book back inside his coat. Aleister wondered what other marvels he might be keeping there.

'As you please, sir,' Mr Wilson said to Mr Rawlins, 'but it really did change my life. I was no better than the lodgers you no doubt met in the lodging house until I read Mr Smiles. He gave me the inspiration to make something of myself. He did indeed, sir. And now here I am.'

'And Doyle?' said Mr Rawlins.

'I thought Eddie Doyle was better than the general run of

lodgers, sir,' said Mr Wilson. 'I did think that. Yes. He'd told me his life story. It comes back to me now. How he'd been a respectable clerk, how he'd worked himself up to that position. How he was glad to prove that an Irishman could do as well as an Englishman. He was proud of that, he was.'

'And then what?' said Mr Rawlins.

'Well, then of course,' said Mr Wilson, 'there was the terrible tragedy with his boy. He was devastated by it. Said it was all because his boy wanted to be English, wanting to join some English gang and take part in the Guy Fawkes festivities with them. He sounded most bitter about that, but mostly he seemed mired in despair. I thought the book would help him out of that.'

'And did it?' said Mr Rawlins.

'Why, indeed, sir,' said Mr Wilson, 'I think it did. Despite the terrible tragedy, Mr Doyle had in him the elements for success. I do believe that. That's why I gave him the book. I wouldn't have given it to just anybody.'

'But somehow it turned him into a murderer,' Aleister blurted out.

Mr Wilson looked at Aleister in astonishment. 'A murderer?' he said. 'What do you mean?'

Aleister felt somewhat abashed, as if he had spoken too hastily. He could see Mr Rawlins frowning at him too, as if to say this was not the way to coax information out of a witness.

'I mean,' said Aleister, 'I mean there's been a murder, and we think Mr Doyle may have had something to do with it.'

'Well, I never,' said Mr Wilson. 'And you want to blame Mr Samuel Smiles and his book on self-help for that. I am shocked, sir. Shocked.'

And with that, Mr Wilson began to take his leave of them.

'Wait,' said Mr Rawlins. 'Mr Wilson, please wait. The boy spoke too hastily. Of course we are not blaming the book.'

'Are you blaming me, then?' said Mr Wilson.

'No, no, of course not,' said Mr Rawlins. 'We simply want

to find Mr Doyle to ask him if he knows anything about what happened to a young man named Palmer.'

'Palmer,' said Mr Wilson. 'Palmer.' He seemed to be musing about the name.

'Do you know Mr Palmer?' said Mr Rawlins.

'No,' said Mr Wilson, 'not exactly. But I'm pretty sure Palmer was the name that Mr Doyle began to mutter about to me.'

'Aha,' said Aleister.

Mr Rawlins glared at him.

'It was after he'd been reading the book for a while,' said Mr Wilson. 'He began to talk about paying someone back, and I think the name was Palmer. I tried to discourage him from that sort of talk, you understand. I told him Self-Help wasn't about revenge. Self-Help is about making yourself better, not about hurting anyone else. And he did seem to grasp the difference, and he was in much better spirits overall by this time, telling me he'd found purpose again in his life, something to persevere in. So I was for the most part greatly pleased. Only he did say a couple of times something about looking up this Mr Palmer.'

'Is that so?' said Mr Rawlins.

'I had no idea he wanted to murder him,' said Mr Wilson. 'If I had known, even with my somewhat difficult relationship with the constabulary, I would have informed the police. I assure you I had no idea.'

'I'm sure you didn't,' said Mr Rawlins in the friendliest tone of voice Aleister had ever heard from him. He wondered if it was quite sincere or if it was just intended to keep Mr Wilson talking.

'He seemed altogether in fine spirits after a while,' said Mr Wilson. 'He even cleaned himself up and said it was time he found some proper employment again. I told him that was an excellent idea.'

'When was this?' said Mr Rawlins.

'Well, let me see,' said Mr Wilson. 'It was around Christmas time that I first met him, and he was very disconsolate then, thinking a lot about his boy and his wife, whom he had left – or she had left him. I did not want to pry, you understand.'

'Of course,' said Mr Rawlins.

'I gave him the book as a sort of post-Christmas gift,' said Mr Wilson, 'and it was within a mere few weeks that he had turned himself around, cleaned himself up, and decided to seek out employment.'

'But he didn't go back to the bank,' said Aleister.

'No,' said Mr Wilson, 'he said he couldn't bear to go back there or to live in his old neighbourhood. He wanted to find work in the city centre and take some rooms there. And I think he said something about going to the YMCA.'

'The YMCA?' said Mr Rawlins.

'Yes,' said Mr Wilson. 'Something about them having an employment bureau. And to be frank, that's the last time I saw him. Back in January or February, it must have been.'

'He never came back to see you?' said Mr Rawlins.

'You may well ask,' Mr Wilson said. 'I who put him on the road to recovery might well have expected a visit, an expression of gratitude. But one mustn't pin one's hopes on others, you know. One must rely on oneself. So I never gave it a thought.'

But it seemed to Aleister that he had given it some thought, and looked a bit sad about it.

'Do you know if he ever found new employment?' said Mr Rawlins.

'That I cannot tell you,' said Mr Wilson. 'But I'm sure he did. He looked so cheerful and positive, confident. That's what one needs to succeed in this world. Confidence. I'm sure he found a new job.'

It didn't seem that Mr Wilson had much more to tell them, and it seemed that, uncharacteristically, he had run out of things to say. Aleister thought he looked quite pensive, as if thinking over everything that had passed between him and Mr Doyle.

And so Aleister and Mr Rawlins took their leave of him.

'What do you think?' said Mr Rawlins.

'I don't know,' said Aleister.

'Put him on the road to recovery?' said Mr Rawlins. 'More like the road to murder. I never trusted that book.'

'No,' said Aleister, but he still thought it might be interesting to read it some day.

'Now what about this business about the YMCA?' said Mr Rawlins.

'I've been there,' said Aleister.

'Really, Lister Smith,' said Mr Rawlins. 'And were you looking for new employment too?'

'No, no,' said Aleister, 'I went with one of the other clerks to hear a lecture. It seems so long ago now. It was an old man talking about Christianity and business.'

'Hmph,' said Mr Rawlins. 'I'm not altogether sure I approve of this mixing of things that belong in different spheres. What on earth do religion and business have to do with one another?'

'I'm not sure,' said Aleister. 'I don't really remember what he said.'

'Well, it doesn't matter,' said Mr Rawlins. 'Let's go and take a look at their employment centre.'

And so once again Aleister went to visit the YMCA.

CHAPTER TWENTY-TWO

Back to the YMCA

As they rode through the streets in a cab, Aleister remembered the last time he'd visited the YMCA. With Robinson on one of his first days in Manchester. How long ago that seemed. He remembered how nervous he'd been, listening to the old man's lecture, worrying if he was being singled out for attention. He felt less worried now. He thought perhaps he had found some of what Mr Wilson had been talking about: confidence. Though he remembered suddenly that it was Mr Doyle who had the confidence, and it had been the confidence to kill someone. He felt suddenly less sure about things.

Up the steps of the building they went, up the stairs inside to the rooms occupied by the YMCA. A young man dressed in brown greeted them.

'Good afternoon, gentlemen,' he said. 'How can I help you?'

Mr Rawlins explained that they were looking for a man named Edward Doyle who might have registered with the employment bureau in the past year.

The young man seemed a bit doubtful at first.

'Mrs Pendleton's in charge of the bureau,' he said. 'I don't know too much about it. We just started it last year.'

'Well, perhaps if we could speak to Mrs Pendleton, then,' said Mr Rawlins.

'She's just gone to tea,' said the young man.

'This is very important,' said Mr Rawlins. 'Perhaps you can show us the bureau yourself.'

The young man hesitated, but Mr Rawlins must have seemed very imposing to him, and eventually he led them down the hall to another room where the bureau was located. He fumbled with a key to the door, then led them inside.

'I think all the files are in here,' he said, and went behind a counter to a large wooden cabinet full of drawers. It was much like the cabinets at the insurance company, Aleister thought.

'Here,' said the young man, 'D. You did say Doyle, didn't you?'

Mr Rawlins nodded, and the young man pulled open the drawer marked D and lifted out a whole stack of papers.

'I'm afraid they're not in any particular order,' he said. 'Just added to when new ones come in.'

Aleister shook his head. The indexing system at the Saviour was much better than this. The young man began going through the papers.

'Dixon,' he said. 'Davis. Douglas. Dougherty.'

A sudden noise behind him made Aleister jump. Someone had entered the bureau and was speaking in a very angry voice.

'Mr Parker,' the voice said.

The young man looked up in sudden fright. Aleister turned around to see a large, middle-aged woman in the doorway. Mrs Pendleton, he presumed.

'Mr Parker,' said Mrs Pendleton, 'what do you think you're doing?'

'Why,' said Mr Parker, 'these gentlemen were looking for a clerk named Edward Doyle. They said he had registered with us, so I was looking to, to – '

'To give them confidential information out of our files?' said Mrs Pendleton.

'Well, yes,' said Mr Parker. 'I mean no, not if that would be wrong.'

'Wrong?' said Mrs Pendleton. 'Wrong? These poor down-trodden men' – she waved her hand at the files – 'these poor downtrodden men come to us in their hour of need, out of work, needing work, ashamed of their lack of work, and you are ready to broadcast their names to any scavenger for information who comes in off the streets.'

'Madam,' said Mr Rawlins, sounding offended, 'I am no scavenger.'

'That is hardly the point,' said Mrs Pendleton.

'It is very important that we find this Edward Doyle,' said Mr Rawlins.

'He may have committed murder,' said Aleister.

'I don't care if he's the King of Siam and has flown to the Moon,' said Mrs Pendleton. 'You won't be looking for him in my files. Put those papers away, Mr Parker.'

Mr Parker hurriedly picked up the papers and began stuffing them back into the drawer labelled D.

Mrs Pendleton shook her head.

'Mr Parker,' she said, 'have some respect for the documents, for the poor men who produced these documents. You will crumple them up, shoving them into the drawer that way.'

She sailed past Aleister and Mr Rawlins, sailed past the counter, removed the remaining papers from Mr Parker's hands, and carefully arranged all the documents in drawer D. When she was satisfied that everything was once again in order, she turned around and seemed surprised to see the intruders still there.

'I'm afraid I cannot help you,' she said.

'But it's so very important,' said Aleister.

Mrs Pendleton just glared at him. Aleister shrunk a little from her gaze. Mr Rawlins tried to take another tack.

'Madam,' he said, 'I sincerely apologise for inadvertently overstepping the boundaries. We had no idea that these were confidential files.'

'Ha,' said Mrs Pendleton. 'No idea? How could you have no idea?'

'I merely meant,' said Mr Rawlins, 'that since Mr Parker seemed willing to show them to us ...'

'I will deal with Mr Parker later,' said Mrs Pendleton, and Aleister thought he could see Mr Parker almost wince.

'Clearly, there has been a misunderstanding here,' said Mr Rawlins.

'There's no misunderstanding at all,' said Mrs Pendleton. 'You are trying to ferret out information that you have no business obtaining.'

'I'm sure you are right, madam,' said Mr Rawlins, surprising Aleister with his apologetic tone. He had never heard Mr Rawlins apologise in the classroom.

Mrs Pendleton made a noise indicating displeasure, but Aleister thought she might be weakening.

'I know how important it must be,' said Mr Rawlins, 'to keep the files in order. I am a great admirer of order myself. And also of keeping one's word, the word one must have given to all the poor gentlemen who have entered their names here. If they have been assured of privacy, then of course that privacy must be respected.'

'I see you are a gentleman, sir,' said Mrs Pendleton, 'and you seem to understand these matters better than some of those who work here.' She glared at poor Mr Parker.

Mr Rawlins merely bowed his head slightly.

'I can't show you the files, you understand,' Mrs Pendleton said. 'But I don't think it would be violating anyone's confidence to tell you that there is no Doyle in them.'

'Indeed, madam,' said Mr Rawlins.

'We hardly ever get Irish job-seekers here,' said Mrs Pendleton. 'We are mostly for clerks, and there aren't too many Irish clerks. I would remember a Doyle. There is no Doyle.'

'Ah,' said Mr Rawlins.

'But, but – ' said Aleister.

'Come away, Aleister,' said Mr Rawlins. 'We have troubled this good woman too much already.'

And with that and another small bow of the head, Mr Rawlins retreated from the employment bureau, taking Aleister along with him.

That evening, Aleister and the others discussed the situation.

'There must have been a paper there for Doyle,' said Aleister. 'Mr Wilson said Doyle went to the YMCA.'

'Perhaps he was mistaken,' said Mr Rawlins.

'Perhaps he registered under a different name,' said Kate. 'Hiding his identity. On the hunt, you know,' she added when the others looked at her with surprise on their faces. 'Wanting to cover his tracks and sneak up on Palmer unawares.'

'But that makes it impossible,' said Aleister. 'He could have changed his name to anything.'

'I still think this is a wild goose chase,' said Mrs Talbot. 'Didn't we establish long ago that the murder was committed with Mr Smithson's pistol? How could anyone outside of work have obtained it?'

'They might have broken in,' said Kate. 'Sneaked in while everyone was at dinner.'

'Or maybe there were two people involved,' said Aleister. 'Maybe Mr Doyle was friends with someone at work, and they took the gun for him.'

'Yes,' said Kate. 'Maybe Mr O'Neill was in on it.'

'Why Mr O'Neill?' said Mr Rawlins.

'They're both Irish,' said Kate. 'They might know each other.'

Mr Rawlins shook his head. 'There are lots of Irish in Manchester,' he said. 'They don't all know each other.'

'Not that many Irish clerks,' said Aleister. 'You heard the woman at the YMCA.'

'Even so,' said Mr Rawlins.

'Regardless of all that,' said Mrs Talbot, 'I think the most logical thing is to return to the insurance company and speak once more to the clerks. Speak to this Mr O'Neill, for instance, and find out where he was on Guy Fawkes Night. We've never done that, have we?'

'And Mr Brooks,' said Kate. 'We haven't spoken to him either.'

'Will Mr Smithson let us keep coming back to talk to the clerks?' said Aleister.

'Under the circumstances,' said Mr Rawlins, 'I think he'll be accommodating. He seemed very sympathetic last time we talked to him.'

'And I really think we must find the true culprit soon,' said Mrs Talbot. 'I went to visit poor Arthur again today, and I fear his mind is suffering too much of a strain from all this. He keeps saying he is guilty, though I know he only means guilty of taking the money, and I've told him that Mr Smithson has been quite understanding about that.'

'Yes,' said Mr Rawlins. 'That is, he didn't say a word about it when I spoke to him. He was focused solely on the murder.'

'That's what I mean,' said Mrs Talbot. 'But Arthur feels he deserves some sort of eternal damnation because of taking a few pennies.'

'I think it added up to more than a few pennies, actually,' said Mr Rawlins. 'More like – '

But he saw Mrs Talbot glaring at him and did not finish the thought.

'However many pennies it was,' said Mrs Talbot, 'he doesn't deserve to be convicted of murder for it.'

'No,' said Mr Rawlins. 'Of course not. Unless, of course ...'

'George!' said Mrs Talbot with anger in her voice, and Mr Rawlins did not pursue that thought either.

CHAPTER TWENTY-THREE

Interviewing

The next day, Mr Rawlins, Kate, and Aleister returned to the offices of the Saviour Assurance Company. Mrs Talbot went again to visit her husband at the Fairfield police station.

This time Mr Smithson was not nearly as accommodating as Mr Rawlins had predicted.

'I do sympathise, my good fellow,' he said to Mr Rawlins, 'but I have a business to run, and can't have you coming in every day playing at detective.'

Aleister could see that Mr Rawlins did not like being called a 'good fellow' or being told he was 'playing', but the schoolmaster kept his temper and eventually convinced Mr Smithson to let them have one more round of interviews.

They called in Mr O'Neill first. He was quite friendly and willing to help. He said how terrible it was what had happened to Mr Talbot and how he hated benefiting from what he hoped was a temporary removal. He meant, Aleister realised, that he felt bad about becoming the chief clerk in this way, as a result of Mr Talbot's being arrested, but Aleister felt almost that Mr O'Neill was trying too hard to convince them that he felt bad.

As to where he had been on Guy Fawkes Night, that was easy, he said. At home with his good lady wife. He was much too old to be running all over town and watching bonfires. Certainly, they could speak to her if they liked.

There was silence for a moment after Mr O'Neill had

answered these questions, and then Kate seemed to have an inspiration.

'Do you know anyone named Doyle?' she said.

'Doyle?' said Mr O'Neill.

'Yes,' said Aleister. 'Edward Doyle. Or Eddie. We've heard he might have been mixed up in the incident with Palmer.'

'Really?' said Mr O'Neill. 'Where did you hear that?'

'Oh, just here and there,' said Aleister.

He wondered why Mr O'Neill should ask such a question. Did it mean he knew Edward Doyle and was suddenly worried they were on the track of his friend? But he didn't look worried.

'I know a few Doyles,' said Mr O'Neill. 'Can't think of an Edward at the moment. There's a Mike and a John and a Richard. I can ask around, though, if you like.'

He smiled in a helpful sort of way, and no one could think of anything else to ask him. He did seem very helpful – perhaps too helpful. Did that mean he was hiding something? Aleister was beginning to become suspicious of everybody, perhaps because he still felt frustratingly far from discovering the real murderer. He looked over at Kate, and they shrugged at each other. It seemed to him that she was feeling the same way.

Then it was time to interview Mr Brooks.

There was something dark about Mr Brooks, Aleister realised when he saw him up close. Dark and mysterious. For one thing, he realised that he'd hardly ever seen him up close before; he'd always been somewhat removed, distant; there, but not there. He looked at him more closely now.

Mr Smithson introduced Mr Rawlins and said that he and 'the children' were asking questions in an attempt to prove that Mr Talbot was not the one who'd murdered Palmer.

'I thought he was the one,' said Mr Brooks, looking gruff and unfriendly.

'We really don't think so,' said Mr Rawlins.

'Actually, we think someone named Doyle might be

involved,' said Aleister, and he noticed that Mr Brooks gave a little start. What did that mean, he wondered?

They asked him where he had been on Guy Fawkes Night.

'Are you accusing me then of doing it?' said Mr Brooks.

The way he spoke made Aleister wonder about his accent. Was it Australian? He remembered that Jack had said that Mr Brooks had seemed more Irish than Australian, though of course there were Irish who had gone to Australia, so one could be both, he supposed. Brooks wasn't an Irish name, though. Or was it?

But he was missing what Mr Brooks was saying. Mr Rawlins had assured him that they weren't accusing anybody, just wanting to account for everyone's whereabouts.

'I don't see that it's anyone's business,' Mr Brooks was saying in response, 'but if you must know, I was at the YMCA that night.'

'Really?' said Aleister.

'That's what I said,' Mr Brooks replied. 'Don't you believe me?'

'It's just that Robinson, the junior clerk, said he was there too,' Aleister said.

'Was he?' said Mr Brooks. 'I didn't see him there.'

'Oh,' said Aleister, and felt suddenly puzzled. Could two people be at the YMCA and not see each other? It wasn't that large a place: just a couple of rooms at the top of that old building in Piccadilly.

After Mr Brooks left, Mr Smithson ushered Aleister, Kate, and Mr Rawlins out of his office.

'I hope that was of some use to you,' he said. 'And now I really must let the office return to its routines.'

It seemed to Aleister that Mr Smithson had lost all interest in helping them. Mr Talbot was gone, and it was time to get on with things – that seemed to be his attitude now.

They made their way through the main part of the office in silence. Aleister noticed that hardly anyone was there – just

Miss Lewisham typing at her desk. Everyone else must be off for the mid-day dinner hour. He wondered why Miss Lewisham wasn't off too. He tried to remember if she always stayed at her desk through dinner.

They could question her, he thought, but what was she likely to tell them? Kate went over to her, though, and he heard her ask Miss Lewisham if she knew anyone named Doyle. He was surprised to see Miss Lewisham blushing. Why was that, he wondered? Did Doyle happen to be the name of her secret husband? Was she married to Doyle the murderer? Was she the mother of little Jimmy Doyle?

But that didn't seem likely. She seemed too young. And Mrs Doyle had gone to Liverpool. Aleister sighed. He was tired of this puzzle, and there was no one to give him the answer.

Kate rejoined them and they made their way out of the main room.

'She said she didn't know anyone named Doyle,' Kate told them, referring to Miss Lewisham. 'Didn't know any Irish, she said – though she said it so nervously, it made me wonder.'

Maybe her secret husband is Irish, Aleister thought. But he was tired of trying to discover the hidden meanings in everything people said.

'I think we should talk to that other clerk,' Kate said. 'The one that Mr Brooks said he didn't see at the YMCA.'

'Robinson,' said Aleister.

'Yes,' said Kate. 'Where is he likely to be now?'

'At the cook-shop, probably,' said Aleister. 'It's dinner-time.'

'Right,' said Kate.

So Kate and Aleister made their way to the cook-shop. Mr Rawlins headed to the police station to meet up with Mrs Talbot and see Mr Talbot. They agreed to meet back at the insurance company at closing time.

Just before they reached the cook-shop, Kate and Aleister saw a boy hurrying up the street in their direction. It was Billy

Cooper, Aleister realised. Billy had his head down and didn't see them at first, so Aleister called out to him. Billy stopped short and looked frightened.

'Hello Billy,' said Aleister. 'Where are you rushing to?'

'Just getting back to the office,' said Billy. 'I can't stay to talk.'

'Are the others still in the cook-shop?' said Aleister.

'I wasn't there,' said Billy. 'I don't go with them any more. One of them could be a murderer.'

It occurred to Aleister that Billy could be right, but it didn't seem too likely. Besides, it didn't seem likely anyone would want to murder Billy.

'You're not going to make me take you back to the gang again, are you?' said Billy.

'I don't think so,' said Aleister.

'I don't have anything to do with them either,' said Billy. 'I have to go now. Bye.'

And he was off.

'What's got into him?' said Kate.

'Scared, I think,' said Aleister. 'He's just a kid.'

'He's as old as you are, I thought,' said Kate.

Aleister just shrugged.

Robinson was in the cook-shop with Crosbie and Jack. Jack smiled at Kate, but she gave him a haughty look and ignored him. Jack turned to Aleister.

'Lister Smith,' said Jack. 'How are you? How goes the great detective hunt?'

'You shouldn't be so flippant,' Kate said, interrupting. 'This is a matter of life and death for my father.'

'You're right,' said Jack. 'I'm sorry. But how does the investigation go?'

Aleister shrugged. 'Lots of promising ideas,' he said, 'but we still don't know who killed Palmer.'

Crosbie looked up and with his mouth half full of a Cornish pasty said, 'It was the Germans, I told you.'

209

'More likely the Irish,' said Aleister, and then caught himself and looked anxiously at Jack.

Jack laughed. 'What do you mean, Lister Smith?' he said. 'Do you think the Republican Brotherhood targeted poor Palmer?'

'What's the Republican Brotherhood?' said Kate.

'The Fenians,' said Jack. 'The Irish rebels fighting for a free Ireland.'

'Oh,' said Kate, 'you mean hooligans. Criminals.'

'I do not,' said Jack, and Aleister suddenly feared there would be an unpleasant argument.

'I didn't mean Fenians,' Aleister said. 'I shouldn't have said the Irish did it. I just meant that there was a man named Doyle who might be the murderer. Only we can't find him now.'

'I still think it must be the Germans,' said Crosbie as Jack and Kate looked at each other in an unfriendly way.

'How did you hear about this Doyle?' said Robinson.

And so Aleister explained about Palmer's gang and Jimmy Doyle and Jimmy Doyle's father.

'But we've come to a dead end there,' he said.

'Yes,' said Kate, 'so we've decided to start again at the other end and find out for sure where everyone was on Guy Fawkes Night.'

'I thought you did that already,' said Robinson.

'Well,' said Aleister, 'there's some confusion about that. You said you were at the YMCA, and so does Mr Brooks, but he says he didn't see you there.'

'I was definitely there,' said Robinson. 'Reading an interesting book on – what was it on, now?'

'Self-help?' said Aleister with what he thought was an inspired suggestion.

Robinson looked at Aleister strangely. 'Mr Smiles's book?' he said.

'Yes,' said Aleister. 'Apparently, this mysterious Mr Doyle was a great admirer of it.'

'Well,' said Robinson, 'it's all right in its way, I suppose. But it does rather neglect the Christian side of things.'

Aleister was tempted to enter into a discussion of Christianity and self-help, but Kate spoke up and said, 'This is all very interesting, but what we want to know is whether you saw Mr Brooks at the YMCA that night.'

Robinson shook his head and said, 'I'm afraid that when I'm immersed in study, I hardly notice anything around me. Mr Brooks may very well have been there, but I didn't notice.'

Kate and Aleister looked at each other in exasperation. This did not settle anything.

'Perhaps we had better go to the YMCA and ask for ourselves,' said Aleister.

'Very good, Lister Smith,' said Jack. 'Get to the root of things. Test our alibis.'

Aleister looked at him sharply. Was Jack laughing at him?

But there was no time to worry about that. He and Kate had to go back to the YMCA.

CHAPTER TWENTY-FOUR

Backtracking

'Mr Brooks seemed very suspicious to me,' Kate said as they walked through the streets on the way to the YMCA.

'Oh, yes?' said Aleister.

'So unfriendly,' said Kate.

'That doesn't prove he's the murderer,' said Aleister.

'No,' said Kate.

They had reached the YMCA building in Piccadilly.

'Let's see if we can find out if he was here the night of the murder,' said Aleister.

'All right,' said Kate.

Inside they met up again with Mr Parker. Mr Parker did not seem at all pleased to see Aleister.

'I can't show you anything from the files,' he said. 'We have nothing here for you. We know nothing about any Mr Doyle.'

'We're actually here to ask about a Mr Brooks and a Mr Robinson,' said Aleister.

'I don't know any Brooks or Robinson,' said Mr Parker. 'I don't know anything at all. I think you are wasting your time here and should probably leave.'

'Perhaps Mrs Pendleton could help us,' said Aleister.

He did not much want to speak to Mrs Pendleton, but Mr Parker seemed committed to telling them nothing.

'Mrs Pendleton is still away at dinner,' said Mr Parker. 'In any case, I am sure she wouldn't tell you anything either. We can't have people looking in our confidential files.'

Aleister felt ready to give up at this point, but Kate suddenly intervened. She put on her winningest smile and held out her hand to Mr Parker, who reluctantly took it.

'My name is Kate Talbot,' she said. 'I don't believe we've been formally introduced. Aleister here is so backward about these things.'

Aleister blushed, even though he could tell she was just saying this to get on Mr Parker's good side.

Mr Parker introduced himself and said it was a pleasure to meet Miss Talbot, but he had work to do and he hoped she would excuse him.

'Oh, of course,' said Kate. 'You must be a very important man with all sorts of things to do that a poor young girl would not even understand.'

Mr Parker, who had been about to move away, paused as if trying to digest what Kate had said: to figure out if it was some sort of mockery or rather a genuine compliment.

'You look like an intelligent girl,' said Mr Parker. 'And what I do is not that mysterious.'

'But very important, I'm sure,' said Kate.

'Well, I am more or less in charge,' said Mr Parker. 'That is, when Mrs Pendleton isn't here. I mean, there is, of course, a board of directors, and a president, Mr Philips, and the head secretary, Mr Hind Smith. But I am the person in charge on the spot, so to speak.'

'When Mrs Pendleton isn't here,' said Aleister.

Mr Parker frowned at him. 'Yes, I said that.'

Kate frowned at Aleister too. He realised he wasn't helping. It was important to make Mr Parker feel valued; then he might tell them something.

'What sorts of things are you in charge of?' Kate was saying.

'Well,' said Mr Parker, 'there's the reading room. Our little library.'

'Is that here?' said Kate.

'Oh, yes,' said Mr Parker, 'just down the hall.'

'It would be so interesting to see it,' said Kate.

And so Mr Parker led Kate down the hall to see the reading room. Aleister trailed behind, though he thought Mr Parker would have been happy if he hadn't.

'Do lots of people come here?' said Kate, looking around the empty book-lined room.

'Oh, yes,' said Mr Parker. 'There were several here just half an hour ago during their dinnertime, and we'll get more in after the offices close up. We get mostly young clerks, and right now they're back in their offices, of course.'

'We know two clerks who come here quite a bit,' said Kate.

'Oh, yes,' said Mr Parker.

'And they're having a silly dispute,' Kate went on. 'They both say they were here on Guy Fawkes Night, but they also both say the other one wasn't. We thought perhaps you could settle the matter.'

'I'm not sure – ' Mr Parker began.

'You must have an awfully good memory,' Kate said, 'to keep track of all these books here.'

'I suppose,' said Mr Parker doubtfully.

'But I don't suppose that's the same thing as remembering people's faces and when they were here,' Kate said.

'I could try,' said Mr Parker. He seemed suddenly eager to please.

'Well, it's that Mr Brooks and Mr Robinson,' said Kate.

Mr Parker's face fell. 'I'm afraid we don't keep track of the names of everyone who comes in,' he said.

'Perhaps if we described them?' Kate said.

Mr Parker shrugged hopefully. Kate gave a rapid description of both Robinson and Mr Brooks. Aleister was impressed; he would never have been able to sum them up as she did. He always forgot what people looked like the moment they were out of sight.

'Oh, the red-haired one is often here,' said Mr Parker.

'Robinson,' said Kate.

'If that's his name,' said Mr Parker.

'And the other one?'

'Why, he's often here too, if he's the one I'm thinking of.'

'And on Guy Fawkes Night?' said Kate. 'Which one was here?'

Mr Parker frowned in concentration. His forehead suddenly turned into a mass of wrinkles. Finally, he shook his head.

'It's over a week ago now,' he said. 'They both often come in, but whether either of them was in that particular night, it's very hard for me to say.'

Kate nodded sympathetically. 'It was the night of the bonfires and fireworks,' she said helpfully.

Mr Parker looked slightly insulted. 'Of course,' he said. 'I know what happens on Guy Fawkes Night.'

It was a misstep, Kate realised, but she seemed unable to retrieve it.

Aleister spoke up to try and save the situation. 'Did they use the reading room?' he said.

Mr Parker looked at him in a not very friendly way, but he answered nevertheless. Perhaps he wanted to show there was an answer he could provide. 'Mr Brooks often came in here,' he said.

'What sorts of books did he read?' said Aleister.

'Why do you want to know that?' said Mr Parker, suddenly suspicious.

'Oh, Mr Parker,' said Kate, 'I'm afraid I haven't told you the full reason why we're here. It's not so much because of a friendly dispute between Mr Brooks and Mr Robinson. It's to do with a dreadful murder, and we think one of them may have been ... involved. Only, if they were here on Guy Fawkes

Night, they couldn't have been. That's why we wanted to know.'

'Well,' said Mr Parker, 'I don't much like being misled like that.'

'No,' said Kate, and Aleister noticed that she seemed to be batting her eyes at the young man.

'No,' Kate said again. 'It was very wrong. I hope you can forgive me. Only, my father has been arrested for this murder, and we are desperate to find the real culprit, or else, or else – well, I don't really like to think about it.'

Now Aleister noticed that a tear seemed to be rolling down Kate's cheek. Mr Parker noticed too, and seemed suddenly quite awkward.

'Oh, Miss Talbot,' he said. 'Please don't upset yourself. Would you like to sit down? Would you like a handkerchief?'

Kate pulled a handkerchief of her own out of her sleeve and patted her eye.

'I'll be all right,' she said. 'And we really mustn't take up more of your time.'

'Oh, no,' said Mr Parker, 'that's quite all right. If there's anything I can help you with ...'

Aleister saw this as a chance to ask his question again, though in a different form. 'If you could tell us what you know about the two of them,' he said, 'even that might help. Especially about Mr Brooks. He's very mysterious.'

Mr Parker turned to look at him. He still didn't seem very friendly to Aleister and acted as if he was tolerating him only as an extension of Kate. Still, he did ponder what Aleister had said and ventured a few thoughts.

'As to Mr Brooks, he was a bit mysterious as you say. He rather kept to himself.' Mr Parker paused and thought some more, then said, 'I don't exactly know what he read. We don't look over the patrons' shoulders, you know, but I think he looked at the Bible a lot.' Something else occurred to him. 'He did ask me a strange question one time.'

216

'Oh?' said Aleister. 'What question was that?'

Mr Parker seemed to be straining to bring a distant memory into focus.

'It was about Cain and Abel,' he said. 'The story in Genesis. That's the first book of the Bible.'

Aleister bit his tongue to keep from saying that of course he knew that. He could tell that Mr Parker wanted to prove himself superior.

'What did he ask about Cain and Abel?' Kate said.

Mr Parker turned from Aleister to Kate almost with relief.

'Well,' he said, 'he asked me if I thought it was very bad of Cain to have killed his brother. Can you imagine such a question?'

Kate nodded sympathetically.

'What did you tell him?' said Aleister.

'Well, of course, I said I didn't think it was right. It was murder, and Cain was punished for it.'

'How did Mr Brooks react to that?' said Kate.

Mr Parker wrinkled his brow again in an effort to recall, then said, 'I think he just sighed and said he supposed I was right.'

Kate and Aleister looked at each other. Mr Parker fell silent.

'That's about all I remember about Mr Brooks,' he said. 'He did rather keep to himself, as I said. Did you want to hear about Robinson?'

Kate and Aleister looked at each other again, and shrugged. After what they had just learned about Mr Brooks, it hardly seemed necessary. But Kate responded politely.

'Please do tell us if there's something you remember about him,' she said.

Mr Parker seemed to be getting interested in this now.

'I think he was the one who was interested in Manitoba,' he said. He strained in concentration, but could say nothing more than, 'I can't remember anything more particular about him, I'm afraid.'

217

'Nothing about Cain and Abel?' said Aleister, and Mr Parker looked at him sharply, as if to see whether Aleister was making fun of him. Kate meanwhile jabbed Aleister with her elbow as if to shut him up.

'Nothing about Cain and Abel,' said Mr Parker. 'Not from Mr Robinson. That was only Mr Brooks.'

Kate made a motion to leave, at the same time glaring at Aleister as if to keep him quiet.

'You've been very helpful, Mr Parker,' she said. 'And I certainly found it fascinating here.'

Aleister thought that Mr Parker almost blushed, but he had no time to think about it, because Kate was hurrying him away.

'It must be Mr Brooks,' she said when they got outside. 'He was asking about Cain and Abel. He wanted to know if killing was all right. He was working himself up to kill Palmer.'

Aleister nodded, but said, 'How do we prove it, though? We can't just go to the police with what we know now. They wouldn't listen to us.'

'They'd listen to me,' said Kate. 'I've discovered I'm quite good at getting men to listen to me. And to talk to me too.'

'Yes,' said Aleister, with a hint of disapproval in his voice, 'but I still don't think the police will do anything about Mr Brooks until we can provide them with some more serious evidence. What, after all, do we have against him? That he was interested in Cain and Abel?'

'He was asking about killing people, and he acted very mysterious, and, and ...'

'That's not really very much to go on,' said Aleister. 'Though he did give that start when I mentioned Mr Doyle.'

'Yes,' said Kate, 'there's your proof.'

'Well,' said Aleister, 'I'm not sure about that.'

'But he must know Doyle,' said Kate.

'Perhaps,' said Aleister. 'Perhaps he just has a twitch or something.'

'Oh, don't be silly,' said Kate. 'Why would he twitch just then?'

'And there is his accent,' said Aleister.

'What about his accent?' said Kate.

'Did it sound Australian to you?'

'I don't know,' said Kate. 'I'm not sure I know what an Australian accent sounds like.'

'I'm not either,' said Aleister, 'but his sounded artificial somehow.'

'Oh,' said Kate, 'he was disguising his real voice.'

'Maybe,' said Aleister. 'Jack once told me he thought Mr Brooks was Irish.'

'Oh, Jack,' said Kate, 'what does he know?' She seemed suddenly caught up in some feeling about Jack; it was only for a moment, however. 'But if he's right,' she went on, 'and Mr Brooks is really Irish, well, then, there's more proof.'

'Proof of what?' said Aleister.

'That he knows Mr Doyle,' said Kate. 'Isn't it obvious? You can be a bit slow at times, Aleister.'

'I think the police will need more than that,' said Aleister. 'Can we prove that he was on the scene?'

'Well, he wasn't at the YMCA,' said Kate.

'Wasn't he?'

'Mr Parker couldn't remember him there that night,' said Kate.

'But he couldn't remember him not there either,' said Aleister. 'And he also couldn't remember whether Robinson was there that night.'

'You're just being difficult,' said Kate.

'I'm suspicious of Mr Brooks too,' said Aleister, 'but we need more evidence. And what exactly is his connection with Mr Doyle?'

'They were in league together,' said Kate. 'An Irish conspiracy. Fenians.'

'I thought it was about Mr Doyle's son.'

'That too,' said Kate. 'Whatever. We need to get the police involved. If they arrest Mr Brooks, then Papa can go free.'

Aleister sighed. Kate seemed suddenly not very rational about all this.

'What we need now is evidence,' he said.

'We have to act,' said Kate.

'Without evidence ...' he said, and shrugged, letting the thought trail off.

'Oh, Aleister,' said Kate in frustration.

'All right,' said Aleister, 'let's stop and figure out what we have so far. On the one hand, we have Jimmy Doyle's father, who was upset about his son's death and blamed Palmer and maybe went out looking for Palmer, maybe to kill him.'

They had stopped walking now. Kate looked at him intently and nodded.

'All right,' said Aleister. 'And then there's Mr Brooks, who seems mysterious and was startled when I mentioned Mr Doyle – '

'And who was asking about Cain and Abel and murder,' said Kate.

'And who was asking about Cain and Abel and murder,' said Aleister. 'Yes. And the gun that was used to kill Palmer came from Mr Smithson's office at the insurance company where Mr Brooks works.'

'Yes,' said Kate, 'Mr Brooks took the gun and, and – '

'And what?' said Aleister. 'Gave it to this man Doyle? Why?'

Kate seemed impatient and excited, as if everything was right there for them to grasp, but just out of reach.

'I don't know,' she said. 'Maybe he was friends with Doyle. Maybe he was Doyle.'

She stopped suddenly, as if surprised by what she had just said. Aleister looked at her. He was surprised too. And yet it suddenly all seemed to fit.

'That's very interesting,' he said. 'Let's see how that works.

Mr Doyle is upset over his son's death. At first he sinks into despair, but then that man Wilson gives him the book about self-help and he finds a new purpose in life. The purpose seems to have been to track down Palmer.'

'And kill him,' said Kate.

'And kill him,' said Aleister. 'But not right away. First he goes and cleans himself up. Leaves that lodging house. Goes to the YMCA employment bureau.'

'And changes his name to Brooks,' said Kate.

'Changes his name to Brooks,' said Aleister, 'and gets a job at the same place as Palmer to keep an eye on him.'

'And then kills him in revenge on Guy Fawkes Day,' said Kate excitedly. 'There, we've figured it out. Papa is saved.'

'Only, we have no proof,' said Aleister.

'But it all makes perfect sense,' said Kate.

'Well, it's an interesting theory,' said Aleister, 'but how do we know that Doyle changed his name to Brooks?'

'What do you mean?' said Kate.

'Maybe he changed it to – to O'Neill or Jack Quinn,' said Aleister.

'But Mr O'Neill's been there for years, hasn't he? And Jack – ' She paused as if thinking why it couldn't be Jack. 'Jack's too young,' she said at last. 'He couldn't be the father of Jimmy Doyle.'

Aleister nodded. 'You may be right,' he said, 'but we still need some stronger way to show that Doyle became Brooks and not anyone else. Maybe your father would know.'

'My father?' said Kate.

'He hired him,' said Aleister. 'Or at least would have done so together with Mr Smithson. And Mr Brooks worked under him all those months. He must know something.'

'I'm not sure,' said Kate dubiously, and Aleister thought she was probably right. What would Mr Talbot know? He thought about Mr Talbot for a moment. Locked in his cell, waiting for the judgement he thought he deserved for a crime he did not commit. Even if he did know something, he might not be willing to tell them. Or able. From what Mrs Talbot had said, it sounded like he was confused. Preoccupied with his own guilt.

'Well, perhaps not your father, then,' said Aleister, 'though he could quickly tell us everyone who was hired since last Guy Fawkes Day.'

'It's as if you want to prove that it's not Mr Brooks,' said Kate. 'Why don't we find some way to prove that it is?'

Aleister thought for a moment. 'Well,' he said, 'the key would be to show that Doyle and Brooks are the same person.'

'Who could do that?' said Kate.

'His old bank manager,' said Aleister. 'We could try and get him to come identify him. But it would probably have to wait until tomorrow. It's getting late now.'

'It can't be much past three o'clock,' said Kate.

'Bankers leave early,' said Aleister, and paused to think. 'There is someone else, though,' he said at last.

'Who?' said Kate.

'It would mean going into Ancoats, and I'm not even sure we can find him.'

'Well, let's do it,' said Kate, 'and if we can't find him, we'll go to the bank tomorrow.'

'It's not a very pleasant part of town,' said Aleister. 'You might not feel safe.'

'Oh, don't be a ninny,' said Kate. 'Let's go now.'

And so they went off to look for Mr Wilson.

CHAPTER TWENTY-FIVE

The Witness

It was surprisingly easy to find Mr Wilson. There he was at the same corner, writing out a betting slip for another customer. He looked at Aleister closely when he approached.

'I know you,' he said. 'You were here yesterday with your father, that big man. Didn't much look like your father, mind you.'

'He's not my father,' said Aleister.

'Well, he's won five shillings whoever he is,' said Mr Wilson.

'I beg your pardon?' said Aleister.

'Idle Fancy in the third,' said Mr Wilson. 'Went off at two and a half to one.'

Aleister looked a bit blank, so Mr Wilson added, 'The horse race. The gentleman made a wager on the horse race.'

'Oh, of course,' said Aleister. 'The horse won? Mr Rawlins won five shillings?'

'That's what I've been trying to tell you, lad,' said the bookie. 'You should have him come down here with his betting slip so's he can collect.'

Aleister remembered wondering what would happen if they won. But he'd been thinking of a big fortune. Five shillings was not a very large amount, not for an adult like Mr Rawlins.

'I don't think he'll care much about the five shillings,' he said.

'You'd be surprised what people care about,' said Mr Wilson.

Kate suddenly spoke up. 'What we care about,' she said, 'is solving a murder.'

'Murder?' said Mr Wilson in an accusing tone, as if Kate and Aleister were the ones who had committed it. 'What is all this talk about murder? The young lad was here yesterday talking about it and besmirching the good name of my friend Eddie Doyle.'

'It's very important,' said Kate.

'And who are you, young lady?' said Mr Wilson. 'The lad's sister, I suppose.'

'No, I'm not his sister,' said Kate.

Mr Wilson eyed Aleister with a hint of appreciation. 'He looks a bit young to have a special lady friend,' he said.

'I'm not his special lady friend,' said Kate. 'I'm the daughter of a man falsely accused of a murder we think your friend Eddie Doyle committed.'

Mr Wilson looked as if he were about to interrupt to protest his friend's innocence again, but Kate hurried on and did not let him.

'We need you to come and identify someone,' she said.

'Identify?' said Mr Wilson.

'Yes,' said Aleister, 'we want you to tell us if a man going by the name of Brooks is actually Eddie Doyle.'

Mr Wilson looked at Aleister in astonishment. 'Well, I never,' he said. 'You've been reading too many adventure stories, lad.'

Aleister shrugged. 'We could be wrong,' he said, 'but we'd like you to help us find out.'

'And how would I do that?'

'Just come with us to the insurance company where Mr Brooks works and – '

'And leave my post here?' said Mr Wilson. 'I can't afford to do that. I have a business to run.'

224

Even in his anxiety to solve the murder, Aleister found it interesting that the bookmaker standing on the street corner used the same phrase as the managing director of Saviour Assurance. But he had no counter-argument ready to persuade Wilson to change his mind.

Kate did, though. 'I'm sure my uncle, Mr Rawlins, will make it up to you,' she said.

'The gentleman who was here yesterday?'

'Yes, yes,' said Kate.

'And how would he do that?' said Mr Wilson.

'He'll give you some money, I'm sure,' she said.

Mr Wilson seemed to ponder this for a moment. 'I suppose it would be all right if I joined you for just a short while,' he said.

'Excellent,' said Aleister. 'We'd better hurry, though, to get there before closing.'

And so they set off through the streets of Ancoats, heading for the city centre and the Saviour Assurance Company.

Aleister led the way up the stairs when they got there. It was still not long after four o'clock. He looked around the main office. There was Robinson. Crosbie too, and Jack at the carding desk. Mr Carruthers's office was empty, of course, with Mr Carruthers suspended. There was Mr O'Neill at the far end of the room emerging from Mr Smithson's office. But where was Mr Brooks?

Kate and Mr Wilson had caught up with Aleister now.

'Where is this Mr Brooks?' said Mr Wilson.

'I don't know,' said Aleister. 'He should be here.'

But he wasn't. Aleister ended up asking Jack, who said that Mr Brooks had not returned after dinner.

'It's all very mysterious,' Jack said. 'Mr O'Neill was just in conferring with Mr Smithson about it, and I heard him say something like "First Talbot, then Carruthers, and now Brooks."'

'What does that mean?' said Aleister.

'Oh, you know,' said Jack. 'All three of them are gone.'

Aleister nodded. He could see why Mr O'Neill was concerned. It must seem as if the company was collapsing. But he didn't have time for the company's problems; he needed to find Mr Brooks and show him to Mr Wilson.

'Who's the funny-looking bloke with the moustache?' said Jack.

'That's Mr Wilson,' said Aleister. 'He's a bookmaker.'

'A bookie,' said Jack. 'Lister Smith, you never cease to amaze me. Who would have thought it? I never took you for a gambler.'

Aleister shook his head impatiently. Jack was just too facetious. These were serious matters.

'He's not here about gambling,' he said. 'He's here to identify Mr Brooks.'

'Identify Mr Brooks,' said Jack. 'What do you mean?'

'Oh, it's too long a story to tell now,' said Aleister. 'We need to find Mr Brooks.'

Jack looked both surprised and offended, as if he couldn't believe that Aleister had more important things to do than tell him the story.

'Do you have any idea where he went?' said Aleister.

Jack shook his head. Aleister felt frustrated. To have figured things out so well and now to have the evidence slip away – he sighed in irritation.

Mr Wilson approached them. 'I really don't think I can stay any longer,' he said. 'I would like to help you out, though I must say I'm surprised poor Eddie Doyle would resort to murder. In any case, I would like to help you and tell you if this Brooks fellow is really Eddie, but I have customers waiting for me back at my corner, and I really can't afford to keep them waiting. They'll go and try some other corner, if you get my meaning.'

Kate, who had kept her distance from Jack, now came over too.

'I think we need to go to Mr Brooks's house,' she said. 'Does anyone know where he lives?'

'Mr Smithson would, I suppose,' said Jack. 'But if Mr Brooks is running from you, why would he let you in to talk to him or identify him?'

'Do you think he's running from us?' said Aleister. 'We didn't even know we were chasing him until a little while ago.'

Jack shrugged.

Kate said, 'What we need is the police.'

'The police?' said Mr Wilson.

'Yes,' she said. 'We need to convince them to come with us to arrest Mr Brooks. I think we should go to the police station immediately.'

'How will we convince them?' said Aleister.

'We'll bring our witness,' said Kate. 'Mr Wilson. We'll tell the police that Mr Wilson can prove that Brooks is really Doyle and that Doyle is the real killer.'

'Just a minute,' said Mr Wilson. 'I came with you to make this identification. I was willing to do that. But you have to understand my position. I can't be walking into a police station.'

'Why not?' said Kate.

'Why not? Because what I do for a living is – how should I put this?' Mr Wilson paused as if searching for words to explain the obvious. 'Let's just say that the members of the constabulary do not look with favour on my profession.'

'We have a murder to solve here,' said Kate. 'We can't be worried about your minor problems with the law.'

'Minor problems?' said Mr Wilson. 'Minor problems?' And for once he seemed rendered speechless.

'I don't see the problem, really,' said Kate. 'Whatever your dealings with the police, they have nothing to do with this case. You'll be going to them to help solve this case. They can only appreciate that.'

Mr Wilson looked a bit dubious. Aleister felt a bit dubious

himself. Would the police really be appreciative? They already had the man they thought was the murderer: Mr Talbot. Would they really want to go chasing after someone else on the say-so of a bookie and two young people?

Kate was speaking again, though. 'First we should find out the address from Mr Smithson,' she said.

'Actually,' said Jack, 'I think Mr O'Neill will probably know it too.'

'All right,' said Kate, 'then let's ask him.'

Aleister admired Kate's sudden decisiveness. Having decided that Mr Brooks, aka Doyle, was the murderer, she seemed intent on tracking him down. And now she seemed on the brink of convincing Mr Wilson to go with them to the police station.

Jack went over to talk to Mr O'Neill, and Mr O'Neill went to a cabinet to look something up. Mr Brooks's address perhaps, Aleister thought.

And indeed it was Mr Brooks's address, and with the address in hand, Kate, Aleister, and Mr Wilson made their way to the police station.

CHAPTER TWENTY-SIX

Talking to the Police

The sun was setting by the time they made it to Fairfield Street, and the police station loomed ominously in the twilight, but Aleister felt somehow upbeat. A lot had happened since the last time he'd been here, as a prisoner. Things had seemed so confused and difficult then. Now they seemed on the verge of being cleared up.

Inside the station, however, it did not seem so simple.

When they walked into the reception area, one of the constables cried out at the sight of Mr Wilson.

'Bob Wilson,' he said. 'Have we caught you at last? Taken the wrong person's money?'

Mr Wilson smiled awkwardly and shook his head. 'I am here on another matter entirely,' he said. 'Come to do my duty to make sure an innocent man is not convicted of murder.'

Aleister thought it was a stirring speech, but the constable just laughed.

'I'm in earnest,' said Mr Wilson. 'We need to speak to someone in charge.'

Still laughing, the constable pointed to the sergeant at the big desk at the far end of the room. Kate, Aleister, and Mr Wilson made their way there, and the stern sergeant looked down at them.

'We're here about a murder,' said Mr Wilson.

'Is that so?' said the sergeant.

'It's the Robert Palmer murder,' said Aleister, and the

sergeant had to lean over his desk to see where this statement was coming from.

'The Robert Palmer murder,' said the sergeant. 'Which one was that?'

'The one on Guy Fawkes Day,' said Aleister. 'You've got Mr Talbot in here for it, but we know he's innocent.'

'Sounds like something for the judge and jury,' said the sergeant.

'But it's more than that,' said Kate. 'We know who the real murderer is.'

Now the sergeant peered over the desk at Kate.

'And what is a young lady like yourself doing mixed up in something like a murder?' he said.

'I am Mr Talbot's daughter,' Kate said.

'Ah,' said the sergeant. 'Well, if you want to visit your father, we can sign you in. I think, in fact, he has visitors with him already.'

'I don't want to visit him,' said Kate. 'Not now at least. We want you to send some men to arrest someone else.'

The sergeant smiled down at her. 'Well, you see, Miss,' he said, 'we can't go off arresting people just like that, even if a pretty young girl asks us to.'

'But we have evidence,' said Kate.

'Oh,' said the sergeant, 'what evidence is that?'

Kate started to say something, but fell silent, for after all what evidence did they have?

Aleister had a sudden inspiration. 'Perhaps if we could speak to Inspector Brown,' he said.

'Inspector Brown?' said the sergeant.

'Yes,' said Aleister, 'he was in charge of the case.'

'He's in charge of lots of cases,' said the sergeant.

'Yes, but he interviewed me and Mr Talbot about this one.'

The sergeant looked more closely at Aleister. 'Why, you're the lad we first thought did it,' he said. 'Have you come to confess that it was you after all?'

'No, no,' said Aleister.

'We already have a confession in the case as I recall,' said the sergeant. 'From this Mr Talbot. Are you just trying to obstruct the course of justice by making a false confession to get your father off?'

'He's not my father,' said Aleister, 'and I'm not here to confess. We think we've figured out who the actual murderer was.'

'But Mr Talbot has already confessed to doing it,' said the sergeant. 'The whole case comes back to me now. Mr Talbot is filled with remorse. He tells us all the time how guilty he is.'

'It's just that ...' Aleister didn't know how to go on. It seemed so complicated to explain, and suddenly it didn't seem like everything was on the verge of being cleared up after all.

A constable brought a slovenly dressed man to the desk. He smelled of alcohol.

'Drunk and disorderly,' said the constable to the sergeant.

The sergeant turned his attention away from Aleister, saying only, 'I have to attend to real business now. No more of this make-believe detective work.'

Aleister stood there feeling helpless for a moment. Then he had another inspiration.

'Come on,' he said to Kate and Mr Wilson. 'Let's go and find Inspector Brown on our own. He'll listen to us.'

'Why?' said Kate.

Aleister didn't really know why. He wasn't sure it was true at all, but he knew they had to do something.

'Let's just go and find him,' he said, and led the way down the corridor beyond the sergeant's desk.

'Just a minute,' said Mr Wilson, peering down the corridor. 'I'm not sure I want to go down there. I've spent my whole life making sure I didn't end up down there.'

'We're not going to the jail,' said Aleister, 'just to Inspector Brown's office.'

'And where is that?' said Kate.

That was a slight problem, actually. Aleister had only the vaguest notion of where it was. He had never been very good with directions or landmarks, and remembered hardly anything about which corridor was which.

He noted a photograph on the wall depicting the early Manchester police force wearing top hats instead of helmets: it looked curiously ancient, but was it near Inspector Brown's office? And over there was a plaque listing all the chief constables going back to 1842 – was that where Inspector Brown's office was?

'We seem to be going in circles,' said Kate after they had been walking for a while.

Mr Wilson seemed increasingly nervous. 'I really think we should just leave and let the police handle this matter in their own way,' he said.

Aleister stopped and sighed. Kate was probably right. He had no idea where they were going. And why was he so concerned anyway? What was this murder to him? He hadn't committed it. Mr Talbot wasn't his father, even if everyone kept assuming he was, or assuming Mr Rawlins was.

He should just go back to Shrewsbury and be a schoolboy the way he was supposed to be. Or maybe he should catch the next ship to Calcutta and go off to find his real father.

They had stopped in a corridor lined with unfamiliar looking offices. Suddenly, they heard some familiar voices: Mrs Talbot and Mr Rawlins. They were coming down that very corridor.

'Mama,' said Kate, running to embrace Mrs Talbot.

'Kate,' said Mrs Talbot, 'what are you doing here?'

'We have figured out who the real murderer is,' said Kate, 'and we want the police to arrest him, but they are being so difficult.'

Mrs Talbot looked at her daughter in silence for a moment as if not fully understanding what she had said.

Aleister spoke up. 'We need to find Inspector Brown,' he said.

'Why?' said Mr Rawlins. 'And why is Mr – Mr ...'

'Wilson,' the bookie said. 'I owe you some money.'

'I beg your pardon?' said Mr Rawlins.

'You won five shillings,' said Aleister. 'On that horse.'

Mrs Talbot looked at her brother. 'George,' she said in a shocked voice, 'have you been wagering?'

'It was just in order to encourage Mr Wilson here to provide us with some useful information,' Mr Rawlins said.

Mrs Talbot shook her head in disapproval. 'Wagering,' she said. 'On a horse. What would our mother have said?'

'Agnes,' Mr Rawlins began, but for the first time in his life Aleister Lister Smith interrupted his schoolmaster.

'None of that is important,' he said. 'The important thing is that Mr Wilson is a witness who can identify the real murderer.'

And then he explained the whole story of Brooks and Doyle, the theory that he and Kate had come up with that Brooks and Doyle were the same person. He was beginning to get tired of going over the story, and also wondered whose theory it actually was. Had Kate come up with the idea first? He couldn't remember.

'Quite fascinating, Lister Smith,' Mr Rawlins was saying. 'How ever did you come up with this idea?'

'It was Kate, actually,' Aleister said.

'Oh, we figured it out together,' said Kate.

'But how do you propose to prove it?' said Mr Rawlins.

'That's where Mr Wilson comes in,' said Aleister. 'He can tell us whether Brooks is Doyle.'

Mr Rawlins nodded.

'And we wanted the police to come along to arrest him,' Aleister added.

'Only the sergeant at the desk was quite rude and wouldn't agree to sending anyone out,' Kate said.

'So I thought we could ask Inspector Brown,' said Aleister.

'Do we need the police at all at this point?' said Mr Rawlins. 'Why didn't you go to the insurance company and have Mr Wilson identify Brooks-and-Doyle there?'

'We tried that,' said Aleister, 'but he was gone.'

'Gone?' said Mr Rawlins.

'Flown the coop,' said Kate.

'I beg your pardon?' said Mrs Talbot.

'He'd run off,' said Kate. 'That proves he's guilty.'

'I'm not sure it does that,' said Mrs Talbot. 'And what does "flown the coop" mean? It sounds vulgar.'

'Oh, I read it in an American novel,' said Kate. 'Lydia Cavendish lent it to me.'

Mrs Talbot shook her head. 'You know,' she said, 'I think I need to go home now. It's been rather a trying day. Your father remains wrapped up in his imaginary guilt, and now I learn that your uncle is betting on horse races and you are reading American novels. It's all a bit, a bit ...'

Mrs Talbot seemed too worn out even to finish her sentence. Mr Rawlins took her by the arm and led her back through the reception area and outside, where he hailed a cab for her and sent her home.

The others followed along behind, and then made their way by foot to the address for Mr Brooks that Mr O'Neill had supplied.

'Not the sort of neighbourhood I would expect a senior clerk to live in,' said Mr Rawlins as they made their way down the street where Mr Brooks lived.

Aleister hadn't been paying much attention to their surroundings, but he looked around now and noted that the buildings were a bit rundown. Not as bad as the neighbourhood where they had last looked for Mr Brooks. No beggars in the street. No one picking at his sores. But not an elegant leafy neighbourhood either.

They came to the right address and began to climb the stairs. Mr Brooks was supposed to live on the top floor. They knocked on his rickety wooden door, but there was no answer.

'He's not here,' said Mr Wilson. 'There's no one to identify. This time I think I really must be going.'

He hurried down the stairs before anyone could stop him.

'What do we do now?' said Aleister. It seemed to him that every time they got close to settling everything, the final resolution receded from their grasp.

'Let's find the landlady,' said Mr Rawlins.

He headed down the stairs. Aleister and Kate lingered at Mr Brooks's door.

'Maybe there's a window we could get in through,' said Kate.

'We should have made sure to bring the police after all,' said Aleister. 'Though if Mr Brooks is not here, then I'm not sure what even they could do.'

He felt suddenly gloomy.

Mr Rawlins returned with the landlady, a large squat woman jingling a large key ring.

'I don't know as I ought to be doing this,' the landlady was saying even as she inserted one of her keys into the lock.

The door swung open, and Aleister beheld the sparsest looking room he had ever seen. There was less in it than in his old jail cell. Just a narrow bed, a table, one chair, and a chest of drawers. The walls were in desperate need of paint and the floor was rough-looking, uncovered wood. Not a rug or carpet in sight.

The only hint of decoration was a photograph on the table of a young boy. Kate went and picked it up. 'Jimmy Doyle, I presume,' she said.

Aleister nodded. His eye had been caught by what looked like a letter lying on the bed.

'What's that?' he said.

Mr Rawlins went and picked it up. He unfolded and read it, then handed it to Aleister.

'Looks like you were right,' he said.

CHAPTER TWENTY-SEVEN

What the Letter Said

Aleister took the letter and began to read. There was no salutation.

'If you're reading this,' it began abruptly, 'then you've found me out. I'm rather expecting to be found out. I think I expected it all along. I don't think I even really cared. That wasn't the point. I wasn't trying to commit some unsolvable crime, just to make the guilty one pay for the death of my son.

'Once the child came to the office asking about Doyle, I knew it was all over. Clever of the child to figure it out, but I expected someone to do it eventually. If no one had, I think I would have stepped forward before Mr Talbot's trial. I had no grievance against him.

'My grievance was with Robert Palmer, the one who killed my son. I know he didn't do it directly or even intentionally, but my son is dead and someone had to pay.

'My poor little son wanted so desperately to be English, to fit in with the English boys, and this is what it got him: fireworks exploding in his face. I blame Palmer for that. I spoke to one of the boys in his gang and heard how Palmer used to taunt my son with being Irish and not really English, how he egged my son on to do things that would prove he was English, and my son – well, I don't want to talk of that any more.

'For a long while after his death, I was simply grief-stricken. I couldn't work. I left my job. I left my wife. I ended up living in the lowest of lodging houses.

'Then one day the grief suddenly lifted. I felt inspired, full of purpose, full of direction for the first time in weeks. I decided the thing to do was to exact revenge for my son's death.

'To do that, I cleaned myself up and sought out a job in the city centre. It was pure happenstance that I managed to get a job in the very office where Palmer worked. I thought that was a sign from Fate saying I was right to go ahead with my plan.

'I wasn't sure I was right, though. I took to visiting the reading room at the YMCA hoping to find guidance. The Christian teachings said to turn the other cheek and leave punishment to God. I thought perhaps that's what I should do.

'But as the anniversary of Guy Fawkes Day approached, I felt possessed, gripped. Part of me knew I was possessed, knew that I was in the grip of something unpleasant, even evil. But I couldn't shake off its grip. It told me to kill Palmer, and I did.

'Now, though, I simply feel numb. I was wrong to have done what I did. It was not for me to judge and execute. And now others will judge and perhaps execute me.

'I have gone down to the cemetery where my little boy is buried. You will find me there this evening.

'If no one comes, I will go to the police station myself tomorrow. It will be a relief to end this masquerade, to give up the false identity of Brooks and return to being Eddie Doyle.'

Aleister handed the letter to Kate and watched as she read it.

'It's proof,' she said, 'the proof we needed.' She sounded more sad than pleased.

'Yes,' said Mr Rawlins. 'And now we really should go to the police.'

They thanked the landlady and hurried down the stairs. This time they didn't walk, but took a cab to the police station. And this time the sergeant, on reading the letter and having the situation explained to him, was much more inclined to help. He summoned Inspector Brown from a corridor Aleister had not even remembered.

The inspector looked at the letter, shook his head, then summoned another plainclothes detective to go with him to arrest Mr Brooks.

'And what about releasing my father?' said Kate.

'In due time,' said the inspector. 'In due time. First let us confirm this confession.'

This statement for some reason caused Kate to burst into tears. Mr Rawlins patted her on the back and said the two of them would go break the news to Mr Talbot and tell him he would no doubt be released soon.

Aleister wondered if he should go with the police to see the arrest. He had a vision of looking on while the inspector laid a hand on the shoulder of Mr Brooks in front of his son's grave, but he realised he had no place there.

He wondered where he did have a place. The murder was solved, the blackmail had been solved long ago; everything was done; he should be happy – but he wondered what he would do now.

'Why, you'll go back to Shrewsbury and be a schoolboy again,' Kate said the next morning when they talked about it.

The police had found Mr Brooks where he'd said he'd be and had confirmed his story (they'd brought in a nervous Mr Wilson to make the identification after all). And Mr Talbot was released, though not without protesting that he should still pay for his crime of theft.

'Mr Smithson is not pressing charges about that, Arthur,' Mrs Talbot said to him. 'As long as you pay the money back, he will forget the whole thing. He will even let you have your job back.'

And so all the mysteries were cleared up, and everything went more or less back to how it had been before: Mr Talbot chief clerk at the Saviour Assurance Company, Aleister and Mr Rawlins back at Shrewsbury School, and Kate and Mrs Talbot at home quilting.

But things had changed subtly. Aleister had learned he could handle himself in a crisis and even help solve a murder. He became a full-fledged monitor at school next term and felt generally more confident about life. He also sat down and wrote a long letter to his parents in India telling them all about his Manchester adventure. His mother wrote back worriedly to ask if he was all right, and his father appended a brief note, just saying, 'Good job.'

Aleister kept in touch with Kate and learned that she eventually convinced her father to let her take a course in how to use a typewriter so that she might eventually become a typewriting lady clerk.

'What about becoming a lady detective?' he wrote her.

'Well, if another murder comes up,' she wrote back, 'perhaps I will get involved in solving it. You could even help me.'

Aleister grinned to himself at the way she put it, but he thought it might be fun to play detective again with Kate. It would certainly be more exciting than studying Horace.

And with that thought he folded up Kate's letter, put it on his night table, and went to sleep.

Acknowledgements

This novel came about in an unusual way. I have long belonged to the wonderful on-line discussion group for Victorian studies started by Patrick Leary and known as VICTORIA. A few years ago the novelist Michel Faber joined the group to ask for help with research for his novel *The Crimson Petal and the White*, which he was planning to set back in 1875. I answered some of his questions and as a result was mentioned in his acknowledgements when the novel came out in 2002.

In the fall of 2002, Michel came to a Vancouver writers festival, where I went to hear him read. After the reading, he thanked me from the stage for helping with his research. Hearing this, a local Vancouver publisher in the audience approached me with the suggestion that I write a murder mystery for ten to fourteen-year-olds set in the Victorian era. He made this suggestion based solely on the knowledge that I was an expert in the period, without even knowing whether I could write.

All very odd – but I'm very glad it happened, because the suggestion got me to write this novel, which I very much enjoyed doing.

In the end, the local publisher decided not to publish the novel, but luckily UKA Press decided that what I had written had merit, so it has been published after all, and I hope it gives as much enjoyment in the reading as it did in the writing.

Once I began work on the novel, I took to showing it to certain select readers a chapter at a time, just like a Victorian serial, and I want to thank all of them for their comments and encouragement, especially my mother, who always read each chapter right away and kept asking me to reveal the solution to the mystery (which I wouldn't do). I would also like to thank her for her suggestion that I put more in about tigers and elephants.

My co-worker Valerie Levens was another enthusiastic reader who kept me on my toes with probing questions and useful suggestions – and she gave me the word 'hoity-toity'.

I would like to thank the members of my screenwriters group (including Margaret Vanderbolt, Bill Marles, Terrie Rolph, Adam Fulford, Belle Mott, and Eric Finkel), who agreed to read my manuscript and offer feedback on it, even though it was clearly not a screenplay. I am especially grateful to the two members, Bon Thorburn and Poppi Reiner, who showed the manuscript to their children so I could get feedback from the intended audience. The same is true of my co-worker Marnie Craft, who showed the manuscript to her grandson Brody Watson (Brody even gave me written comments). I would also like to thank another of my young readers, my cousin (once removed) Eve Mozur, who told me she thought Aleister was 'so cool'.

My co-worker Paramjit Rai urged me to put some quilting in the novel, which I did. Peter Wood, whom I met through the VICTORIA list, provided me with useful information about train schedules and railway stations. Ellen Jordan, another member of the list, provided information about Victorian-era clerks, and I also received assistance from the following list members: Susan Hoyle, Neil Davie, Emelyne Godfrey, Beth Sutton-Ramspeck, Cathrine O. Frank, June Siegel, Annette Wickham, James M. Cornelius, K. Eldron, Sue Doran, and Alan Mountford.

Doris Meriwether, also a member of the VICTORIA list, was an eager and enthusiastic reader from afar who urged me on when it looked like I was slowing down. Cindy Hanna came up with the subtitle and made several other useful suggestions.

I consulted numerous books and websites on the Victorian

era as part of my research into the novel's background. I cannot possibly cite them all here, but Gregory Anderson's book on Victorian clerks was especially useful, as was Alan Kidd's book on Manchester, J. Basil Oldham's history of Shrewsbury School, Kellow Chesney's entertaining study of the Victorian underworld, and Molly Hughes's fascinating memoir of her Victorian girlhood. I found out about William Makepeace Thackeray's discussion of a murder in a railway carriage from Richard Altick's book on Victorian murders, soaked up some useful background information from the collection of letters by the Reynolds family (an Irish family in Victorian Manchester), edited by Lawrence W. McBride, and learned many things about Manchester from the Manchester UK website.

I would like to thank the Inter-Library Loan Service of the Vancouver Public Library for obtaining books for me that were not available in Vancouver's libraries. And I must send out special thanks to Graham Hobbs, the Chief Executive of the Manchester YMCA, for kindly sending me a brightly coloured little book detailing the history of that institution.

I should also mention Professor Ira B. Nadel, my former supervisor at the University of British Columbia, who invited me to hear Michel Faber read at the Vancouver writers festival, and so in a sense started the process that culminated in this novel.

Finally, I would like to thank Don Masters, the acquisitions editor at UKA Press, for his boundless enthusiasm over *Remember, Remember* and for his accommodating attitude in our many discussions about style and usage.

— Vancouver, British Columbia, Canada
August 2004

Printed in the United States
29357LVS00002B/151